A Gain For A Loss

By: Darrell Bracey, Jr.

First print 2018 July

ISBN- 978-0-9823880-2-0 (Trade Pbk.)

Bout Dat Lyfe Publications, LLC
Bloc Extension Publishing, LLC
Attn: Byron R. Dorsey or Darrell Bracey, Jr.
Email: blocextension007@gmail .com
Email: authordarellbracey@gmail.com
Phone: 301.313.0272

Library of Congress Cataloging-in-Publication Data
1. Darell Bracey, Jr., African American, Contemporary, Urban Crime, Washington D.C. - Fiction

Book Production Credits:

Book Production: Crystell Publications
Edit: Darrell Bracey Jr. & Byron Dorsey
Revised Edit By: Darrell Bracey Jr. & Byron Dorsey

Printed in the USA

Praises for - *A Gain For A Loss*
By: Darrell Bracey, Jr.

"Author Darrell Bracey, Jr. is quickly becoming a fan favorite in the urban fiction arena. With his page turning debut novel, *Concrete Jungle*, acquiring the supportive reviews it has, our team at Special Needs X-press expected nothing other than a well-crafted second effort. His sophomore title, *A Gain For A Loss* effectively delivers, and is a bonafied trailblazer that's packed with plenty of action and spell-bounding suspense that will engage the readers from beginning to end."

-Dwayne - Co-founder of Special Needs X-press

"True to form, Darrell Bracey, Jr. pushes the envelope in repeat fashion with a first-rate follow-up to his coming out. He's a natural at building compelling, relatable, characters, and plausible plots, which anchors this must read with captivating appeal."

-Angel Williams - Author of *Raven's Cravings & Love On Lockdown*

Praises for – Concrete Jungle
By: Darrell Bracey, Jr.

'This gripping, authenitic fictional account serves it's audience compelling twist and eye-popping suspense that epitomizes the opposite side of the law from a firsthand point of view, while strategically narrating the deathly reality of the street life."

- Jason "J Rock" Poole
Author of *Larency, Victoria's Secret & Prince of the City*

"Thrilling ...Gritty...Graphic...Bracey delves deep into the soul of Washington, D.C. and cooks up an illustrious plot with interesting characters, which pose for a supurb cinematic street tale."

- Eyone Williams - Author of *Fast Lane & Lorton Legendz*

By: Darrell Bracey, Jr.

ACKNOWLEDGEMENTS

First and foremost, I'd like to thank the man upstairs for blessing me to originate yet another masterpiece. Next, I'd like to salute these new supporters for showing me love from the beginning: Angel Williams CEO of Star City Publications, thanks for all the sound advice that you gave me since our first encounter. Your acumen has been very supportive and appreciated. You single handedly penned over twenty books, learned how to write movie scripts and executive produced your very own project. Your dedication led to your success, which only motivates me to go harder so that one day, I too can accomplish at least half of what you've succeeded in doing thus far. Looking forward to doing business with you in the near future. Lastly, I want to say (R.I.P) to your child's father, Eric Gwynn, who blessed you with your beautiful daughter, Kady. Keep your head up and continue to strive toward prosperity.

To James Preston III, CEO of Uptown Music and Film Group, from man to man, I am extremely honored to have someone such as yourself to read, believe, and take a chance on my project. You're the first to afford me the opportunity of having my creative thoughts brought to screen. For that I am forever loyal, meaning, no matter what I put out you will always have first dibs on any of my projects. That's my word as a man. Can't wait to see the finished project. Much Luv.

To my main man, Columbian "Black" Thomas. My bad, bruh. I don't know how in the world I didn't mention you in my debut novel. You already know how far we go back, from being neighbors running back-n-forth from house to house playing hooky in middle school with all the females. Man, had my folks known how much company we were bringing through their house back then, they would've killed us (LOL). I miss them days, Slim. Remember we threw our first party in your shed? We were young dudes with big dreams. Til this day people still talk about that party. Those were lifelong, priceless, and memorable times. Love you, bruh!

To Erica Hicks, even though I met you only recently, I feel as though I've known you for years. I'm a good judge of character, and from what I've seen, you are one-in-a-million. I really do appreciate and value our friendship. Thank you much for the necessary support that you provide.

To Special Needs X-Press Book Division. By your company accepting my book and making it a part of your highly notable catalog that includes many other great urban authors such as, K'Wan, Jimmy Dasaint, Ca$h, Al-Saadiq Banks, Silk White, Seth Ferranti, and Ashley-n-JaQuavis, just to name a few, is like a dream come true. To have my book listed in the same directory with those authors, who are considered staples in the Urban Book Industry, is awe-inspiring in itself. That alone further propels me to showcase my talent and prove to others as well as myself that I deserve to be on the same platform alongside of prominent writers in the game. I believe I have my foot in the door, and I plan to take full advantage of the moment, because sometimes in life there's no next time or second chances. In some cases, it's either now or never! So thanks Dwayne of S.N.X Book Division and my business associate Byron "B-Bo" Dorsey for making this dream a reality.

I would also like to express my appreciation to, in no particular order, and for different reasons: Lamar Grey (Luv ya cuzz), Ranada Parker, Cornell Smith, Tavon Brown, Gabbie Moe and his "Top Notch" crew , Latosha "Peaches" Nicole, Jarrell "Pimp" Elliott, Raquel "Cookie" Jitta, Kenneth "K-Dog" Hampton, Australia Smith, Elijah Phillips, Kiana Perry, Aaron "Pat" Jones, Lil' Mama, Da'Quon Jones, Lowell "B" Lamont, Mark Credle, Larry "L" Thomas, Gerald Andrews, Kee- Kee Miller, Alex (A-Rod) Rodriguez, "My typist," Adam "A-Rod" Jackson, David "Dave G" Gutierrez, Tashiek "Nubian" Champean Sr., and my beautiful-n-loving aunt, Nee-Cee. Luv you all, and hope you enjoy this book just as much as my first.

Current Contact Info:
Darrell Bracey, J.R. #39673-007 Rivers Correctional Institution
P. O. Box 630
Winton, NC 27986

DEDICATION

First, I would like to thank my higher power for looking over ME
AND keeping me focusED on my
journey to stardom.
Second, I would like to dedicate my sophmore novel to all my
doubters who became the driving force behind my hard work, and
determination, to prove to not only them, but to myself that I can
achieve any undertaking
I set my mind too.
Lastly, any project that I produce will always and forever be
devoted to my mother
Robin M. Motley
and my son
Darrell Bracey III
the future football star.

Love y'all more than anything.
Be there soon!

By: Darrell Bracey, Jr.

PROLOGUE

The Year 2007...

"Michael! Michael!" the voice came echoing from his mother's room.

"Ma'am!" the young teen responded, jumping up, thinking that he had overslept.

"Boy, get your tail up, and get you and your sister ready for school, so that y'all won't be late!"

"I' m getting up now, Ma!" he assured her.

It didn't take them long to get dressed because they usually took their showers and laid their outfits out the night before. Michael, being the oldest, had to make sure that they both made it to and from school promptly and safely. It was also his responsibility that they ate and that the house was clean before their mother got back home from work. Due to their mom working two jobs, the pair didn't spend much time roaming the neighborhood, so the little time they spent walking home after school was their leisure time.

"Michael, I'm working late tonight, so I left twenty

dollars on my nightstand so that y'all can order pizza or carry out for dinner. I don't want to have to worry about you trying to cook and burning my house down. Okay!" their mother commented.

"Okay!" he replied.

"It's time for me to get out of here, so you two come in here and give me a hug and a kiss before I leave," she ordered. Seconds after, her kids strolled into her room. "Now look, you two be careful walking to school. It's messy outside," she said, making sure her kids were aware of the weather conditions before heading out.

Ten minutes later, they were leaving as well. Michael made sure his sister stayed close, given the hazardous weather. It was one of those days that he wished school was closed, but sadly it wasn't.

"What do you wanna eat for dinner, since Ma left us some food money?" he asked his sister.

"I want pizza, big brother!" she shouted excitedly, jumping up and down.

"It's too messy out here for you to be jumping around like that," he warned. "So please stop, before we both fall, and yes, we can order pizza, if that's what you want," he assured her.

"Thank you! Thank you, big brother, you're the best!" she beamed, rising up on her tippy toes to give him a peck on his cheek.

"Oh, now I'm the best, huh?" he smiled.

"Yep!" she confirmed, nodding her head.

"Well, if I'm the best, then let's hurry up so we don't be late."

As they approached the intersection of Piney Branch Road and Butternut Street, halfway across the road, out of nowhere, a vehicle came screeching in their direction, swerving uncontrollably. Like the ice that coated the street, both brother and sister froze from terror at the sight of the vehicle bearing down on them. At the last minute, Michael tried to grab his sister and jump out of the way, but stuck like a deer blinded by headlights, he reacted too slowly, and the intractable car collided into the both of them.

Chapter 1

Six Years Later...

"Michelle!" shouted Michael, sweating profusely.

He sat up and shook his head, waking from one of the many nightmares that had haunted him on an almost daily basis since the death of his little sister. Michael stumbled when he tried to stand and sank back into his bed. The crash had caused him to have a limp for the rest of his life, so he was still sometimes unsteady on his feet. As he lay in bed, his mother dashed into the basement to console him, knowing that he was having another bad dream.

"Michael! I know! I know, baby," she said with compassionation. "It's been difficult, but we gotta stay strong!" she said, cupping his head in her arms, rocking back and forth, fighting back tears of her own.

"Why, Ma? Why her and not me!" he cried out.

"Don't say that! Don't you even think of talking like that! God called her home early for a reason. She's in a better place where she can watch over us and guide us in the right direction. She can't suffer no more, and though we must endure the pain of it, the both of us have to be resilient for the sake of us!" she wept, trying to ease her son's pain as well as her own.

"I gotta get out of here!" he snapped, breaking his mother's embrace, storming into his bathroom, slamming the door.

Michael (Mike-Mike) Gardner had never gotten over the death of his sister and vowed that if he ever were to find out who was behind the wheel the day of the tragic accident, they would pay with their life. Period!

At the age of seventeen, Mike-Mike had already established himself throughout his area. He was respected mainly because of how he conducted himself. He never once picked on anyone or started unnecessary conflicts, which was a positive feat considering how his sister's death had left an indelible stain on his heart that often caused a negative shift in attitude.

Even after the incident, Mike-Mike and his moms still resided in the same two-bedroom, three level, single family home as before, located on Whittier Place, Northwest, Washington, DC. Mike-Mike and his sister had shared the same room up until her passing. Once he was rehabilitated from his injuries, he moved all his personal belongings into the basement, leaving everything of his sisters in the room they shared as if she had never left. After all the adversity, he still managed to graduate from Calvin Coolidge Senior High School and had developed into his own man.

He finally got dressed and headed out the door, hopping into his older model Chrysler *LHS* that his mom purchased for him due to him completing school. His mom was oblivious to the fact that the car she brought him was mostly used to get to and from one of the two luxury vehicles that he kept stored in a secret place until needed. The two vehicles he owned included an all-white mirror-tinted, rimmed-out, Lexus *GS Sport,* and a silver Cadillac *DTS,* both 2013 editions.

Although he had the titles for both vehicles, they weren't legally purchased. They were flipped to perfection and as long as they weren't serviced at the dealership he was in the clear. No one other than the individuals who were responsible for the vehicles being chopped and his partner Slick, who owned one as well, knew of their illegitimacy.

Slick was Mike-Mike's partner, who he'd met shortly after his sister's early departure. Slick was actually the person who introduced him to stealing cars, but Mike-Mike quickly grew out of the habit and commenced to snatching vehicles for anyone who needed parts or accessories. It was cool at first, but he didn't start seeing any decent money until he met the same individual who was responsible for switching the numbers on his two vehicles who went by the name of Zoe.

After the introduction, it didn't take long for things to start progressing. Zoe was paying Mike-Mike something more comfortable just to steal vehicles he requested and drop them off at a designated spot. Zoe would then switch the numbers and sell them for profit. The money that Mike-Mike would get from Zoe was split with his partner Slick for his assistance. It wasn't difficult for Mike-Mike to conceal his wrongdoings from his mother because her fiancé, Anthony, was occupying a lot of her time. She had met Anthony two years after her daughter's casualty. As of recent, the two decided to take their relationship to another level. Mike-Mike was happy for his mother and even convinced her that she was doing the right thing, as far as marriage. In his eyes, Anthony was a good man for his mom. Plus, he helped her with a lot of the stress that she was enduring.

As Mike-Mike drove to Fourteenth and Luzon Street to switch cars, he thought about purchasing something to relieve his stress as well. That thought alone led him to retrieve his cell phone and placing a quick call to his weed man as he parked his Chrysler and hopped into his Lexus. He turned his key in the ignition, and the rapper Yo Gotti blared through the speakers. Nodding his head to the music, he casually opened the sunroof to let out some of the stuffiness from the combination of the heat and the scent of the leather seats. He pulled off making a right turn onto Aspen Street, driving toward Georgia Avenue. Out of nowhere, he started having reflections of his sister's face the day of the accident, which instantly got his blood boiling.

Unknowingly, he stepped on the gas pedal, rapidly gaining speed on a straight and narrow street. He floored the Lexus until he was within twenty feet of the upcoming intersection then slammed on the brakes just in a nick of time to avoid sliding into the busy intersection. Sweating, heart pounding and breathing ragged, he sat frozen at the traffic light, gripping the steering wheel, until he gained his composure. Once he calmed down, he wiped the sweat from his forehead, closed the sunroof, and turned on the air conditioning.

He took another long breath, then changed the CD to Musiq Soulchild to help further relax his mind, after feeling as if he were on the verge of self-destruction. Back in control, he made a right turn onto Georgia Avenue, cruising past Aspen Courts Apartment Complex, which was where he hung at in Northwest, D.C. Aspen Courts was a group of housing buildings that consisted of seven 12-unit apartments. Seconds after driving past his safe haven, his cell phone alerted him to a call.

"Slick, wassup?" Mike-Mike answered, turning down the volume on his radio.

"What's good, bruh? You just rode past?" Slick asked.

"Yeah, dat was me," he confirmed.

"Where you on ya way to?"

"I'm 'bout to go down Kennedy Street and holla at Jamaican Eric to cop some of dat loud right quick."

"Shid, I need some of dat in my life too, so you need to swing back around and scoop me up, so I can ride wit' you."

"I got you. Where were you standing, cause I didn't see nobody out there when I rode past?" inquired Mike-Mike, making a U-turn heading back towards his neighborhood.

"I was standing in Monique's building wit' Lil' Chico."

"Tell dat nigga I said wassup. Look I'm pullin up now, so go ahead and come out."

"Bet! Let me stash this shit real quick."

Mike-Mike and Slick were like right-hand men, partners in crime, brothers from another mother, or whatever else you choose to call it; that was them. The two became close after an altercation between Mike-Mike and some other neighborhood dudes who tried to jump him. Slick, witnessed the dispute, and went over to help out and ended up with a worse beating than Mike-Mike. Since then, the pair just clicked, becoming best of friends. Mike-Mike was a teenage version of Blair Underwood, while Slick was the spitting image of the singer J. Holiday when he had cornrows.

Shortly after Mike-Mike pulled up, Slick came out and slid into the car.

"I see you on ya slow shit, huh?" questioned Slick about his partner's selection of music.

"Yeah, I was on my laid-back shit, but you can switch it if you want to," he told Slick, not wanting to reveal the real reason he had the soul music playing.

"Good, cause it's too early for dat slow sensitive shit," Slick countered, reaching for the CD case under his seat, and then flipping through it.

"What was Lil' Chico doing?" asked Mike-Mike.

"Nothin' fo' real, 'bout to get Moe-Moe to do his hair, dat's all," he replied.

"I should've known, 'cause you two red niggas ain't leaving da 'hood wit' out y'all's shit braided."

"You better know it," Slick shot back, "'cause ya never

know who we might run into. But fo'get dat. Did you holler at Zoe 'cause a nigga's funds runnin' low, ya dig?" he inquired, changing the subject to a more pressing matter.

"Not since I told you we talked da last time, but he should be hittin' me up soon," Mike-Mike responded, riding past Rittenhouse Street, tapping the horn at Worl-n-Scrap, who was standing in front of Food Barn convenient store, chatting with three females. (A Scene from *Concrete Jungle*, also written by Darrell Bracey, J.R.)

Slick finally found a CD to his liking, which was *Bag Of Money* by Wale (feat. Rick Ross, Meek Mill & T-Pain).

"Every time you get in here you play dat same joint!" Mike-Mike voiced.

"Cause dat's where my mind set is. A nigga tryin' to get dat bag, and live comfortable, ya feel me!"

"Yeah, I feel ya," Mike-Mike smiled, already knowing his right-hand man was filled with cupidity.

When Mike-Mike came to the intersection of Georgia and Missouri Avenue, he made a left turn, driving toward 7th and Kennedy St.

"What you coppin' anyway?" Slick asked.

"A quarter," he confirmed, pulling up to his destination, and parking.

"Grab me da same then," replied Slick, handing his money over.

"I got you," Mike-Mike stated, pocketing the money, prior to hopping out to conduct his business.

"Wassup, Beez?" he greeted, walking up to a group of males standing near the alleyway. "You see Jamaican Eric?"

"I think him and Lil' Dee walked down by Yum's Carry-Out not too long ago," Beez replied.

"Dat nigga can't stand still fo' nothin', I just told 'im I was on my way," he commented, not wanting to hang around the heavily trafficked drug strip for too long.

"If you want dat loud pack we got da same shit if you not tryin' to sit and wait on'im," Beez stated, sensing Mike-Mike's uneasiness.

"Let me hit him and see where he at first since I already told 'im I was comin.'"

"Do you, I wasn't tryin' to step on his toes, I was just lettin' you know just in case you didn't feel like waitin', dat's all," he clarified.

"Naw, it's cool, 'cause if he's not close by, I'ma cop from you," assured Mike-Mike, pulling out his phone to make the call.

"Matter of fact, dat's them comin' out da corner store wit' them two broads," pointed Beez.

"I see 'em... Man, I swear y'all keep plenty of females out here," he chuckled slyly.

"All hoovers," Beez responded, "them broads ain't tryin' to do nothin' but smoke a nigga shit up."

"Dat's all, huh?"

"Ya know it."

"I'll catch up wit' ya later. Let me go holla at slim so I can get outta here."

"Make sure ya do dat, so we can go grab a bottle or somethin.'"

"Bet," stated Mike-Mike, heading down the hill to meet up with Jamaican Eric.

Mike-Mike shouted his name to get his attention. Jamaican Eric quickly turned around after hearing his name called. Noticing who it was, he immediately went to meet him.

"Mike-Mike, wassup?" he greeted as he approached. "How long ya been waitin', mon?" he asked in his Jamaican accent.

"Not dat long, but ya know how I am 'bout standin' out here."

"Me know, me know, so let's handle our business, 'cause I know ya tryin' to get outta here."

"We can hop in my car real quick," Mike-Mike said. The pair then walked back up the hill towards his vehicle.

Jamaican Eric instantly greeted Slick, once the two got into the car, "My main man Slick, how ya been, me bloodren?"

"Ya know me, just coolin' as usual," Slick replied. He turned halfway around to dap him up. "Wassup wit' you?"

"You know me, mon, just takin' a hard life easy," he retorted, smiling as he pulled out a Ziplock bag full of that sticky.

"Man, dat shit strong as shit!" Slick exclaimed.

"You know I keep nothin' but the finest," Jamaican Eric bragged. "So what y'all need?"

"Two quarters," Mike-Mike replied, handing him the money.

"Wassup with them two broads y'all walkin' wit'?" Slick inquired, nodding his chin at the two young ladies who were standing on the corner with Jamaican Eric's homie Lil' Dee apparently waiting on Jamaican Eric's return.

"That's Garnisha, and Shanetra," he answered, passing Mike-Mike the two quarters he purchased. "Why you ask, ya like what ya see?" he broadly grinned, showing off a set of large white teeth.

"They definitely look good from a distance."

"Try ya hand, they not our folks or nothin', just some round da way girls," he confirmed.

"You sure, 'cause I'm not tryin' to be on no disrespectful shit, ya feel me."

"Yeah, I feel ya, but if dat was da case then I would've corrected you when ya asked who they were," he assured him.

"Say no more."

"A'ight, we'll get up wit' you and you be careful out here walkin' 'round dirty like dat," said Mike-Mike.

"I'm straight, plus I'm 'bout to go put this shit up anyway," Jamaican Eric replied, dapping the pair up before getting out.

Mike-Mike pulled off and drove to the corner where Lil' Dee and the two females stood. When they reached them, Slick respectfully spoke to Lil' Dee first before directing his attention to the two females standing next to him.

"Wassup wit' ya?" asked Slick.

"Same shit, tryin' to get this money. I see y'all ridin' good," Lil' Dee spoke, complimenting the vehicle.

"Just trying to keep up wit' good men such as ya'self," Slick shot back. "I see you standin' wit' two lovely ladies," he commented, throwing the bait out there, hoping they'd catch.

After a moment, judging by the way they blushed, Slick knew he had them.

"Yeah, they standin' wit' me but they free to do as they please," Lil Dee responded, letting him know that the two women weren't taken.

"Well, in dat case, y'all two ladies think my partner and I could have a moment of y'all's time?" Slick inquired, in a respectable tone.

"Sure, if y'all don't mind getting out. We don't walk up to strangers' vehicles," spoke Shanetra alluringly.

"I like her lil red petite ass, and she don't seem shy. I think I'ma get her," Slick whispered to Mike-Mike as he stepped out of the Lexus.

"Dat's even better fo' me 'cause you already know I like 'em dark and thick in all da right places," responded Mike-Mike just as his phone started it's familiar hum. "Damn, you must've spoke slim up 'cause this Zoe right here callin' me", he conveyed, glancing at his incoming call.

"Shid, dat's more important. You handle dat while I go holla at them," Slick said.

He shut the car door and left Mike-Mike behind to take his call as he made his way over to the group.

While Mike-Mike took care of his business on the phone, Slick handled his with the two females. A few minutes later, Slick got back into the car with a smile on his face. Mike-Mike gave Lil' Dee the thumbs up and waved at the females before pulling off, still talking on the phone.

"What you cheesin' fo'?" Mike-Mike asked after he disconnected his call.

"I was smilin' at shorty. She cute as shit close up, too.

She damn near looks good enough to eat," Slick boasted.

"Weak-ass nigga! One thing 'bout me, I ain't eatin' nothin' dat can get up and walk away unless it's my wifey or Erykah Badu."

"Yeah, dat's what ya mouth say."

"Dat's what I know."

"Yeah, I hear you," Slick shrugged. "So what Zoe talkin' bout?" he asked, quickly changing the subject.

"I'm 'bout to go 'round Langdon now and see what's what."

"Dat's wassup, 'cause I damn sure need some extra bread."

"You too," Mike-Mike added. Twist some of dat loud up," he insisted.

"Bet," Slick said in agreement, glad to know that some money was soon to be heading their way.

CHAPTER 2

Mike-Mike's mother Gloria and her fiancé Anthony were in their bedroom conversing about Mike-Mike's endless nightmares of his sister's death and his generally distant behavior. She was afraid of losing him to the streets, especially after having lost one child already. She was a good mother who at times worked two jobs just to support her children. Though it was overwhelming at times, she did what she had to to ensure that her children didn't need for anything. She became a single parent after their father left home one day, and never returned, due to his street dealings. She knew that her son was holding in a lot of anger from his sister's and father's deaths, and it worried her. She had seen what that kind of anger could do to people.

Anthony was also feeling the effects of these matters since Gloria hadn't been in the mood lately for anything except sleeping, but considering the circumstances he dealt with it. He got up, walked to the edge of the bed, removed his lover's slippers, and gently began to massage her feet. He stayed quiet and let her vent. Once she was finished, he looked her in the eyes and gave her his point of view.

"The last thing I want to see is you stressed out and hurting, 'cause what's affecting you is affecting me. What I'm about to say is merely from a man's perspective."

After she nodded her head in agreement, he continued, "Michael's lashing out at times is just a reflection of what he's been going through. He's a young man who's starting to make his own decisions. Give him some room to allow himself to vent, and if you ever think his actions are getting out of hand then I'll have a man-to-man talk with him. Okay?"

"Okay," she agreed, giving him that puppy smile he was accustom to, and so in love with.

"There goes that smile I've been missing," he flattered, causing her to smile even wider.

"I just worry so much," she confided.

"That's understandable. You're a concerned parent whose witnessed firsthand the loss of a child, and that's one thing no parent wants to ever experience. But you must try not to stress yourself. Michael hasn't done anything yet to make you speculate that he's going down the wrong path."

"I guess you're right. I just want what's best for him," she concluded.

"And you should, but stop worrying, and give your future husband a kiss!" he stated, dropping his tone to a deeper register.

Anthony eased up from massaging her feet, so he could receive his requested kiss. Afterwards, he casually moved down and repeatedly sucked on her neck until a crimson hickey appeared. That's when he laid her back on the bed and allowed the electricity between them to spark a flame of passion that quickly comforted her and quelled the stressful thoughts she had been absorbed in.

CHAPTER 3

Mike-Mike and Slick finally made it to their destination, which was near Langdon Recreation Center. As Mike-Mike turned on his designated street, the first person they saw was an associate by the name of Andy, who was standing on the front porch of the corner house.

Mike-Mike pulled over briefly to see what he had been up to. When Andy saw who it was, he immediately left the front porch to holla at Mike-Mike and Slick.

"Wassup fools!?" he exclaimed animatedly as if they hadn't seen each other in years.

"What's good wit' you fool!?" Mike-Mike shot back.

"It's too early to be all hyper and shit!" Slick added.

"Y'all know me, I'm out here gettin' it while it's good," Andy replied. "Damn, it smells like y'all just finished burnin' down a weed branch or something!" he commented.

"Yeah, dat's dat 'loud pack' we just finished smokin'," Mike-Mike confirmed. "You want a jay of this shit?"

"Hell yeah! Y'all know I ain't turnin' nothin' down, but

da music when I'm dirty, and da police around, ya dig!"

"I can dig it," Mike-Mike responded. "Ay, you seen Zoe, 'cause I'm s'posed to be meetin' him?"

"Yeah, he just pulled off before y'all drove up. He should be on da next street over."

"You straight, 'cause I'ma push over here, so I can holler at him real quick."

"Yeah, I'm straight, and good lookin' on da smoke. I'll catch up wit' y'all later," replied Andy, giving them both a pound.

"Dat's a bet," Mike-Mike replied, pulling off driving over to the next street, so he could meet Zoe.

Once he turned on to the street, he immediately spotted Zoe standing next to a burgundy 2013 *SL500* Mercedes Benz. He parked, then waited patiently for Zoe to finish his conversation with someone else.

"Dat nigga keeps a different whip!" commented Slick, admiring the Benz from a distance.

"Anybody wit' eyes can see dat," Mike-Mike shot-back just as Zoe signaled for him to come on over. "I'll be right back," he informed Slick.

"Bet!" said Slick, leaning his seat back, waiting for his partner's return.

"Slim, you killin''em wit' that Benz, plus you dressed like you 'bout to be nominated for an Oscar or somethin'," Mike-Mike complimented, extending his hand.

"Yeah, I'm on my way to a business meetin', so a nigga had to get fly for that. You right on time though. Now I shouldn't be late," he responded, returning the handshake.

Zoe was decorated in an Ermenegildo Zegna Couture

dark-grey, tailor-made suit that hugged his physique perfectly, giving him a distinctive appeal fit for a businessman. Slyly passing Mike-Mike a piece of folded paper, he inquired, "Do you know how to get out to Briggs Chaney?"

"Yeah, I know my way out there," Mike-Mike validated.

"Good, 'cause that needs to be taken care of tonight, and I have somethin' extra for you when it's done. A'ight!?"

"Say no more. I'll hit you when it's done."

"A'ight, that's cool. Talk to you later," Zoe replied, ending their brief discussion.

"That's a bet, slim," Mike-Mike responded, heading back to his vehicle.

Slick lifted his seat back up, right away asking what Zoe had said once Mike-Mike got back into the car. Mike-Mike simply pulled out the piece of paper that Zoe had given him and passed it over to him.

"It's an address for a green Yukon *XL*," conveyed Slick, after reading what was written on the paper.

"A Green Yukon, huh?" Mike-Mike suspiciously thought out loud.

"Dat's a first. He ain't never gave us no address before, just a make, year, and a model," said Slick.

"I was thinkin' da same thing, plus he said he'll give us somethin' extra when it's done."

"Shid, that's all I needed to hear, 'cause like I said, I need some extra bread. Hopefully, da extra he's talkin' 'bout is worth the extra I need to handle all this extra shit, besides, we ain't doin' nothin' no different from what we been doin'. Takin' da vehicle and droppin' it off like any other time; work ain't hard."

"You might be right, plus I doubt if slim will put us in harm's way," Mike-Mike summarized.

"I doubt it, too."

"Let's get this money then. Twist some more of that dat 'loud' up!" Mike-Mike shot back while driving onto South Dakota Avenue, heading back towards their neighborhood.

CHAPTER 4

Shortly after Zoe departed from his brief meeting with Mike-Mike, he met up with an associate of his at Loriol's Mexican Restaurant, located off 18th and T Street, Northwest, DC. Loriol's Mexican Restaurant was probably one of the most low-key, elegant dining spots in DC, which to some degree, attracted a select group of people. Zoe had already made reservations beforehand, so by the time he arrived, his associates were already there and seated.

"Good evening, Zomil," greeted Mr. Beanson as he stood up to embrace him.

"Mr. Beanson! How are you this evening?" Zomil replied, returning the friendly gesture. "Sorry to keep you waiting, but you know how the traffic can be."

"Sure, no problem," Mr. Beanson responded, unbothered. "This here is one of my colleagues, Mr. Leaman. Mr. Leaman this is a good associate of mine, Zomil," he said, introducing the two of them.

"Pleased to meet you and this is my business partner Herm," Zoe politely made the introduction before they all shook hands and sat down.

"This is a lovely place!" admired Mr. Beanson.

"Thank you. A lady friend of mine introduced me to this spot some time ago."

"She definitely has good taste."

"I would like to think so," Zoe smiled.

The two parties conversed for almost an hour before getting to the heart of the matter.

"So, I take it that my order was fulfilled?" inquired Mr. Beanson.

"Have I ever let you down before?" Zoe shot back. "We do live in reference to our past experience, and not our future events, correct?"

"Point taken," Mr. Beanson agreed.

"I like to look at our business relationship sort of like a vehicle, neither one can function without human assistance," stated Zoe. He flashed Mr. Beanson a tiny smile and then passed him a set of car keys and a valet ticket.

Mr. Beanson surreptitiously grabbed the set of keys and slid them to his colleague Mr. Leaman, who got up and left to inspect the vehicle. Moments later, Mr. Beanson received a call indicating that everything had checked out. He instantly reached into his inner blazer pocket and pulled out an envelope. He passed it over to Zoe, returning the smile from earlier.

"I take it that your needs have been met," said Zoe, receiving the envelope.

"As always," he assured him. "It's all there, like you

requested."

"I don't have to count it to make sure, do I?" Zoe threw back at him.

"If you like, but like you stated, we live in reference to our past experience, and not our future events," he reminded.

Zoe smiled and said, "Point taken!" He extended his hand to complete their business deal. "It has always been a pleasure doing business with you, but now that our dealings are done, I do have other matters to which I must attend," he stated, having just sold the same burgundy *SL500* Mercedes Benz that Mike-Mike had seen him standing next to during their brief meeting.

"My time is also up," Mr. Beanson admitted, glancing at his watch. "I guess you don't need for me to drop you off anywhere?"

"I'm okay, but if you ever need anything else, don't hesitate to call, and I hope you enjoy your new toy."

'I'm sure that I will.''

"I'm sure that you will, also," Zoe replied, as he stood and shook Mr. Beanson's hand once again before departing and going his separate way.

Zoe and his partner Big Herm left the restaurant, found the valet attendant, and passed him another ticket. Zoe always stayed five steps ahead. When he'd made reservations earlier that day, he also had Big Herm follow him to stash another vehicle in the garage just in case everything went as planned, which it did. Shortly after the valet received the ticket, he emerged from the garage driving an all black-on-black *CL550* Mercedes Benz. Once the attendant pulled up, he got out with the biggest smile on his face, from admiring the luxury vehicle. "Nice ride," he complimented while holding the driver's door open so that Zoe could get in.

"Thanks!" Zoe smirked, giving the valet a decent tip before getting in, followed by Big Herm, who jumped in the passenger's side, and pulling off.

CHAPTER 5

Later that night, Mike-Mike and Slick were on their way to complete their assignment. It was 11:30, and the first thing they did after finding the address they were looking for was to wait for the right opportunity to accomplish their goal. After circling the block several times, the pair patiently waited until the coast was clear, so they wouldn't be detected while performing their task. Once they were satisfied, the two began what they set out to do. They had stolen a Nissan *Maxima* earlier that evening to use while driving to the Yukon S.U.V. that they were about to take. Slick immediately reached under his passenger seat and retrieved a screwdriver and a "slim jim" to equip himself for the task at hand.

"Them white boys in dat movie, *Gone in Sixty Seconds*, ain't got nothin' on me!" Slick bragged. "Watch this!" he said before getting out.

"Yeah, I hear you!" Mike-Mike replied. "Just hurry up. I'll be on da corner waitin' for you, so I can follow behind."

"Bet!" Slick confirmed, closing the door and heading towards the S.U.V.

Mike-Mike pulled off, parking near the corner as promised. Once Slick approached the S.U.V., he quickly whipped out the "slim jim", slid it between the crease of the window seal and the door panel, then moved it around until he found the spot he was searching for.

"Bingo," he whispered, unlocking the vehicle.

But when he pulled forward, the alarm system sounded shutting the power down. After several attempts of trying to open the door, he finally realized that the alarm system was causing the door's lock to automatically re-engage. It didn't take him long to figure out a way to time it perfectly, so he could get in. However, by the time he did, a man was standing in his doorway pointing a handgun directly toward the S.U.V., demanding that he move away. Slick looked up after hearing the man's voice, and his heart rate jumped as his eyes locked in on the weapon in the man's hand.

He tried to jump into the S.U.V. just as the owner opened fire, letting off several rounds. The shells that struck the truck nearly panicked Slick, but somehow, he quickly gained his composure, started the truck, and sped off as the owner continued to hit the truck with a rain of bullets. Mike-Mike heard the shots and was on his way to make sure that his partner was okay when he noticed the Yukon bending the corner, hurtling toward him. Mike-Mike was relieved to see Slick driving past. He took a deep breath and trailed behind him. Once Slick made the left turn onto Colesville Road, he immediately observed the damage that was done to the side of the vehicle. Mike-Mike instantly knew the S.U.V. wasn't any good to Zoe in that condition, and to make matters worse, Slick was speeding on a heavily patrolled Colesville Road with no headlights.

"Shit!" Mike-Mike shouted, knowing if they didn't get off the main road that they were sure to be seen by the authorities.

He quickly started to click the headlights of the stolen *Maxima*, hoping to get Slick's attention so that he could at least turn on his headlights, but he never responded. After speeding past several vehicles, Mike-Mike decided to take a different approach by speeding up next to him to get his attention, but as soon as he proceeded to do so, just as predicted, a police cruiser emerged on the opposite side of the road. Slick, speeding without any headlights, immediately caught the officer's attention, who also must have seen the damage to the S.U.V. The squad car wasted no time switching on its sirens in hot pursuit. The officer sped to the nearest intersection, made a U-turn, and headed in their direction.

"Shit! Shit!" Mike-Mike cursed, watching how quickly the police went into pursuit. "Slick, you drive dat mutha-fuckin' truck!" he barked to himself while noticing that Slick too was slightly swerving on the road.

Mike-Mike glanced through his rearview and saw that the squad car was slowly gaining on them. Mike-Mike continuously started tapping his horn and flickering his lights once more to get Slick's attention, so he would speed up. At the rate they were driving, the two were surely going to get caught. He saw that the police cruiser was rapidly approaching and started to panic, not from fear, but from not knowing what to do since his partner was driving as if they weren't being chased.

"Dat truck gotta be faster than dat!" he shouted, knowing that it was only a matter of time before other squad cars joined the pursuit.

Once again, he decided to pull alongside of Slick to tell him to abandon the S.U.V. and hop in with him so that they would have a better chance of getting away. Suddenly, out of nowhere, the truck drifted into the far-left lane, then back into the middle. The sudden shift in driving caused Mike-Mike to brake, and the police to get even closer.

"This can't be happening," Mike-Mike spoke out loud, damn near riding on Slick's bumper.

The next time Mike-Mike glanced through his rear-view mirror, the squad car was about thirty yards behind and closing in fast. By the time he focused on what was ahead of him, Slick was swerving off the road and onto an open field on his right-hand side. He came to a complete halt as he collided with a brick sign and a bundle of bushes. At that very moment, with no other option, Mike-Mike braced himself and slammed on the brakes, causing the speeding police car to smash into the rear of the stolen *Maxima*. The impact from the collision sent the *Maxima* spinning out of control about forty feet from where Slick had crashed.

After about fifteen seconds of blacking out, Mike-Mike suddenly sprung up, got himself together, and exited the wrecked vehicle. Safely, out of the car, he glanced over towards the police cruiser but didn't see any signs of movement. He sprinted over to the S.U.V. that Slick was in, pulled the driver's door open, and saw that Slick was passed out, slumped halfway over in the passenger seat. He wasted no time moving Slick's body all the way over to the passenger side. Then he jumped into the driver's seat, threw the truck into reverse, and peeled rubber. When he was clear, he slammed the gearshift back into drive and skidded away from the scene.

Mike-Mike fled just in the nick of time because shortly after several police cruisers swarmed the area. But, luckily for them, they managed to escape the scene without further incident.

CHAPTER 6

At 12:42 a.m., a continuous pounding came from the back door of the house.

"What in God's name!" shouted the male individual, awakening from out of his sleep.

"Someone's banging on our back door, honey!" his alarmed wife spat back, obviously shaken.

"Go in the room with the kids and stay there!" he instructed.

Without waiting for her to comply, he jumped up from his bed, rushed over to the closet, and retrieved his .38 revolver from the top shelf. Exiting the room, he headed for the back door, his pistol leading the way.

"Dr. Whitaker!"

Bang! Bang! Bang!

"Dr. Whitaker!" a voice sounded from the opposite side of the door.

Who is that at this time of night, Dr. Whitaker thought thinking the voice sounded familiar, but he couldn't quite place who it belonged to. He stood next to the door as if he were Malcolm X himself, and with one swift motion, he swung the door open and aimed his gun.

"Michael!" Dr. Whitaker exclaimed as he focused in on Mike-Mike and the wounded person he had in his arms.

"Dr. Whitaker, please, we need your help!" Mike-Mike anxiously uttered, stepping into the house.

Dr. Whitaker tucked his handgun away and ushered the two into his basement.

"What happened?" inquired, Dr. Whitaker.

"My friend's been shot!" Mike-Mike replied frantically.

In the midst of everything that had taken place, Mike-Mike had panicked and driven straight to Dr. Whitaker's home. Hysterical from the chain of events, he assumed that he was doing the right thing, but what was wrong was the fact that Dr. Whitaker wasn't a surgeon. He was a dentist who knew nothing about treating gunshot victims.

"Why did you bring him here?" the dentist questioned. "This boy needs to get to the hospital right away!"

"You're a doctor, right?" Mike-Mike nervously asked.

"I'm a dentist!" he corrected. "Time is wasting. If you don't get him some help soon, he might not make it!"

"Is there anything you can do?"

"Yeah. Call an ambulance!" he shot back.

"I don't think dat's a good idea," Mike-Mike sadly remarked.

"I don't think you have a choice, Michael."

"Honey, is everything alright down there?" Dr. Whitaker's wife yelled down from the top of the stairs.

"I can't be around when they get here," Mike-Mike

admitted.

"Look! You get out of here, and I'll think of something to say to them when they arrive, but we're running out of time. He's already lost a great deal of blood!"

"Honey, is everything okay!" his wife shouted for the second time.

"Yes, baby!" Dr. Whitaker answered. "And call 911 for an ambulance! Quick and don't come down here!" he ordered.

"Okay," she responded, rushing off to do as she was told.

"You can't tell my mother about this!" Mike-Mike expressed with profound concern in his voice.

"I won't, just as long as you promise to never show up here at my home again under these circumstances," he ordered. "Do we understand each other?"

"Yes sir," he confirmed.

"Good. Now get out of here, before they show up."

"Thanks," Mike-Mike replied.

Taking one last look at his partner and telling him to hang in there, he stormed out of the house. Shortly after, an ambulance showed up along with the authorities, asking all sorts of questions.

Mike-Mike sat in the play yard of his old school looking on as the police ushered Slick off into the ambulance. Dr. Whitaker stayed directly across the street from Takoma Elementary, which was within walking distance from Mike-Mike's house. He stayed put until the police left and then went on his way.

Afterward, Mike-Mike found a stash spot that was

inconspicuous enough to temporarily park the damaged S.U.V. then hiked back to his house. Finally making it home, he crept in through the back door to avoid being seen by his mother who would've surely thrown a fit if she saw the blood-stained clothes he had on. Once he made it in safely, he immediately snatched off his bloody clothing and threw them in a trash bag, promising himself to get rid of them the following morning. After changing, he found himself pacing the floor, wondering about his right-hand man. He continuously paced back and forth, worry nagging at him, causing him to be stressed. Before long, his head began to thump so hard that he predicted a severe migraine might be coming on. What would he do if Slick didn't make it? About an hour later, questions still unanswered, he eventually sat down and just stared at the wall until he ultimately passed out from mental exhaustion.

CHAPTER 7

When Mike-Mike woke up the following morning, he quickly freshened up and rushed out of the house to hit the street. A block away he ran into his mother who was walking home from the grocery store.

"I didn't know you were in the house, 'cause I didn't see your car outside," she told him.

"That's because Slick dropped me off last night, but I'm about to go get it now," he quickly lied, kissing her on her cheek before speed walking down an alley toward Georgia Avenue.

Once he entered his safehaven, he walked straight to Monique's apartment. She was one of the little females in the neighborhood that everyone was cool with. She wasn't the prettiest, but her attitude and the way she carried herself made her alluring. She had brown skin, silky dark, shoulder-length hair, stood about five-foot-seven, and weighed around 140 lbs. One thing for sure, her door was always open to the main folks in the neighborhood. Mike-Mike was hoping she would be home, so he could ask for a ride to pick up his vehicle.

He walked up to her place and knocked on the door.

"Who is it?" she asked from behind the door.

"It's me, Mike-Mike!"

"Boy, what you want?" Monique asked when she opened the door with a smile on her face.

"Who you callin' boy?" he teased as he stepped in. "Stop playin' wit' me. Look where's your car, I need a ride to where I left my car."

"First of all, where's your manners? And second of all, my car is parked on the side, because I'm not going nowhere. I'm trying to enjoy my me-time, since the kids are over their father's house for the first time since God knows when!" she replied, throwing her hands in the air as if to say, *Thank you, Jesus!* "And I'm trying to relax while they are gone. Thank you!"

"Look, I'm sorry for interrupting your me-time, but this is jive like an emergency," Mike-Mike responded sternly.

It didn't take Monique long to give in after seeing the seriousness in his eyes.

"I can't stand your ass," she hissed, a tidbit annoyed from being barged in on. "Where's your car at? And you better have some gas money!"

"Damn, I love you too. Anyway, I parked it by Rhode Island and Eastern Avenue on the Mount Rainer side near an alley directly behind where Bass liquor store used to be."

"Why you leave your car all the way over there!" she said, making more of a statement than a question.

"You' actin' like it's far. It's only about fifteen minutes away. Plus, I had my man B-Bo keep an eye on it for me while I took care of somethin'."

"I'ma hurt you! Let me grab my keys," Monique said, walking into her room to get her purse.

"Don't act like dat," Mike-Mike said to her, after seeing her facial expression once she came back from the room, storming past him like she had an attitude.

"Come on!" she spat back as they left her apartment.

Once the two got in her vehicle, he glanced at her and saw that she looked bothered. So he asked her if she was mad at him.

"Not if you said it was an emergency," she replied. "I just barely get any time to myself. You know with the kids and all," she continued as she pulled out of her parking spot.

"I'll make it up to you, and dat's a promise."

"I'ma hold you to that," she laughed, glancing at him with that friendly smile he was so used to seeing from her.

Feeling somewhat relieved, Mike-Mike laid back after realizing she wasn't holding any grudges toward him. As soon as he started to relax, his mind focused back on his partner Slick's well-being. The unknown kept him silent for most of the ride. His absence of sound made Monique inquire whether he was alright or not.

"Yeah, I'm cool, just got something heavy on my mind, dat's all," he conveyed to her.

"Anything that I could help you with?" she inquired.

"Naw, you doin' enough by takin' me to get my car," Mike-Mike assured while pulling his phone out to make a call.

Thinking about Slick made him think to call Zoe, who

answered almost immediately.

"I been waitin' to hear from you," Zoe answered.

"We need to talk, 'cause things ain't go right."

"Where are you now?"

"By Mount Rainier, gettin' dropped off at my car as we speak," Mike-Mike informed him.

"You not even ten minutes from where I'm at. Come to the Stadium Club, off Bladensburg Road," he instructed.

"Bet! I'll be there in a minute," Mike-Mike confirmed.

"I'll see you when you get here."

Mike-Mike was hanging up simultaneous to pulling up to his vehicle. He handed Monique twenty dollars, then thanked her for the ride as he got out.

"Hey, you're welcome, and when are you going to let me drive that pretty car of yours?" she asked.

"I got you soon."

"I'ma hold you to that, too," she smiled.

"I'm a man of my word, so you won't be holdin' on too long," he countered, shutting the door and walking over to his own car.

Mike-Mike knew where the Stadium Club was located, but before today he had never stepped foot in the establishment. As he made it to his destination and found a parking spot, he called Zoe to inform him that he was outside and that he didn't have any identification on him. Zoe told him that he would meet him out front and not to worry. Once Mike-Mike got to the door, Zoe was already standing there to usher him inside. As the pair took a seat, Zoe immediately inquired about what transpired the night before.

"Everything went wrong," Mike-Mike confided.

He was reluctant to go into detail until he was done checking his surroundings for potential eavesdroppers.

"So y'all didn't get the truck?"

"Yeah! I got da truck. But..."

"But what? It's okay, you can talk freely, no one can hear us from here," Zoe assured, noticing Mike-Mike's uneasiness.

Mike-Mike nodded, then went into detail about the prior night's events, especially in regard to what happened to his partner.

"I most definitely didn't mean for anything to happen to you or your man, but you must understand that this is a game where anything can transpire at any moment. You just have to be prepared for it," Zoe explained.

"How we s'posed to be prepared for somethin' we wasn't put on point about?" he countered. "We was basically left in the blind, and dat could've cost one of us our life. Til this very moment, I still don't know da outcome for my man!"

"I clearly understand where you comin' from, but I can't change what happened. So my question to you is, what is it that you want from me, 'cause I still need that truck, shot up or not."

"What I want..." Mike-Mike let the thought hang until he realized that the truck must have some type of value for Zoe to still want it, and that's when he decided to tell him that he wanted half of whatever dealings he had with the

Yukon, or else he'd burn it and leave it where it was. He expressed it just like that to Zoe before he added, 'Cause whatever business connection you have with dat truck ain't more valuable than me or my man losin' our lives over!" He fixed his attention on Zoe with an uncompromising stare.

Zoe gave him an expressionless glare as he absorbed everything Mike-Mike had just conveyed to him. Finally, he spoke, "I like you and always have," he said, leaning back in his seat. "You basically leaving me with no choice, but now what I want to know from you is, are you sure that you ready to jump into the big league?" Zoe stared deep into Mike-Mike's eyes, searching for certainty.

Mike-Mike felt a bit jittery at Zoe's question because he wasn't sure of what Zoe was actually into, but he stood his ground, nodding his head in approval.

"It's official then, you asked, you receive. No more petty car stealing," Zoe declared, extending his hand to seal the deal.

"What's next?" Mike-Mike asked, returning the handshake to confirm his readiness.

"Can you get the truck to my body shop off Bladensburg Road?"

"Yeah, but I have to wait until late night to be on the safe side."

"Cool," Zoe agreed, passing him an envelope.

"This feels a lil' thicker than usual," he commented.

"I got to keep my word, I did tell you that I was going to look out for you once the task was done. Plus, now that we are going in a whole different direction, I need for you to buy yourself something nice to wear and meet me at Sequoria's Restaurant on the waterfront in Georgetown tomorrow night. Be there by nine o'clock, and I suggest that you bring a lady friend. It'll be nice," Zoe smiled.

"I'll be there," Mike- Mike assured him. "You think you can order us a drink before I leave?" he asked, feeling as if too much was coming his way; way too fast.

"No problem," Zoe responded, signaling for the waitress to come over.

"Thanks," Mike-Mike said. *'Cause I could sure use it,* he mentally added.

CHAPTER 8

On his way back uptown, Mike-Mike was feeling a bit inebriated after sharing a few drinks with Zoe. As he was leaving the Stadium Club, he received a call from one of Slick's female friends, who told him that Slick had pulled through and was doing fine. She tried to ask Mike-Mike what happened, but he quickly denied knowing anything. Hearing that his road-dog had pulled through was music to his ears, and now he was hoping to have a clearer viewpoint on what was in store for him in the future with his recent commitment to Zoe.

As he turned onto Brentwood Road from New York Avenue, he started thinking about the meeting he had the next day and who he was going to allow to accompany him to the restaurant. He did a mental inventory, and his mind landed on this one female by the name of Tia, who he had known since middle school. Tia was petite, light skinned with short dark hair, and stood 5'7", at least. She closely resembled the singer Keri Hilson. Since middle school, her personality had always remained the same, which was sweet, sexy, and classy and Mike-Mike had always admired her for those traits. What you saw is what you got, and what you saw was definitely someone you would want to get with. He chose her to be his date because he knew that she would know how to conduct herself no matter what. He pulled his cell phone out to give her a call and invite her to dinner the following night.

"Hey you," Tia purred, picking up the phone.

"How you been, beautiful?" Mike-Mike complimented.

"Working and looking forward to finally getting my own place."

"So, how's dat coming along?"

"What, as far as my job, or finding my own place?"

"Both."

Tia laughed. "Well, as far as my job goes, everything's been going perfect, because can't too many people actually say that they have a job they enjoy. I love doing what I do, so for me, it's perfect. But as far as finding my own place, it's a slow process because I'm not sure what area I want to actually move to," she explained.

"So you ready to be on ya own, huh?"

"I'm grown and it's time for me to have my own space. That's all."

"You going to invite me over?" he asked.

"Why wouldn't I?" she questioned.

"Maybe 'cause one of your male friends might be tryin' to handcuff you."

"Handcuff me," she scoffed. "You should know me better than that. Can't nobody handcuff me unless I allow them to, and right now I'm not trying to be shackled down. I'm focused on me," she expressed. "But enough about me.

Why haven't I heard from you, stranger?"

"It wasn't on purpose. It's just dat a lot's been goin' on lately, dat's all, but I want to make it up to you by takin' you out tomorrow night for dinner if you not busy!" he invited.

"So are you asking me out?" she inquired, just to make sure.

"Yes, I am," he confirmed.

"Well, let me see," she said, contemplating for a few seconds.

"I think that would be nice, and hopefully we can get each other caught up on what's been happening with one another since the last time we talked."

"I was thinking da same thing."

"Well, I guess it's true when they say two great minds think alike," she quoted. "What did you have in mind, and what time should I be expecting you?"

"It's a nice spot in Georgetown that someone put me up on. You should be expectin' me around eight o'clock," he informed.

"Sounds nice. I'll make sure to be ready by the time you get here," she assured him.

"I guess I'll see you tomorrow then."

"Guess so," she replied, her smile bleeding through the phone.

"Call you when I'm on my way."

"You do that," she said seductively.

"I most definitely will," Mike-Mike shot back. "Bye, beautiful."

"Bye," she said, before hanging up.

Once he hung up, his next thought was what he was going to wear. Then he quickly remembered Zoe passing him an envelope stuffed with U.S. currency. But how much was the question, so he pulled over to check the amount inside.

"Five stacks!" Mike-Mke mouthed to himself. *It's definitely time to do some shopping*, he thought.

Mike-Mike considered rerouting to Georgetown to shop, but quickly dismissed the idea after deciding to drive to Neiman Marcus on Wisconsin Avenue. It was a closer drive and had a better, more unique selection of what he had in mind at the moment. With his decision made, he drove the back streets until he got to Military Road, taking it straight to Wisconsin Avenue. Finally, making it to his destination, Mike-Mike parked in a parking garage and made his way into the store. Within minutes of walking in, he bumped into a Caucasian female in her mid-twenties. She worked there in the store and asked him if he needed any help finding anything. He stared momentarily, her attractiveness catching him off guard, before responding to her question.

"Sure, why not," Mike-Mike responded.

"Anything particular you're looking to buy?"

"Umh…," he said as he briefly thought. "Somethin' soft but noticeable," he hinted, showing her some casual pieces he was interested in.

"Well, that depends on your spending limit," she said, brows arching upwards, with a tiny smile playing on her lips.

"Ugh!" he grumbled.

"What's that supposed to mean?" she asked, drawing back.

"Oh, dat's just my Master P impersonation, simply 'cause there's no limit to da money I'm spending," he tossed back at her, trying to play big, not knowing that she was about to knock a huge dent in his pocket. "But I will say, never buy what you want just because it's cheap, 'cause it won't mean anything to you," he smiled.

Though he looked young, she still admired his style and couldn't help but smile at his comment.

"Well then, right this way, Master P," she said, turning to lead the way.

As she turned her back toward him to lead the way, Mike-Mike lustfully gazed at her voluptuous figure. She had long, silky brunette hair that stopped at the tip of her curvy rear end that was built to stand next to any competitor and give them a run for their money. The tight fitted dress she wore hugged her hips and dipped low in the front, exposing enough cleavage to entertain any man. She led the way to different sections, picking out various items, piecing everything together, starting with the shoes. Once everything was finalized, he ended up with a pair of all black Prada high-top perforated sneakers, a matching perforated belt, a black short sleeve Michael Kors Edition shirt, some faded blue denim jeans, a black Prada light-weight nylon jacket, and a black Brera Round Digital Sport watch with a perforated band to help complement the other accessories. The second outfit consisted of a pair of brown and red striped suede Prada low-cut sneakers, a W. Kleinberg suede crocodile belt, and a Red Band Burberry chronograph watch to furnish the second outfit.

"Hope you like what I picked out for you," the floor assistant politely remarked.

"I must say dat you have good taste," Mike-Mike complimented.

"I'm glad that you like it. So will that be all today?"

"Yeah, unless you think dat there's a good chance dat I could at least get your name, and hopefully your number?" he slid in, trying to make his move.

"My name is Emily Widger as stated on my name tag," she said, pointing to the nameplate. "But my number isn't an option. Besides you seem a little too young for me."

"Too young," he repeated. "So you going to do me like dat?" he asked, looking at her somewhat disappointedly. "I'll tell you what...," he paused briefly, "let me go find my parents and see if they willin' to pay for these lovely outfits. You know, the ones you took the time to pick out for me. 'Cause I'm sure someone my age shouldn't be walkin' around with enough money to pay for them," he calmly remarked, turning to leave.

He watched her facial expression go from simple to deflated after thinking that she had just wasted her time choosing those items for nothing. But then he turned around, telling her that he was only joking. A sense of relief stretched across her face when he ordered her to take the items to the counter so that he could pay for everything.

When the two reached the counter, she rang up everything, which came up to a grand total of $4,493, only to get a vacant expression out of him.

"It's 4,493 dollars for two outfits!" he blurted out. "Sweetheart, at first I was jokin', but this time I'm serious. I can't afford this," he uttered seriously, noticing her displeased reaction as he turned to walk away for the second time.

"Sir, are you serious!" she clamored.

"Naw, I'm just messin' wit' you," Mike-Mike smiled, turning back around, "but I would've been wrong if I was serious, huh?" he questioned. "Just like you wrong for assuming dat I'm too young for you, but it's cool 'cause I think you afraid of da dark anyway. Plus, without me buyin' all this name brand stuff, I still sport da world's most eye-catchin' attire."

"And what may that be?"

"A look of confidence," he responded, then paid for the items and calmly walked away, leaving her standing there with a curious look on her face.

CHAPTER 9

Shortly after Mike-Mike left from meeting Zoe, his partner Big Herm showed up to accompany him at the Stadium Club. After being seated they held a discussion about an earlier conversation between Zoe and Mike-Mike. As they were chit-chatting, a female by the name of Viagra approached their table, wearing little to nothing, flirting, hoping to entice one of the two men that stood before her. She stood between them, spun around, then used her ass muscles to make her juicy butt bounce up and down as if each cheek had its own heartbeat.

"You sure know how to work them ass muscles, huh!" Big Herm flirted, giving her a tip.

"I know how to work this tongue even better," she commented enticingly, licking her lips.

"Is that right?"

"Mmh...hm," she assured him, giving him that seductive look that women do when they are ready to give into the man of their choice.

"I'm definitely trying to be the judge of that someday."

"You know how to find me," she told him before

directing her attention towards Zoe.

"How you doing today, Zoe? You not speaking?"

"How you doin', Viagra? I didn't want to be rude and interrupt what you and Fat boy had goin', that's all."

Zoe chatted with her for a few more seconds, then sent her on her way so that he and Big Herm could finish their discussion.

"So like you was saying, you sure youngin' can handle being put in that type of position?" Big Herm inquired once Viagra was out of earshot.

"I think he's hungry as a hippo and got a heart of a lion," Zoe replied.

"I hear you, but life is a game you don't get a cheat sheet for, you feel me?"

"I hear you, but any movement requires a team, and if your team is structured right, then the sky's the limit."

"I'm all for it since you seem to have your mind already made up, but what happens if he messes up?"

"You of all people should know that I don't believe in second chances, 'cause if you mess up once, then you'll fuck up again. I'm basically placing the ball in his hand to see if he gon' fumble or hold on and run wit' it. The good thing about all of this is if he just happens to fumble, we not taking a loss regardless."

"Ho... ho...hold up just a minute. Let me stop you right there!" Big Herm cut in. "Free or not, that's a lot of product to throw away!" he corrected. "I could've dumped that shit A.S.A.P. and made us a quick 300 stacks apiece."

"Yeah, but I'm not thinkin' about the now, I'm thinkin' 'bout da later, and you know what else?"

"What's that?"

"Youngin jive stepped to me gangsta like he had control. I liked that shit, but what he didn't know was what he was asking for. I had already planned on givin' him more to do in the first place," Zoe enunciated.

"Shorty got potential, huh?" said Big Herm.

"Yeah, I think so," Zoe assured him.

"Only time will tell then."

"I guess so, but what's done is done. Let's get outta here, so we can get everything in motion before he drops that truck off later," Zoe instructed as the two got up from their seats and proceeded to leave the establishment.

CHAPTER 10

Mike-Mike's mother was in a good mood. She had already finished cooking dinner and had her oldies-but-goodies playing as she cleaned the house. She had already straightened up upstairs when she decided to go into the basement to clean Mike-Mike's room.

"This boy got stuff everywhere," she muttered to herself, picking up some of his clothes that were lying around on his bed and floor.

She couldn't believe how messy his room was, it was as if a tornado had passed through. As she was cleaning, she stopped and looked at some old photos of him and his sister and couldn't help but get teary-eyed as she reflected on her precious daughter and the memorable times they had. After a brief moment of sorrow, she went back to cleaning his room when she stumbled across something that not only rattled her, but deeply disturbed her as well.

CHAPTER 11

Later that evening, Mike-Mike went to switch vehicles. He parked his Lexus, then hopped back into his Chrysler and found himself back at Monique's apartment. Nightfall was nearing, and he was basically killing time until he was comfortable enough to transport the stolen Yukon to its destination. His main concern was changing locations of the damaged SUV without being detected by the authorities. So while he sat there in Monique's living room he tried to figure out the safest route to take. After Mike-Mike offered Monique $200, she was more than willing to follow him to his destination. They'd gotten so caught up in their conversation that Mike-Mike hadn't realized how much time had passed.

"Damn, it's ten-twenty already," he remarked, glancing at his watch. "You ready?" he asked Monique, to which she answered by nodding her head and simply getting up to retrieve her keys.

He had the stolen truck stashed away in a secluded parking lot that only a handful of residents used off of

Butternut Street. Shortly after, the two of them pulled up to the corner where the truck was located.

"It's a green Yukon, so when you see me flick my headlights, just stay close behind and don't allow no one to separate us," he directed before getting out.

"Okay," Monique replied.

Moments later, he appeared in the Yukon, flicked his lights twice and then pulled off into the night.

"What in the hell!" Monique exclaimed after seeing the damaged vehicle, but she kept her thoughts to herself as she trailed behind like she was asked to do.

Mike-Mike cautiously drove on the back streets to avoid any encounter with the law. He knew Monique was probably a bit nervous after seeing the dismantled SUV, so he made sure to take precautions while they traveled. Everything was going smoothly until they got halfway to their destination.

Out of nowhere, just as they came upon a four-way stop sign, a police cruiser came to a halt on Mike-Mike's right-hand side. Luckily for him, the officer couldn't see the damage from that angle. Mike-Mike calmly drove through the stop sign, hoping the officer continued straight through. Unfortunately for him, the officer made a right turn behind him, he and there wasn't anything Monique could have done to prevent the situation because the officer had the right-of-way. After observing the officer turn behind him, immediately became a bit nervous, and started rubbing his perspiring hands against his jeans while trying to decide whether he should run or just see what would happen. After driving a few blocks with the officer never turning off, he figured that he might be running his tags. That thought alone caused his heart to slam against his chest so rapidly that it was no wonder it wasn't visible through his shirt.

"Shit!" he cursed, getting ready to step on the gas and try to elude the police before more showed up.

Then, just as he expected, the officer must have run his tags, because he turned on the red and blues indicating for him to pull over. As he came up on the next stop sign, he heard a loud crash out of nowhere. His eyes shot to the rear-view mirror, where he saw that Monique had rammed into the back of the police cruiser.

The officer immediately stopped, and Mike-Mike took the opportunity to quickly turn off the street, speeding away from the scene, hoping that everything with Monique would turn out okay. He instantly called Zoe to inform him of what had just happened, and also to convey to his people at the garage to have the door open so that he could pull right in.

I owe her big time for that, he thought as he rushed towards the lot. Minutes later he was turning onto the street and whipping the truck into the garage unnoticed. Zoe's workers immediately closed the door after allowing Mike-Mike to enter. Once inside, he hopped out and tossed the keys to one of the workers, who quickly told Mike-Mike to follow him into one of the offices. The worker called Zoe on a secure line and passed the phone over to Mike-Mike. Zoe got all of Monique's information, then told him that he was going to handle everything from there. He also informed him that one of his workers would take him wherever he needed to go.

"Good lookin," said Mike-Mike, feeling a bit relieved that Zoe was so quick to get on top of the situation.

"Don't mention it," Zoe replied and then hung up so he could find out if Monique was apprehended or not.

As one of the employees took Mike-Mike to his destination, the others went to work on the truck. The first thing they had to do was remove all the seats. When that was done they used the proper tools that were needed to cut into the SUV's floor panel. Shortly after, the crew found what they were looking for.

"Bingo!" declared one of the workers, pulling its contents, then tossing each one to another worker who then placed each item into a miniature trash bin.

The head worker called Zoe to relay the end result and was told to complete two final tasks before they closed up shop.

CHAPTER 12

Mike-Mike rushed into his mother's house to use the bathroom. On his way, he saw his mother sitting in the living room with the light out, which seemed kind of odd to him. Once he finished using the bathroom, he immediately went to check on her, to make sure she was alright.

"Ma, are you a'ight?" he asked concerned. "Why you sittin' in the dark?" he pried as he sat on the ottoman across from where she was sitting.

That's when he noticed that she had tears in her eyes. She rose her head slowly before speaking, "It's been times I worked two jobs so that you and your sister wouldn't need for anything. I raised y'all practically by myself. I put my wants and needs to the side for the better of you two like I was supposed to do as a mother," she wept, looking towards him with questioning eyes.

"Where is this coming from?" he quizzed, unclear to her reasoning for bringing the conversation up.

"It comes from you lying to me and I don't appreciate it!" she countered sternly.

"Lied to you about what!" Mike-Mike wanted to know,

narrowing his eyes.

"This morning I asked you where your car was, and what did you tell me?"

"I told you it was over Slick's house, and that he dropped me off last night. Is dat what this is all about? Me leavin' my car somewhere?"

"This doesn't have anything to do with you leaving your car someplace else, because it's your car to do as you please. But, this has everything to do with you lying to me with no remorse," she scolded, standing up.

"Ma, I have no idea what you talkin' 'bout," he responded, not understanding her point.

"How can you explain this!" she questioned, storming out of the living room, returning a minute later with a trash bag in her hand before tossing it toward him.

At the first sight of the bag, Mike-Mike immediately knew the contents inside. He instantly felt foolish for being careless by rushing out of the house and not cleaning up behind himself. He just stared at the bag, speechless.

"Now do you want to revise your statement, 'cause not only did I find these clothes, but I talked to Slick's mother, and she told me that he's been hospitalized from gunshot wounds. So, I'm wondering, what's the connection between him being shot and these bloody clothes that are in my house," she chastised, waiting on his response.

Guilt caused him to simply shake his head, but even though he was caught red-handed, the fact of the matter is that he still couldn't reveal the truth to her. He looked up at her and made up a fabricated story about how someone tried to rob them and ended up shooting Slick in the process. Although, him not giving her eye contact, only led her to believe that he was lying once again.

"Boy, I raised you, so don't think for a second that I don't know when you're lying to me. So since you can't be straight with me, I only have one thing to say to you," she hesitated as a river of tears once again began to pour from its bank. "If you're careless enough to make decisions with consequences that could possibly put us in jeopardy, after what we've been through with your sister, then you're grown enough to be on your own," she fussed, contorting her face with every word that came out of her mouth, causing her to look like a totally different person. "I want you out of my house by the end of the week!"

"Ma, don't..."

"Don't you Ma me, 'cause this house isn't a home for anyone who welcomes the devil with open arms!" she fumed.

"Where I'ma go?" Mike-Mike nervously replied as the tears started to form in his eyes as well.

"You should've thought about that before you made those decisions," his mother countered before walking out of the living room leaving him there in his own thoughts.

CHAPTER 13

The nightmare that jolted Mike-Mike awake was frightening. The realism of the dream made it more terrifying than fending off evil demons. Once again, the flashing images of the vehicle smashing into he and his sister woke him up drenched in sweat. It seemed as if each time he'd jump up around the same time, which was always right before the impact. He quickly rushed into the bathroom to splash some water on his face. Mike-Mike momentarily stared at himself through the mirror, reminding himself of how much he loved his sister, and that he'd also promised to one day avenge her death. His thoughts quickly reverted to his conversation he and his mother had the night before.

He knew that his mother loved him dearly, but he also knew that he devastated her by allowing her to find those bloody clothes in his room. His poor decision led him to getting kicked out of his home and getting put out of his home was leading him further into the lures of the streets. His mother was his everything, which caused him to briefly think about backing away from his street dealings, but his commitment to Zoe led him to think differently.

"Shit, Monique!" he thought out loud, after thinking about Zoe.

He wondered whether she made it out alright from the incident with the police. He rushed out the bathroom to grab his phone when he noticed that he had fifteen missed calls, and ten messages, all from Monique's and Zoe's phones. He called Monique's phone first, only to get her voicemail the two times he tried calling her, then he decided to call Zoe, who instantly answered. After speaking with him briefly, he found out that she was safe and sound. He was informed that the officer had taken it light on her, being that she wasn't under the influence, and didn't have a prior record, but she did have to pay for the damages. Zoe told him that he had someone drop her off.

"Thanks for everything," said Mike-Mike.
"No problem," Zoe retorted before the two ended their call.
Once Mike-Mike hung up, he proceeded to get dressed. After showering and throwing on some clothes, he headed out the door. He hopped in his Chrysler, then drove up the block, parking in the motel parking lot, before footing it across Georgia Avenue into his safe-haven. As he entered, he noticed a few of his associates gathered in the rear of the apartments congregating.

"What's good y'all?" Mike-Mike spoke as he walked up.

Everybody greeted in unison as Lil' Chico continued to roll up his weed.

"Ay, Lil' Chico let me holla at ya?" Mike-Mike called out.

Lil' Chico got up and headed over toward Mike-Mike as he continued to put the finishing touches on his Sour Diesel- filled backwood.

"Yeah, wassup?" replied Lil' Chico as he walked up.

Out of all the adolescents that were gathered, he was considered to be the most developed one who jumped off the porch early. He bought his first car at the age of eleven and was barely tall enough to look over the dashboard. His grandmother, Ms. Welch, was the resident manager of the apartment complex, so Lil' Chico basically did as he pleased in the neighborhood and got away with it. Besides what he got away with, his street credibility was signed, sealed, and stamped.

"Look, I think I got something in the making that's gon' hopefully put us where we need to be," stated Mike-Mike.

"Something like what?" Lil' Chico asked, firing his weed up.

"You a know real soon, but for now I need for you to holla at ya folks and see if I can get one of these vacant apartments," Mike-Mike requested in an all too easy tone.

"I'll see what's up," Lil' Chico replied, blowing out a cloud of smoke.

"It's jive an emergency so get on top that a.s.a.p. fo' me."

"Bet! I'll ask her, right when I go in," Lil' Chico assured him. "You wanna hit this?" he asked, trying to pass him the backwood.

"Yeah, let me tap dat right quick," Mike-Mike accepted, taking the backwood from Lil' Chico and inhaling the intoxicating leaf.

"Dat shit hit good don't it?" smiled Lil' Chico.

"Hell yeah! Good lookin' and let the rest of da homies know I'll holla at 'em later."

"A'ight," he confirmed. "Ay, where da fuck Slick been at, 'cause I haven't seen 'im around?" Lil' Chico questioned.

Mike-Mike didn't want to lie to him, nor did he want to expose the truth, so he threw him out some facts, most of which were fabrications of the truth before he stepped off.

"I'll see you later on," Lil' Chico said as he went to join his homies.

Mike-Mike walked straight to Monique's apartment, hoping that she was there. As he entered the building and headed up the stairs, he started to hear a heated conversation coming from one of the apartments. The closer he got to her door, the more clear-cut the noise became as he was about to knock on her door. After listening for a few seconds, he knew that the person she was arguing with was her baby's father. Since it was a bad time, he decided to just come back to talk with her later. As soon as he turned to walk back down the steps, the door abruptly swung open.

"I don't have time for this shit! I told you something

came up and I'll be back next week to pick them up!" Monique's children's father shouted as he stormed out of her apartment. He made eye-contact with Mike-Mike, giving him a once over before heading down the stairs.

"You sorry son-of-a-bitch! You haven't spent no time with your kids in over three months, and when you finally decide to come to get them, you only kept them for one day, and ain't buy them shit! Fuck you! Don't worry 'bout coming back next week you good for nothing, cheap, sorry excuse for a father!" Monique yelled as he was walking out her building.

"I see I came at a bad time," Mike-Mike said, hating to see her so upset.

"Sorry you had to see that," Monique said, in a faraway tone, feeling a bit embarrassed.

"It's cool, just as long as I didn't walk into no bloodbath, 'cause I know how you can get," he replied, jokingly, trying to soften the blow. "Can I come in?"

"You sure can 'cause you about to get it next!" she threatened, stepping aside to allow him access.

"Shit, I don't know if I want to come in now."

"Boy, get in here!"

"Where da kids at?" he inquired, as he walked in.

"In the room. I hate to act like that around them, but that baby daddy of mine got me mad as shit. He's lucky I'm not one of those females that believes in taking these men to court, 'cause if I were, I would've been hit his ass for child support. I don't ask his ass for nothing except to spend some time with them and buy them things from time to time. He can't even do that," Monique vented.

"Damn, dat's messed up."

"Yes, it is, but you not getting off the hook that easy mister. Because of you, I don't have a car," she quickly announced putting him in the hot seat while waiting on his response.

"I mean dat's da reason I'm here; to not just tell you how thankful I am for what you did but to also tell you dat I owe you big time. I'm goin' to make it up to you real soon. I promise," he said meekly.

"So, I'm just supposed to sit around and wait on you, huh!" she said, waving her hands as if swatting flies. "What if I have an emergency, or my kids get sick or something, huh!" she folded her arms defiantly.

"Trust me, I know, and I understand all of dat, just give me a couple of days," he assured her.

"A couple of days, huh," she replied, trying to sound offended as she hid the grin on her face, knowing the whole time she wasn't really mad at him. She knew that he was going to find a way to rectify the situation, so instead of continuing to give him a penetrating look, she formed a smile on her face.

"So, you not mad at me?" he asked in nearly a whisper, noticing the grin on her face.

"No, 'cause it's not the end of the world. We only human with mortal flaws. I'm just glad that I didn't get hurt, and you didn't go to jail. My car can be replaced."

He immediately felt relieved after hearing her remark.

"You got a credit card?" Mike-Mike asked her.

"Yeah, why?"

"'Cause tomorrow I'ma take you to get a rental car," he

told her. "I would take you today, but I have a lot of things to get on top of, plus I have an important meetin' later on dat I don't wanna be late for," he explained.

"Tomorrow's good, plus I don't feel like going nowhere right now anyway."

"Until then, take this," he said, reaching in his pocket and handing her about three-hundred dollars.

"What's this for?" she asked, taking the money.

"That's for you and the kids after I take you to get the car tomorrow. Take them someplace and get out for a minute. I'll add some more to it tomorrow."

"Thank you," Monique replied, giving him a hug and a kiss on his cheek.

"No, thank you for everything," Mike-Mike politely replied before turning to leave back out the door.

"Mike-Mike?"

"Wassup?" he said, partially turning around.

"Never mind, just make sure you call to check up on me," she whispered in a sensitive tone.

"I got you," he assured her, then headed out the door.

When he left her building, he walked back over to the Motel Six parking lot where his CAA was and decided to get a room for a few days. He knew that after their date, Tia would more than likely want to spend some time with him.

He didn't want to use his ID, so he quickly scanned the area for someone to reserve it in their name when he noticed Hubb, the most known crack fiend in the area, standing on his front porch.

"Ay Hubb...Hubb!" Mike-Mike called out to get his attention.

Hubb was trying to figure out who was calling him until he saw Mike-Mike in the Motel Six parking lot, flagging him to come over. Hubb quickly obliged, knowing whatever it was, that there was something in it for him.

"What's goin' on Mike-Mike?" he greeted after rushing over.

"Ain't shit. You got ya ID on you?"

"Sure do! I keep that. Bam!" he responded, whipping out his ID card.

"Good, 'cause I need you to get a room for me."

"Cool, where's the money?"

"Here… get da joint for three days," Mike-Mike instructed, handing over the money.

"You gon' look out for me, right?" Hubb asked while smacking his lips and rubbing his hands together.

"Nigga stop geekin' and get da room!" Mike-Mike shot back.

"A'ight. A'ight man. I'll be right back," fumbled Hubb, storming off.

Mike-Mike sat in his vehicle while waiting for Hubb to return. Minutes later, he came back out and handed over the keys to the room. "Good lookin". How much change was left over?" questioned Mike-Mike knowing the amount already.

"Twenty-four and some change."

"You keep dat."

"Boy oh boy, you on time. I swear I needed this. Umh… Umh…. Umh… Let me know if you need anything else," Hubb replied with a huge smile on his face, stepping off in a hurry so that he could go purchase some crack.

"Yeah, I bet you would say dat," Mike-Mike mumbled to himself.

He walked to the trunk of his vehicle, retrieved his items that he'd purchased from Neiman Marcus and then headed into the motel room.

Once he entered the room, he placed his bags on the bed and opened the windows to allow some fresh air to circulate throughout the room. He then sat down on the bed to try and get his thoughts together. The breeze from the fresh air helped to ventilate his flow of ideas. In the process of him doing some mental inventory, he decided to roll up some weed while meticulously giving some thought to his future. About forty-five minutes later, the mixture from the weed, the cool breeze that flowed throughout the room, and his constant line of thoughts caused him to fully relax before passing out.

CHAPTER 14

Hours had passed since Mike-Mike's mother watched him leave the house from her bedroom window. As she sat and watched, she hoped that her only son would make the right decision of staying home instead of falling victim to the streets. When she told him that he had until the end of the week to get out, she was hoping that would scare him into not wanting to make the wrong choice. Gloria didn't want to put her child out into the streets, because she knew what the streets had to offer, and that wasn't something she wanted for him.

A parent's greatest fear is losing a child, and that was something that Mike-Mike's mom had already experienced. The pain from her daughter's death was as if someone had pierced her heart with a knife and left it there. That, along with Mike-Mike's current situation was messing her up mentally, and her lack of eating properly and rest was physically showing.

Her fiancé was trying to do what he could to help her ease some of the stress, but the fear of losing another child was overpowering his support. Seeing how distraught she was made Anthony decide to have a talk with Mike-Mike when the time presented itself in hopes of convincing him to do the right thing. He and Mike-Mike had a good relationship, mainly because Mike-Mike saw how happy his mother was since he'd come into her life. Anthony was in the street at one time himself and knew first-hand the outcome of that fast life.

Once addicted, prison or death was the end result. His intentions were to give Mike-Mike some cautionary advice, being as though he had been where Mike-Mike was headed. If he couldn't convince him to change his mind about driving in the fast lane altogether, then at least he might give it some thought. Anthony also knew that it was hard to shift one's mind once committed, so he had to think of the most appropriate way to approach Mike-Mike without seeming too candid. He figured that he would deal with that when the time presented itself because at the moment he had other priorities to tend to. Which were to give his woman his attention, love, and support to assure her that he was there for her through thick and thin.

CHAPTER 15

Later on that evening, Zoe stopped by the shop to make sure that all his demands had been met. After entering and checking out everything, he was satisfied and passed his head worker a stack of bills for finishing the job.

"Anything else?" questioned the worker.

"You've done enough, Fred," replied Zoe.

"Well just let me know, 'cause I'm always available for you," he offered, gathering his belongings before exiting the shop with his helpers trailing behind.

"So, you sure about this," Big Herm questioned, once the workers left the building.

"Positive. I thought we talked about this already," Zoe remarked in an irritable manner.

"A'ight then, what's done is done," he concluded. "It's on to the next chapter."

Zoe glanced at his watch, noticing the time was nearing for them to head to Sequoia's Restaurant. He tossed Big Herm a set of car keys so that he could follow him to their next destination. The thought of his meeting with Mike-

Mike made him pull out his cell phone to reach him. Mike-Mike answered, sounding drowsy just as Zoe was about to hang up.

CHAPTER 16

Mike-Mike was stretched across the hotel bed sound asleep when suddenly the ringing of his phone awoke him.

"Who this?" he answered sluggishly, disregarding the phone's caller ID.

"If I didn't know any better, it sounds as if you just waking up," said the caller, brushing off Mike-Mike asking who it was.

"I did," Mike-Mike replied, immediately picking up on the voice on the other end.

"You not going to sleep past our meeting, are you?"

"Of course not," he assured him. "What time do you have?"

"It's seven on the nose."

"Seven!" he yelped, hopping up. "Let me get myself together, 'cause I didn't realize I'd slept that long."

"You have to give the body it's proper rest for the mind to operate. I need you to be fully rejuvenated, so that you clearly get a full understanding of what's at stake once you commit, 'cause you entering a family that's bonded for life."

Rubbing his head, Mike-Mike briefly stared at the motel room's ceiling, wondering what he was getting himself into before conveying to Zoe that everything was cool. He blamed his sleepiness over actually having a lot on his mind.

"It's not too late to back out if you have other things that could possibly hinder our future plans."

"I'm straight."

"You sure?"

"Yeah," he confirmed.

"See you soon then."

"Dat's a bet," Mike-Mike said before ending the call, getting up to get himself situated.

The first thing he did was call Tia to inform her of the time he'd arrive at her place. The next thing was removing his outfits from the bags, spreading them across the bed and deciding which one to wear. Once he made his choice, he went to take a shower. Shortly after, he hopped out and splashed himself with some Prada Infusion O'Homme Cologne and then got dressed. He threw on his Michael Kors Editon short sleeve shirt, some faded blue jeans, and his black perforated belt with the matching black perforated hi-top Prada sneakers before topping his outfit off with his all black Brera Round Digital Sports Watch with the perforated band.

"Damn, I'm lookin' good," he complimented himself, glancing in the mirror as he threw on his black Prada lightweight nylon jacket, then headed out the door. Once he walked outside, he thought the evening was the perfect time to pull his Cadillac out the cut. Soon after making up his mind, he was pulling alongside his silver 2013 Cadillac. Looking at the vehicle, he immediately knew his next stop was the carwash.

After briefly warming the luxury vehicle, he pulled off, heading to Mr. Wash on Georgia Avenue, across from Emery Heights. As he waited for his vehicle to come out the wash-through, he noticed a medium-build brown skin female standing next to a Toyota *Solara* peeking in his direction while waiting for her car to get dried off. He admired her from a distance in her light tan waist-length jacket, her cream sweater dress that hugged her curves perfectly, and a cute pair of Camel Platform Boots.

She wearin' that dress, he thought as his Cadillac was coming out the wash. He quickly decided to walk over to speak with her before it was too late.

"How you doin' young lady? Hope you didn't mind me walkin' over to speak to you, 'cause I wouldn't have been able to forgive myself if I didn't," he macked in his smoothest voice.

"No, I don't mind," she replied, giving him a once-over, admiring what she saw.

"By da way, my name's Mike-Mike, and yours is?" he said, extending his hand to greet her.

"My name's Makiya," she replied with a smile on her face that showed off a beautiful set of white teeth that would've been perfect to advertise in a bleaching commercial for teeth, returning his handshake.

"It's a pleasure to meet you," he responded before commenting on her smile, causing her to blush a bit more. "You goin' out this evenin'?"

"What made you ask me that?" she countered.

"I'm assumin' basically by da way you're dressed."

"So just because a woman dresses nice means she's going out?" she asked sternly.

"I didn't mean it like dat, I just figured since you were so well dressed dat you were probably on your way someplace, dat's all," he explained, trying to clean it up.

"I see you a quick thinker, 'cause you cleared that up pretty fast!" she smiled, "but to answer your question, I'm actually on my way someplace, so you were correct."

"So, I was right, huh?" he smiled back. "You almost made me feel like I insulted you."

"Well you didn't, I was just joking with you," she smirked.

"It's good to know dat you have a sense of humor, so where you on ya way to?"

"To meet up with my girlfriends, then to this happy hour spot," she conveyed.

"Ma'am, your car is ready," stated one of the employees that were drying off her vehicle.

"Thank you," she told the worker before directing her attention back towards Mike-Mike with a glowing look.

"I'm not tryin' to hold you up, but do you think it's possible I can give you a call some time?"

"It depends," she countered.

"On?" he questioned.

"You're not a stalker, or a serial killer, are you?" she

grinned.

"Of course not," he grinned back at her.

"Well, in that case, I wouldn't mind you giving me a call," she told him, reaching into her car to grab her phone, giving him a clear view of her curvaceous shape.

Damn, he thought, as she was retrieving her phone, "What's your number," she asked.

She dialed the numbers as he called them out to her. When he finished, his phone rung.

"Now that's my number, call me sometime," she said while getting in her driver's seat.

"Sure will," he assured her, closing her driver's door. "You be careful at dat happy hour spot, 'cause you can best believe there are a few stalkers there," Mike-Mike said, then walked back to his car.

He glanced at his watch, noticing it was a quarter to eight, and knew he had to step on it to pick Tia up so he wouldn't be late for his meeting with Zoe. Fifteen minutes later, he was calling Tia, telling her to come outside. Simultaneously as he was pulling up, she was walking out the door. She looked very chic in her red Gucci dress, black thin waist belt, and a pair of black-n-gold trimmed heels, also courtesy of Gucci.

She keeps dat fly shit on, he thought as she slipped into the vehicle. "How you been stranger? Men don't open the doors for women no more?" she inquired, staring at him in disappointment.

"My bad, I'm sorry, I'm rushin' dat's all, don't be mad

at me," he replied, leaning over, giving her a kiss on her cheek.

"Yeah, I bet," she smirked.

"You lookin' good as usual," he complimented, pulling off.

"Don't try to change the subject," she countered, cutting her eye at him, "but thank you anyway," she grinned. "You lookin' handsome yourself, and whose pretty Cadillac is this? This is really nice," she admired, doing a brief inspection of the interior.

"I had this for a minute. I just don't be drivin' it like dat."

"What happened to the white Lexus?"

"I still got it," Mike-Mike confirmed.

"Doin' big things, huh," she commented.

"Not really, just doin' me."

"I see," she replied, blushing.

The pair continued to converse as he headed to their destination, catching each other up on what had been going on since the last time they saw one another. Before they knew it, he was parking and calling Zoe to inform him of his arrival.

CHAPTER 17

The spacious Sequoia's Restaurant was known for hosting some of the largest, most unforgettable fundraisers in the nation's capital for over two decades. Plus, the inside was enormous enough to seat twenty-five hundred comfortably.

"This place is really nice," Tia admired when they entered.

"It sure is," Mike-Mike agreed. "You never been here before?"

"This is my first time," she admitted.

"Mines too," he confessed with a smile.

"And you going to ask me like you a regular or something," she said, tapping his shoulder.

"I know right," he replied, scanning the area for Zoe.

The place was slightly dimmed but lit-up enough to view the scenery. A waitress was approaching seconds ahead of Zoe.

"Welcome to Sequoia's my name is…"

"Mrs. Purdom, I'll take it from here, they're with me," Zoe interrupted.

"Well, you two are definitely in good hands. Enjoy your evening," she said, walking off."

"I see you on time, that's a good sign," he said, extending his hand to greet Mike-Mike, "and who's the lovely young lady that you have accompanying you this evening?"

"This is my friend Tia, and Tia, this is a soon to be business partner of mines, Zoe," Mike-Mike said, introducing the two.

"Please to meet you, and I must say that you are a sight for sore eyes," Zoe complimented, expressing his approval, shaking her hand.

"Thank you," Tia replied, glowing.

"You lookin' sharp yourself," Zoe remarked, directing his attention back towards Mike-Mike.

"Thanks to you."

"Don't thank me, 'cause you earned it," Zoe threw back. "Follow me."

Zoe also looked fashionable in his grey two-button cotton jacket and his flat-front pants, both made by Theory. He was also sporting Tom Ford glasses, an all black Prada leather belt, and black Prada loafers. Once they reached their table, Zoe politely introduced everyone. His partner Big Herm was seated with their dates. The roundtable was huge with couch like seats that were soft as silk. Purposely, Zoe chose a table that was in a far corner, out of ear utterance of others. Moments after getting acquainted, and some casual talk, the group finally decided to order their food. Zoe signaled the waitress over to place their orders.

"Please, order anything you choose, my treat," he assured them. With that being said, the group ordered everything from lobster, oysters, mussels, to black spaghetti with lump crabmeat.

"Will that be all?" asked the waitress.

"Yes, and bring us three bottles of my usual," Zoe concluded.

"Coming right up," replied the waitress, walking away to fulfill their orders.

The group immediately continued having social intercourse while waiting for their meals to arrive. From time to time, Mike-Mike would catch Big Herm staring at him oddly, but he acted as if he didn't notice it. Making a mental note, he figured that he would ask Zoe about it at a better time. Besides that, everything seemed to be going well. Before they knew it, the meals and bottles were arriving. The waitress correctly placed everyone's order in front of them, leaving the bottles in an ice bucket on the food cart beside the table. The group wasted no time pleasing their stomachs. Their meals were so good that it was hard to not ravenously eat the food as if it were their last meal.

"I can't believe y'all ate that food like that," commented Zoe, knowing he had done the same.

"Us! What about you, look at your plate! You didn't leave a crumb on it!" Big Herm shot back jokingly.

"I know right, I was starvin'," Zoe admitted, holding his stomach and then popping the cork on one of the bottles.

Champagne flowed as the group continued to share a few laughs. By the time they realized it, two more hours had zoomed past.

"They say time fly past when you havin' a good time," Zoe acknowledged.

"I thought that was a good thing," replied Zoe's female friend while she rubbed his chin.

"It is," he responded, glancing at his David Yurman Belmont watch, and then turning towards Mike-Mike letting him know that he needed to speak with him privately. "Do you mind if I borrow your date for a few moments?" Zoe asked Tia.

"Not at all," she replied in her sweetest voice.

"I promise not to keep him long," he said, standing up for Mike-Mike to follow. "Big Herm, keep the women entertained."

Zoe and Mike-Mike walked to a secluded area of the restaurant before Zoe commenced to speaking his mind. "They say action without thought is like shooting without aim. We do as we are and become as we do. Our worst enemy is ourselves, and I say this, 'cause I'm placin' the ball in your hands. Can't no one mess this opportunity up but you. With that being said, I'ma ask you again…" he advised as his words trailed off. "Do you think you ready to play in the big league, 'cause this is a lot more dangerous, and definitely riskier than stealin' cars? You gotta watch out for the cops, robbers, and most of all, the people that are close to you," he concluded with a stern look.

"After givin' it some thought, I know I'm ready," Mike-Mike assured.

Looking into his eyes and seeing the sureness, Zoe pulled out a set of car keys from his inside pocket and handed them over to him.

"What's these for?"

"It's your half, plus the extra I promised," he smiled.

"My half," Mike-Mike reiterated, confused.

Sensing his confusion, Zoe pulled out a piece of paper from his inner pocket, also handing that to him, before clarifying the situation.

"Don't open that until you get to a safe destination. Even if you just so happen to get pulled over for whatever reason, make sure you dispose of that piece of paper. I don't care if you have to swallow it," Zoe sternly remarked. "What's on that paper is your introduction to the big league," he confirmed.

Mike-Mike simply understood, tucking the paper away.

"You drove that sleek Cadillac of yours?" said Zoe.

"Yeah, how you know?"

Zoe just smirked at him, then told Mike-Mike to leave his car keys with him while he drove the other vehicle, and they would meet up the next day, so he could pick his Cadillac back up.

"Where's this car parked at?" inquired Mike-Mike.

"Directly behind your Cadillac."

"How did you know where I parked at?" Mike-Mike grinned. Smiling, Zoe just pointed at his head like he knew everything.

The two conversed a bit more about the do's and dont's

of the game before wrapping things up so they could return to their table, but before they did Mike-Mike wanted to ask Zoe one last question.

"What is it?" Zoe replied.

"What's up with Big Herm?"

"What do you mean?"

"He don't like me, do he?"

"What made you ask that?"

"'Cause he be givin' me a funny look," he explained.

Zoe smiled before saying, "Don't worry about him. Big Herm just being Big Herm, that's all. Unlike me, he thinks I'm makin' a big mistake, so don't prove me wrong," Zoe deduced.

"I won't," he responded with assurance, shaking his hand. Then the pair headed back to join everyone else.

Shortly after, the group ended their gathering. They said their goodbyes and went their separate ways. When Mike-Mike and Tia exited the restaurant, the night's breeze instantly rushed them.

"It's chilly out here," Tia complained, rubbing her arms.

Mike-Mike immediately removed his jacket and wrapped it around her.

"Thank you."

"Dat's what a gentleman s'posed to do," he smiled. "So, you had a good time?"

"I had a wonderful time, and the food was delicious," she validated.

"Well I'm glad you enjoyed ya'self, 'cause I did too," he agreed, as they came close to his vehicle.

Once his Cadillac came into view, Tia tried to rush to

the car to escape the night's breeze.

"Unlock the door so I can get in," she called out, speed walking ahead of him. "It's cold!" she murmured, approaching the passenger side.

"We not ridin' back in dat," he replied.

"This is not the time to be playing, 'cause it's freezing out here," she shot back in a whining manner.

He never responded, he simply took the keys out of his pocket and hit the unlock button on his latest toy and hopped in. She was briefly stunned, watching him get in the all black Mercedes Benz *SLK*. She quickly went to join him after realizing that he wasn't joking about not driving his Cadillac.

"Guess you were serious, huh?" she playfully asked.

"Oh, you thought I was playin'?" he smiled, starting the luxury vehicle.

Seeing you Remind Me, by David Hollister harmoniously flowed through the speakers. Once he gave the coupe its idle time, he pulled off in disbelief that Zoe actually gave him a bad new Benz. Tia was in the passenger seat having her own thoughts as well. Especially after eating an aphrodisiac, combined with some champagne, and now she was in the luxury of an expensive, elegant coupe.

This Benz feels like I'm driving on air, he thought, turning off on P Street into Rock Creek Park. He chose to take that route because it was a shortcut to his destination, though a lot more dangerous, because of the park police that patrolled the park. After warming up, Tia started feeling a little excited. She removed Mike-Mike's jacket from around her and placed it in the back. After doing so, she leaned over, unfastened a few buttons on his Michael Kors Edition shirt, and commenced to rubbing on his chest. She seductively licked her lips, then asked him if he could do two things at the same time, unbuckling his belt. Sensing her intentions, he thought about reneging since he was driving through a heavily patrolled area with an undisclosed quantity of drugs in the car, but that thought shot out the window just as soon as it entered his mind.

"I was taught how to chew gum and walk at the same time when I was young," he responded unable to resist the urge of receiving an oral examination from her for the first time.

"Well I guess there's only one way to find out," she flirted, freeing his manhood, unhesitant to welcome him into her mouth.

"Oh, shit!" escaped from his mouth after she absorbed him fully.

The warm sensation caused his foot to slightly slip off the gas pedal. She showed no mercy, working her tongue and jaw muscles like a pro. She was sucking and jerking his firm erection so vigorously that he almost veered off the road. He caught himself just in time so that he wouldn't miss his exit. Her skills were unexpected and briefly had his eyes wide-open.

When he came off the exit, he stopped at the traffic light that was on 16th Street. Tia continued her fellatio attack as a dark-colored SUV pulled up alongside of them. The driver of the truck glanced over, catching the oral stimulation in clear view. Being that the SUV sat so much higher than the Benz coupe, the female driver was able to look straight into the vehicle witnessing the whole ordeal. Mike-Mike glanced over, noticing the woman driver glued to the event that was unfolding right before her eyes.

Feeling mischievous, he purposely pulled up Tia's dress, exposing her plump red ass before giving it a slight squeeze and a smack, causing it to jiggle a bit. At that point, he gave the woman a player's head-nod and accelerated through the light. Not only did that brief episode boost his ego by having another woman watch him receive oral stimulation, it also boosted his adrenaline. The excitement had him to the point that had him ready to shoot out Tia's wind-pipe with his semen.

"I'm 'bout to cum!" he warned, but she continued picking up her pace.

His body tensed up, then he exploded, serving her with a mouthful of his creamy nutrients. She gagged for a second, but she caught every drop of it, licking him dry. He was speechless because he didn't know that her head game was on that level.

Damn, that was good, he thought, as he looked over at her, he said, "Look, I'm not tryin' to be funny, but girl you got dat porn star head!" he exclaimed.

"Boy, you silly," she giggled, lying back in her seat with a smile on her face.

Shortly after, Mike-Mike was pulling into the hotel

parking lot. After he parked, he handed her the room key telling her he would be right up in a minute.

"Don't take too long," she remarked while licking her lips and getting out the vehicle.

"Trust me I won't," he assured her.

Once she entered the hotel, he immediately retrieved the piece of paper that Zoe had given him, which was a set of instructions. He followed the steps as he read along. Once he finished, a hidden stash spot revealed itself. He leaned in the back, reaching his hand inside the compartment before pulling out brick after brick until it was empty. All in all, he ended up pulling out 15 kilos.

Damn, he thought, realizing how many there were. He sat for a few moments, taking in the amount he was holding at the time while contemplating his future come-up. Feeling a bit jittery, he began to place the bricks back into their nest one by one. He glanced across the street at his safehaven, noticing Monique's light was still on and decided to give her a quick call before going to his room.

"Hello," she answered.

"I see you still up, huh?" he responded.

"Yep, sitting in here by my lonesome watching *Friday*."

"Which one you watchin'?"

"The first one, 'cause Chris Tucker's ass is a trip. For some reason, I can never get tired of watching it."

"Yeah, dat joint is a classic," he agreed.

"You want me to come over and keep you company?"

"Sure, I'ma leave the door unlocked," she blushed.

Mike-Mike was just fooling around, but after noticing her willingness, he quickly decided to not lead her on 'cause he already had company to tend to.

"Naw don't do dat, 'cause I'm jive in the middle of somethin', but I'ma hold you to dat next time."

"Next time the door might be locked," she shot back.

"Now why would you do dat?"

"'Cause you keep playing, that's why," she replied.

"Playin' how?"

"Never mind, what do you want, 'cause you messing up my me-time," she griped with a bit of attitude.

"Don't act like dat, 'cause we better than dat."

"Unh...huh. I hear you."

"I thought so," he joked.

"Boy, stop playing with me!"

"What I tell you about callin' me, boy! I'm all man."

"Yeah, that's what your mouth says," she countered.

"Dat's what I know."

"Bye, 'cause you don't want nothing," she blurted out, about to hang up on him.

"Hold up!" Mike-Mike yelped, sensing her getting impatient. "All jokes aside," he said, getting serious. "I need you to call everybody and tell them to come over tomorrow, so I can discuss a serious matter," he declared.

"Why don't you call 'em?"

"'Cause I told you I'm kinda busy. Could you just do dat for me, and tell 'em to be there by noon," he instructed.

"I'ma hurt you, 'cause you must think I'm your personal secretary or something! Anything else, Mr. Gardner?" she ridiculed, being sarcastic.

"Naw dat's it, and thanks. I promise I got you."

"Interrupting my personal time, you better," she uttered, then hung up.

Satisfied, Mike-Mike hopped out of his newest toy, heading into the hotel. When he walked into the room, Tia was taking a shower, so he chose to twist a jay of "loud" that he'd had since earlier. Once he finished rolling the "loud", he turned the radio on, laid back on the bed, then fired up his backwood. The radio was playing all slow jams, which was perfect for his mood. The timing couldn't have been more ameliorated, 'cause as soon as Tia appeared from the bathroom door wearing a red thong and matching bra, *Baby I'm Ready*, by LeVert flowed through the speakers. Knowing the lyrics to the song, she began to sing along while strutting over toward Mike-Mike as if she were a professional runway model. She stopped for a brief second and spun around, giving him a full view of her sexy frame.

She lookin' too good, he thought, relaxing while taking puffs off his backwood. When she reached the foot of the bed, she slowly bent over, touching the bed so she could crawl on top of him. The mirror that was positioned behind her gave him the perfect view of her plumpness, causing him to instantly get aroused. Tia smiled seductively after noticing the bulge in his pants. She was pleased, knowing she had his full undivided attention. Once she got near his face, she leaned toward his left-side, whispering soft moans in his ear. Having his full attention, she moved in closer, licking on his earlobe then motioned down to his lips as if she were about to kiss him. Stopping just short of their lips touching, she commenced to sucking on his bottom lip like it was a piece of nectarine. Getting moist and wet, Tia removed his top garments, immediately going back to sucking on his lip and neck before easing down to his chest. She stopped just above his navel, so she could unbuckle his pants. Once his pants were removed, she massaged his shaft through his boxer briefs. Extremely aroused she began moaning and licking her lips as if she couldn't wait to absorb him for the second time that night.

Taking his last few puffs, he laid back, allowing her to continue her foreplay. Tia never freed his manhood from his briefs, instead, she nibbled on Mike-Mike's penis through them. Never experiencing oral sex through his drawers, he had to sneak a peek, wondering how she was making the encounter feel so good. She had his stick hard as a bat, and he was about ready to use it to beat her pussy up. Not to mention, he didn't want to rush the relishing moment. Shortly after pleasing him through his boxer briefs, she finally freed his love muscle. Tia tried to gulp him fully but found herself gagging on his thickness. She got watery eyed from trying to perform her magic and make it disappear. Realizing that it was a bit too much for her to absorb all at once, she decided to switch up her tactic. So, she skillfully jerked and sucked while allowing the saliva from her mouth to run down his penis like a waterfall.

Mike-Mike was in a sexual trance from her pleasing aggression. He was holding his hand over his mouth just to keep from blurting out something foolish. Glancing at her and seeing how in tune she was, almost made him tell her that he loved her. Refraining from making a fool of himself, he laid there and continued receiving the satisfying punishment.

Soon after, she freed her lips, then hopped on top of him reverse cowgirl style easing down on his stiff penis. Mike-Mike admired the eye-catching view of her petite frame furthering down his shaft. Once the feeling subsided, she mounted her hand on his ankles and went to work, riding him like a professional jockey. In his mind he didn't know which one was better, her oral game or the sex cruise she had him on, because her wetness surely had his mind afloat. She gyrated her hips in all directions as if she were a human joystick.

Eventually, Mike-Mike decided to take charge and show her who was boss. He flipped her over, laid her on her stomach, placed both hands behind her back as if she were being arrested. Then penetrated her, leaving her helpless to any kind of running, just pleasurable punishment.

"Ooh.... Ooh... Poppi. Ooh.... Poppi. Mmh... It's....all yours," she cried out.

Tia's cries caused him to go into overdrive. He used his left hand to mount her arms still behind her back, then his right to bend her right leg up toward her shoulder. Somehow, he locked his hand on his wrist, twisting her in some kind of pretzel position. She started losing control as he long-stroked her, grinding into her swollen womb.

"Daddy!" she shouted, biting her bottom lip, climaxing all over his saluted soldier.

Mike-Mike glanced through the mirror, noticing her enticing facial expression and really commenced to pounding her harder and harder. Suddenly he got up off the bed, stood there and bent her over, making her grab her ankles while he spread her ass cheeks and went deep-sea diving. He continued to thrust her in that same position, until he felt that familiar build-up.

"Daddy cumin', baby!" he conveyed before releasing a heavy load of cum juice all in her welcoming love tunnel.

Afterward, the two collapsed onto the bed speechless from their intense encounter. Soon after, they rested a short time and then decided to go get cleaned up. Tia led the way to the shower, and Mike-Mike followed. When they finished, he quickly twisted another jay of "loud", turned the volume up on the radio, and laid back while contemplating the 15 kilos he had stashed in his new Benz.

CHAPTER 18

The following day marked the era of Mike-Mike officially being in the big league. Selling drugs was a lot different than stealing vehicles. Though he'd stuck his hand in the game before, the question was, was he ready to convert from minor to major league overnight with very little know-how of prices, weight, and recognition of transforming powder to hard, if need be.

Big Herm thought not, but Zoe thought different. Zoe's mentality was that he knew quite a few teenagers that were knee-deep in the game at some point in time, so why not Mike-Mike? He was smart, mature, a thinker, on top of that, he had heart. With those four qualities, Zoe strongly believed that he had what it took to make it on a higher level, especially with little guidance. Zoe was a pretty good judge of character, and he was willing to gamble on Mike-Mike's ability to hold his own. Zoe had taken a liking to him and thought that this was a perfect opportunity to further his situation. Zoe once told Mike-Mike that he knew more about him than he realized, and he meant every word.

They say that some things are best left unknown, and

what he knew could possibly wake a sleeping giant. With that thought, it was best to leave well enough alone. He was content with taking the info to his grave, unless a situation surfaced that would call for the unknown to be known. Zoe shook off the thought as he focused back on his current situation.

Zoe was taught that early to bed and early to rise makes a person healthy, wealthy, and wise. That quote was something that he planned to embed into Mike-Mike's memory, he reasoned with himself before continuing with his daily routine.

CHAPTER 19

"Get up, Mike!" Tia suddenly uttered, shaking him.

"Umh…What!" he replied, springing up, ending his bad dream.

"Are you okay? You must be having a bad dream."

"Yeah, I'm good, why you say dat?" he responded, wiping his sweaty face.

"'Cause not only are you sweating like crazy, but you almost knocked me off the bed," she informed him.

"You fo' real!"

"Yeah, I'm for real," she assured him.

"My bad," he apologized, "but sometimes I be havin' these bad dreams about…" he stopped mid-sentence.

"About what?" she inquired, a bit concerned.

"Never mind, I don't wanna talk about it. What time is it?" he asked quickly, changing the subject.

"You got your watch on," she pointed out, sensing that whatever it was must've been a touchy subject, so she didn't press it.

I'm trippin', he thought, glancing at his watch. "Damn! It's almost 12 o'clock," he said, hopping out of bed, "I have someplace to be in a little bit.''

"Well, if you in such a rush, just call me a cab, I don't mind."

"Don't insult me, just get dressed, so I can drop you off right quick."

They didn't take long to get themselves freshened up before heading out the room. Reality set in once Mike-Mike stepped outside, seeing his latest gift looking well polished under the radiance of the sun. He stopped briefly, glancing at the sky with a smile on his face, absorbing the moment.

"You okay?" voiced Tia, noticing him stopping and drifting into space.

"Yeah. Yeah. Everything's good," he relayed to her, snapping out of his short daze.

Grinning, he placed his arm around Tia, then continued toward the coupe. Hitting the unlock button, he opened the door for her, allowing her to get in, remembering what she ranted about when he picked her up the day before.

"Thank you," she smiled.

"I only did dat, so I don't get cursed out this mornin'," he joked, causing her to hit him on his arm.

After closing her door, Mike-Mike walked around to the driver's side and got in, starting the vehicle up. Giving the Benz its idle time, he put on Rick Ross' latest CD, opened the sunroof and pulled off, feeling as if he were driving on air. Mimicking the words to *Aston Martin Music*, he casually zipped through traffic, making it to Tia's house in as little as ten minutes.

"Thank you for a wonderful time last night, I really

enjoyed myself," she commented graciously.

"Me too," he agreed.

"When I'ma see you again?" she inquired, opening her door.

"More sooner than later," he relayed.

"I swear you are something else," she commented, shaking her head.

"Why you say dat?"

"'Cause what kind of answer was that? More sooner than later," she reiterated.

"I didn't mean for it to sound so dry," he smiled. "I'm basically just sayin' soon," he corrected. "I have a few things to handle, then I'ma make it my business to reach out to you," he assured her.

"Well until then, don't be no stranger, at least pick up the phone to call," she replied, leaning over and kissing him on his cheek.

Tia got out and went into her house. Mike-Mike waited until she cleared her front door before pulling off and then quickly called Monique to inform her that he was coming by.

"Boy, it's almost 12 o'clock!" she immediately answered. "Where you at, 'cause we all up here waiting on you?"

"Damn Ma, is dat the way to answer ya phone?" he shot back before continuing, "But to answer ya question, I'll be there in 'bout fifteen minutes," he said with certainty.

"I got your ma, just hurry up, 'cause people have other things to do," she said prior to hanging up.

Everything was going as planned, but now Mike-Mike

was questioning himself about how much he should reveal. After some deliberating, he decided to disclose very little while at the same time informing everyone that it was a chance for them to finally make some real money. Shortly after he arrived and parked on Whittier Place, he headed towards Monique's apartment building. He knocked on Monique's door. Already knowing who it was she instantly opened it.

"'Bout time!" she announced with a smile on her face.

"You actin' like I took fo'ever," he stated, looking at his watch. "It's only 12:30," he conveyed, walking past her, entering the apartment.

"True, but when it comes to your so-called meetings, you need to be on time. Lead by example," Monique advised.

"Know what, you absolutely right," he agreed and turned his attention toward the others. "What-up y'all!" Mike-Mike greeted, dapping them up one by one.

"Shit, tryin' to see what's good wit' you," claimed Lil' Chico, who was like Mike-Mike's and Slick's younger brother.

Lil' Chico was of slim build, light skinned and weighing at no more than 140 lbs with long cornrows. He resembled the rapper Bizzy Bone from the group Bone Thugs-n-Harmony. The three others present were Kurt, Tre, and Nose, a few other good associates who were a part of their circle.

"Tryin' to move on up like, *The Jeffersons*," Mike-Mike replied, referring to the 70's hit sitcom.

"Who?" asked Lil' Chico.

"Neva mind," he said, not wanting to waste time explaining to a late 80's baby about an early 70's show, even though he was a late 80's baby himself.

Mike-Mike quickly converted his attention to the matter-at-hand after gaining everybody's attention.

"Listen up y'all," he spoke, looking around at everyone before continuing, "a good associate of mine, basically placed me in a decent position to make some real money. And of course, I'm includin' y'all in da plans, so we can all get this bread together," he explained.

"Sounds like a come-up," said Tre, rubbing his hands together as if he were trying to warm them.

"True, but what are we dealin' wit'?" asked Lil' Chico.

"Hope somebody knows how to cook, 'cause we dealin' wit' powdered coke," Mike-Mike revealed.

"I don't know how to cook, but I bet I know who does," Kurt chimed in.

"Who?" Mike-Mike quizzed.

"Hubb's crackhead ass," he suggested.

"Hell yeah!" Mike-Mike agreed. "Plus, he goin' to make sure dat shit butter 'cause he smoke."

"You better know it!" co-signed Tre. "How much work we talkin' bout anyway?"

Mike-Mike briefly considered how he wanted to respond without sounding so personal.

"Look, don't even trip off da amount, just know dat it's enough to get us all right."

"Dat's good enough fo' me," Tre approved.

"So, what we need to do to get da ball rollin'?" questioned Lil' Chico.

"Fo' starters, Kurt, you could go find Hubb and let'im know dat I need to holla at him. Nose, it might be useful if you could grab all da coke bags you can get. And Tre, I need you to spread da word dat da Courts' 'bout to have da best coke for da low," he instructed.

Mike-Mike then turned his attention toward Lil' Chico and asked if he'd gotten on top of what they'd previously spoken about the day before.

"Yeah, I mentioned it to her, but she blew me off. You may have to talk to her yourself," he recommended.

"A'ight, cool, just let her know dat I'm tryin' to holla at her."

"Bet," Lil' Chico said just before there was a knock at the door, causing everyone to freeze for a slight second.

"You expectin' someone?" Mike-Mike whispered to Monique, who shook her head no. "See who it is," he told her.

"It's me, Slick," he announced, from the opposite side of the door.

"Where da hell dat nigga been at?" Tre inquired.

"Don't know," replied Monique, opening the door.

"I figured y'all was probably up here," Slick said, entering with his left arm in a sling.

"What da hell happened to you?" asked Monique after he brushed past her.

Mike-Mike was standing behind everyone, giving Slick the slice-across-the-neck signal, indicating to not say anything.

"This ain't bout nothin'," he said, hesitant to speak on the situation. "The ole boy good," he commented, picking up on his partner's hand gesture.

"Mmh...umh... I bet," Monique responded, sensing Slick was holding back something, but she didn't press the issue.

Slick greeted everybody, and when he made it to Mike-Mike a huge smile spread across his face.

"What's good, baby boy!" he commented, giving him a brotherly hug.

"Bruh, what's up?" he replied. "How you feel?"

"I seen better days, but I'm here, nigga," he said, his voice low, almost under his breath.

"Dat's wassup. I got something to holler at you about, so take a ride with me."

"Is it good, or bad?"

"I'll let you decide," Mike-Mike told him.

He then turned his attention back to the group and communicated to them that they should get on top of what they'd just discussed so that they could get the ball rolling.

"Bet," said Lil' Chico, standing up. The rest of the crew rose to their feet behind him.

They talked amongst themselves a few minutes more before exiting the apartment.

"Slick, let me put a bug in Mo-Mo's ear right quick and I'll meet you downstairs."

"Dat's a bet," Slick replied, saying goodbye to Monique, then exiting the apartment.

When everybody was gone, Mike-Mike turned to Monique with a solemn look and verbalized the thoughts running through his head.

"Look, I'm a man of my word, and when I told you I got

you, I meant dat."

"I know, I never doubted you."

"But what I'ma need fo' you to start doin' from here on out is to stop the traffic from runnin' in and out the apartment. I have somethin' serious goin' on and I'ma need you to hold somethin' fo' me from time to time. I don't want nobody makin' ya spot hot," Mike-Mike said point blank.

"I got you," she agreed in an all-too-easy tone.

"Thanks," he replied, forming a smile on his face and then headed out the door.

Slick was standing in front of the building when Mike-Mike came out.

"When you get out da hospital?" Mike-Mike inquired.

"I got discharged this mornin'," he confirmed.

"Let's walk and talk, 'cause I gotta holler at you."

"Bruh, let me say somethin' first, 'cause I have to get this off my chest," Slick interjected.

"I'm listenin'."

"I don't know how you done it, but I owe you big time fo' savin' me. 'Cause what you did a lotta folks wouldn't have," Slick said with conviction.

"Owe me?" Mike-Mike chimed in, sounding a bit insulted. "Bruh, you don't owe me nothin'. What I done I would've expected da same in return if da shoe was on da other foot. I'm just glad dat you a'ight," he responded genuinely.

"Real talk, I don't remember anything after I blacked-out, but wakin' up in da hospital," he acknowledged. "Oh, and not bein' hand-cuffed to da bedpost."

"Just remember one thing, we brothers, and I always got ya' back," Mike-Mike promised.

"Likewise," Slick confirmed as the two once again exchanged pounds.

"Bruh, guess what?" Mike-Mike asked.

"What is it?"

"Ma Dukes found the bloody clothes I had on da night of da incident," he informed Slick.

"You serious!"

"Dead azz," he assured him.

"What she say?"

"She basically told me dat I had til da end of da week to either straighten up or get out her house," he explained as the pair approached the Benz.

"Damn, slim, dat's messed up!" he responded, shaking his head. "How you plannin' on dealin' wit' da situation?"

"Lord knows I luv Ma Dukes to death, but I guess I'ma have to find another spot, 'cause it's time fo' us to stack this bread," he concluded.

Mike-Mike immediately hit the unlock button, catching Slick by surprise. He then walked around to the driver's side.

"Slim, who Benz is this? This muthafucka nice as shit!" Slick expressed excitedly.

"This my shit!" he confirmed. "It's a gift from Zoe, but wait until you see what's on da inside," he grinned, getting in.

Slick eagerly hopped in, wanting to find out what it was that his partner had to show him. Mike-Mike started up the Benz while Slick snooped around, trying to figure out what his man was referring to, but he didn't see anything out of the ordinary.

"What you lookin' around fo'?" asked Mike-Mike.

"I'm tryin' to see what you talkin' 'bout."

"Just fall back, I got you."

"Say no more," Slick stated, leaning back in his seat.

As the song *Bad,* by Wale (feat. Rihanna) sounded through the speakers, a huge smile spread across Slick's face.

"What you smilin' fo'?" Mike-Mike inquired.

"You, 'cause you always seem to have da right song fo' da occasion."

"I got dat from you," he informed Slick.

"True dat…True dat," Slick bragged.

Mike-Mike simply smiled at him. Then he peeled off and drove toward 14th Street.

"Your pussy count 'bout to go to the moon wit' this bad boy," Slick boasted, getting comfortable in the passenger seat.

"You know what ya know, 'cause I got hit off ten minutes after I got in it last night," he added.

"Oh yeah! Who was da victim?"

"Do you remember Tia's lil red sexy azz?"

"Do I!" he confirmed. "Shawty bad, plus she be dressin' like shit."

"Exactly! You definitely know who I'm talkin' 'bout then."

"What she do?"

"She swallowed me up, and dat's not it…"

"What else is it nigga, spit it out," Slick said, interested in what he was about to say.

"It's funny you said dat, 'cause she damn sure didn't," he chuckled slyly. "And you want to know what else? I was caught at a red light gettin' hit off, when a bad azz broad, drivin' a Lincoln *Navigator* pulled up right beside us, goosin', smilin' and lickin' her lips and shit!" he boasted in an arrogant manner.

"No bullshit!" Slick grinned.

"Nigga, no bullshit," he assured him. "I feel like I was the director and da star of da same movie."

"Slim, you was fakin' like shit!" Slick laughed, dapping his partner up.

"Was I," he admitted, "and before da light turned green, I pulled up her dress, exposed dat plump red azz of hers, then saluted shawty before pullin' off!" Mike-Mike went on, all animated. "On some real shit, you probably sittin' in some pussy juice right now," he joked.

"Oh yeah! Well, let me sniff this seat then," Slick shot-back foolishly as the pair shared a laugh.

After a few more minutes of clowning around, Slick noticed how his partner's demeanor had changed.

"What's on ya mind?" Slick asked.

"On a more serious note, look at us from an outside view. We ain't doin' too bad fo' ourselves," he acknowledged, turning the music all the way down before continuing. "We not even eighteen yet and we ridin' 'round in big boy shit, ya feel me," he glanced over, seeing Slick agreeing with the nod of the head.

"Regardless of how we obtain it, we makin' it happen. Dat's all dat matters. This is da life dat I always envisioned fo' us, but at da same time, I want to be able to live long enough to enjoy our come up. A lot of people don't get da opportunity, then you have da ones dat do and mess it up, 'cause they get too big-headed, greedy, or careless."

"Where all this comin' from, bruh?" Slick asked, sensing his man trying to make a point.

"What I'm tryin' to say is dat money changes people, some fo' da good, some fo' da bad, and my reason fo' sayin' all of this is 'cause I don't never want this paper we 'bout to get to come between our brotherhood," Mike-Mike revealed, speaking from the heart before pulling into a secluded area.

"Bruh, I'll never allow something dat's replaceable to come in between something dat's not," Slick sincerely vowed.

"Good," Mike-Mike responded, matching his tone. "Remember I told you dat I had somthin' to show you?" he continued, shutting off the engine on the coupe.

"Yeah, I'm still wonderin' what you was talkin' 'bout."

Mike-Mike stared at him for a few seconds before saying, "Bruh, it's fifteen bricks in here as we speak and if we continue to do as we should, we'll never have to look back again," he confided with assurance.

"So, you tellin' me it's fifteen bricks in this Benz wit' us right now?" he inquired, trying to determine whether Mike-Mike was joking or not. Needless to say, the look on his face said it all. "I can't believe you ridin' around wit' seven and a half bricks like it's legal!" Slick replied in astonishment.

"Nigga, I said fifteen," he corrected.

"Naw nigga, like I said seven and a half, 'cause if da po-po's pull us over and find dat shit, I'ma have to take half dat shit!" he joked, causing the two of them to share a laugh.

"One thing 'bout dat, they ain't findin' nothin' due to da secret compartment," Mike-Mike boasted. "Man, we steppin' our game all da way up," he continued, hitting a few buttons and switches, revealing the hidden stash spot.

Slick's eyes lit up when the stash spot opened, revealing its contents.

"I gotta get one of those put in my whip a.s.a.p!" acknowledged Slick, admiring the stash spot.

"I'll get on top of it," Mike-Mike replied, pulling one of the kilos out, handing it over.

Slick examined the package with admiration, then passed it back.

"It's on, bruh," he smiled.

"Fo' sure," Mike-Mike agreed, placing the bird back in its nest. "Can you drive?"

"Of course," Slick confirmed. "My good arm still intact, and if it wasn't, I'm still an expert with my knee," he teased.

"I almost fo'got who I was talkin' to," Mike-Mike added, boosting his partner's ego even further. "Anyway, I need you to drive my Cadi back, I left it with Zoe last night," he explained.

"Bet."

"In da meantime, while we headin' over there, I'ma catch you up on everything dat transpired while you were in da hospital."

CHAPTER 20

When the pair made it to their destination, Mike-Mike told Slick to go ahead and that he'd catch up with him later. Mike- Mike wanted to stay back so he could pick Zoe's brain about a few things pertaining to the game. Being a quick learner, it didn't take long for him to acquire the must needed information to attain the desired end. Though he had never done any of it hands-on, he felt strongly about his future.

Once he left Zoe, he headed back to his neighborhood. He was pleased to discover that everyone had carried out their tasks. Kurt had hollered at Hubb, so he could cook the product for them; Nose purchased enough coke bags to last them for the next month; Tre had spread the word about Aspen Courts having good quality for the low; lastly, Lil' Chico had talked to his mom about Mike-Mike renting an apartment, and this time she actually agreed with only one exception, that Mike-Mike handle everything himself. She also informed him that she could have one available as soon as he came up with the information of who the apartment was going to be leased to, the $1,680 for the first month's rent, and the security deposit. Mike-Mike already had that amount on standby, so it wouldn't be much longer until he had his very own spot.

Once he and Slick hooked back up, they found Hubb so that they could get the process started. Hubb was more beneficial than not, especially since he already had his own place. Hubb surely didn't mind cooking the product at his spot. Mike-Mike only took one kilo over to be cooked. Mike-Mike's first mission was to have that one brick cooked and on the market, so they would know for sure what they were dealing with.

"Damn, dat shit strong!" Slick complained of the aroma as Hubb continued to put his whip game down in the kitchen.

"No bullshit!" Mike-Mike added. "It seems like I'm catchin' contact, just sittin' here."

"You probably are, 'cause I know I am," said Hubb.

Having all that product in his presence, and having not yet taken a blast, had him definitely fiending for a hit. It was evident by the way his lips slanted as if he were Bobby Brown. Mike-Mike made sure to tell Hubb to put fourteen grams of baking soda on every two ounces that he cooked, which ultimately made the coke come back looking like a block of cheese with holes in it. Mike-Mike was being very observant, taking mental notes as Hubb cooked. Figuring he had seen enough, he decided to try it out for himself. He took the last two ounces and followed the steps he'd observed from watching Hubb, and to his surprise, his came out similar, if not better. Finally, in his desire to test the product, he told Hubb to take a piece and try it out.

Hubb quickly went to retrieve his coke-stem, broke a piece off the block of coke and took a blast. Mike-Mike and Slick witnessed firsthand the power of crack cocaine. The blast immediately made him sit down, then knocked him into a trance for about fifteen seconds before he commenced to blinking continuously and biting on his bottom lip.

"This nigga trippin'," said Slick, watching Hubb's high take effect.

"Hubb, you a'ight?" inquired Mike-Mike, staring at him strangely.

Hubb was stuck for a few more seconds, then out of nowhere he just started stuttering, "youn...youn...young... youngin' dat...dat shit must've come straight from Iraq!" Hubb blurted out.

"What da fuck is you talkin' 'bout?" voiced Slick.

"Maaannn, dat shit is da bomb!" he bragged, wiping sweat from his forehead.

"Oh yeah!" exclaimed Mike-Mike, excited about what Hubb just conveyed.

"Hell yeah, dat shit had me stutterin'. Y'all know damn well I don't stutter. Look give me what y'all promised me, so I can do me, fuck dat! I hope y'all remember how to cook it, 'cause this might be da last time y'all see me."

"Why you say dat?" asked Slick.

"'Cause I'll mess around and be done O.D.'d by tomorrow. I'm 'bout to have a crack party and probably get my dick sucked by three women at da same time, fuckin' wit' this good shit."

"Yeah well, before you go overboard, just make sure you spread da word 'bout us havin' dat good shit fo' da low," reminded Mike-Mike.

"Say no more," he assured with his hands out, waiting to get compensated for his services.

Hubb had a smile on his face as if he hit the mega millions when Mike-Mike placed a whole ounce in his palms. They didn't dispute the amount because they knew he was serious about throwing a party. With a party full of fiends and good crack, the word was sure to circulate in no time. Once they gave Hubb his fair share, the two gathered everything they came with and headed out his back door.

"Don't fo'get," said Mike-Mike.

"I won't," Hubb replied, shutting the door.

Once out back, the two briefly discussed their next move. They agreed for Slick to disperse the product to their men while Mike-Mike went to stash the rest. They were sure to blow after deciding to sell ounces for seven hundred when the going price was a thousand. At that price, Mike-Mike estimated they would accumulate a lump sum of two hundred twenty thousand five hundred apiece, and that was without including the brick that Hubb had already cooked for them.

Once they finished conversing, they went their separate ways. Mike-Mike immediately went to stash the remainder of the drugs in Monique's apartment, then footed it to his mother's house to grab the money he needed to give to Lil' Chico's mom so he could rent the apartment. Nearing his mother's house, he noticed that his mother's fiancé's vehicle was parked in the driveway. He tried to creep in, grab the money and then sneak back out without being detected, but he bumped into Anthony on his way out.

"I thought I heard something," said Anthony.

"Hey, wassup, it's just me," Mike-Mike replied.

"You think you have a minute?"

"Yeah," Mike-Mike agreed, even though he was actually in a rush to handle his business.

Anthony always treated him and his mother with the utmost respect, so it was only right for him to listen to what he had to say.

"Come in the living room for a second, I won't be long," Anthony told him as the two walked into the living room and took a seat.

"I'm not the one to preach, but I will address a situation if it calls for me to do so," he sternly stated. He fixed Mike-Mike with a hard stare. "Be mindful of the choices you make, because the lifestyle that you're choosing over your family is heartless. Trust me, I know, the people that you think are your friends will be the same ones to backstab you. That dollar you chasin' is the root of all evil. Folks always want to be in your face when you feedin' 'em, but as soon as that stops, that's when you'll start seeing the change in 'em for the worst," he advised straight-faced.

"I'll make sure I keep dat in mind," he assured him, returning the gaze, letting Anthony know he was taking what he said seriously.

"You do that, and one more thing."

"I'm listenin'."

"Always remember that the art of leadership is being able to tell a person that you deal with on a constant basis no, 'cause it's too easy for us to say yes even when we're not in the position to do as we say. Also, know that every land has its own law, so should man," he concluded, removing a chain from around his neck that held a scroll with a quote that he lived by embedded on it. He then passed it to him. "Take this," he offered.

"What does it say?" asked Mike-Mike, admiring the gift.

"It says that knowledge will give you power, but character will give you respect," he conveyed, hoping he understood the message.

Taking in the content, he simply placed the chain around his neck. Then he stood up and shook Anthony's hand before heading out the door.

CHAPTER 21

When darkness fell, Aspen Courts had people roaming around like South Beach on Memorial Day weekend. Hubb's word must've spread like a wildfire because fiends were all over. Because of Aspen Court's good product and cheap prices, Mike-Mike's crew was able to sell a larger amount at a faster pace. The word must've also circulated to some of the local dealers because they were also out there trying to purchase several ounces, especially at seven hundred a piece. After making a few runs and taking care of some immediate concerns, Mike-Mike showed up in the neighborhood and instantly noticed all the traffic in the vicinity. He quickly found and went over to Slick.

"Where'd all these people come from?" inquired Mike-Mike.

"Slim, let me holler at you right quick!" Slick said animatedly, pulling his partner to the side.

"What's good?"

"They lovin' this shit, this shit butter!"

"Shid, dat's wassup."

"What you tryin' to do, 'cause I already got crooked-eye Shawn-n-Whop from down 14th-n-Somerset tryin' to cop like six ounces, plus red Alex-n-Kenny from up Fern Place tryin' to get a few of 'em."

"Shid, you already know what it is, where them niggas at?" responded Mike-Mike, quickly adding the numbers up in his head. *That's a quick forty-nine to fifty-six hundred,* he thought to himself.

"They just pulled off not too long ago, but I have their numbers in my phone," Slick validated.

"Go 'head and hit'em while I go grab that shit."

"Say no more," replied Slick, retrieving his phone so he could make the necessary calls.

From that moment on, all that was relevant seemed to have changed for the better, because their product started selling quicker than a *New York Minute*. Three days later, the two had already piled up close to thirty-five thousand, and their clientele was rapidly increasing. Mike-Mike was finally able to rent an apartment from Lil' Chico's mom and had already grabbed his personal things from his mother's house. His spot quickly became the hang-out spot for his men, so he could decrease the traffic in and out of Monique's apartment. Her place was where he was momentarily keeping his work stashed, and he didn't want any unwanted attention directed her way. The only time he had any drugs present in his house was when he was cooking product as he was doing at that very moment.

"Slim, you need to bring ya ass in here and watch me do

this shit, 'cause I'm not gon' to be da only one whipping this work up!" asserted Mike-Mike from inside the kitchen.

"Shid, nigga, I thought you had it since you ain't never said nothin'," Slick answered sluggishly, getting up off the living room couch and strolling into the kitchen.

"Yeah, I bet ya did. You better pay close attention, 'cause da next batch you whippin' up and if you mess it up, it's comin' out your half," he warned.

Slick made sure to be very observant after his partner's comment. He watched as Mike-Mike placed the amount of powder he was cooking into the pyrex pot and then placed it on the stove with a low flame. As the powdery substance began to oil-down, Mike-Mike used the digital scale to weigh out the amount of baking soda that he would add. Slick observed how the crystal-like substance melted down into an oily brown liquid form before Mike-Mike added the baking soda that caused it to temporarily foam up.

Afterward, he grabbed the egg beater using it to mix the two raw materials together. Soon after, the powder began to harden. Once the floury substance became solid, he put a little bit of cold water in the pyrex and played with the edges until it started twirling around. At that point, he then drained out the water, turning the pyrex upside-down over a stack of napkins while tapping the sides until the flat, smooth, solid substance fell out.

"Voila!" he boasted. "Now, dat's how you make crack," he grinned.

"Slim, you jive like did dat muthafucka," Slick said,

matching his tone.

"Shid, work ain't hard. It's all in da wrist," he added.

"Yeah, I bet ya wrist strong as shit from all dat late night jackin'," Slick joked.

"Whatever nigga, I got too many women for dat," Mike-Mike corrected.

"Dat's what ya mouth say."

"Nah, dat's what I know," countered Mike-Mike. "But instead of you runnin' ya mouth 'bout some broads, you need to be baggin' this shit up, so we can hit da block," he said rather frankly.

"I got it, where da bags at?"

"Come on bruh, tighten up! You know where da bags at, ain't nothin' changed since da last time, but da time," he interjected. "Stop being lazy, and handle dat while I go get dressed."

Shortly after, the two went outside to see what was going on. Almost immediately, Hubb popped up and rushed towards them.

"Youngins, where y'all been? One of you two gotta leave me a number or somethin' 'cause I been tryin' to catch-up wit' either one of y'all for a minute. Everybody out here seemed to have amnesia when I asked for the two of you."

"Hubb!" Slick barked. "Slow da fuck down so a nigga can understand what you sayin'."

"My bad, but I got some folks parked in front of my buildin' that's tryin' to cop some weight," he calmly stated.

"Who is it?" Mike-Mike inquired.

"Some dealers that I cop from, from time to time," he

informed him. "But they good peoples."

"What they tryin' to cop?" asked Mike-Mike.

"Don't know, I tried to ask'em, but they wouldn't say. It gotta be somethin' proper 'cause they wouldn't put the money in my hand."

"They wouldn't put da money in ya hand, and they s'posed to be good peoples," Slick suspiciously remarked.

"Man, I'm a crackhead. I wouldn't trust myself wit' my own money," Hubb reasoned.

"Hold-on fo' a sec," said Mike-Mike, pulling Slick to the side.

"What's up?" asked Slick once the two were out of range for Hubb to eavesdrop.

"Watch my back, while I go holler at these folks."

"I got you," assured Slick. "Here, take this just in case," he stated, passing his pistol to his partner.

"Bet," replied Mike-Mike, taking the gun and tucking it away before walking back over to Hubb. "You ready?" he asked him.

"Ready when you are."

"C'mon, let's go."

As the two approached Hubb's building, he quickly signaled in the direction of the buyers with a head gesture.

"That's them over there in that green explorer."

"How many of'em in there?"

"There's three of'em."

"And where you say you knew these dudes from?"

"Man, I'm an international crackhead. I know people from all over. I been smokin' this shit way before you was born. Way before Conan was a barbarian, back when folks thought Grace Jones looked like Beyonce´. I done jumped from spot to spot way more than snitches jump from block to block…"

"Hubb, shut da fuck-up wit' all dat bullshit and answer my fuckin' question, fo' I punch you in ya damn mouth and have somethin' else comin' out of it besides dat bullshit you spittin'!" scolded Mike-Mike, interrupting Hubb's animated rambling.

"You right, but like I said before, I bought coke from the dude plenty of times," he explained. "So when he contacted me, askin' me why I hadn't been to holler at'im, I told'im that the dudes around my way got some way better coke fo' cheaper. After I told'im that, he inquired 'bout the prices 'cause he wanted to buy some weight if the price was right, and that's when I told'im y'all had seven-hundred-dollar ounces. Once he heard that, he flew-up here to cop somethin'. How much, I don't know," he briefed.

After hearing Hubb's explanation, he agreed, though he was a bit hesitant.

"Look, I'ma deal wit' da dude on da strength of you being so persuasive, but I swear on everything dat I luv, if these niggas on some dumb shit, I promise you'll regret it. Ya heard me," he warned with a stern look.

"There are no worries 'cause he's straight," Hubb assured, somewhat hesitant.

"A'ight look, go tell da one you been dealin' wit' to come holler at me by himself," he directed. "I'ma be standin' in ya buildin'."

"Got you. You think dat you can maybe look out fo' me if he buys somthin' proper?"

"Look out fo' you," he frowned. "You ain't doin' me no favors," he retorted defensively. "If anything, you need to be askin' dude fo' somethin' 'cause he's da one you lookin' out fo', plus, I just gave you damn near an ounce not too long ago!"

"Man, I'ma chain smoker. I smoked dat shit back to back like a re-run, but I'm good, I just thought I'd ask. Let me go get'im so y'all can handle ya business," he stated, walking off.

The small cemetery the three dudes were parked in front of was located in the middle of the block. That same exact cemetery was the neighborhood dealer's hangout spot at night because it camouflaged their presence after nightfall. Plus, it was easily accessible for a quick getaway when necessary.

Minutes later, Mike-Mike observed a tall, medium-build, dark-skinned individual who emerged from the passenger side of the Ford *Explorer* and crossed over a busy Georgia Avenue, headed toward the building. Once he was close, Mike-Mike pushed the building door open to allow him in while quickly scanning the area for Slick who was nowhere to be found.

"Moe, wassup?" the male customer asked as he entered the building.

"Moe" was a term that was mostly used by locals on the south or northeast sides of town, so immediately he knew that the dude was from one of the two areas.

"Wassup," Mike-Mike spoke back. "Hubb said you tryin' to do some business."

"Yeah. He said you had some good product for da low."

"I guess you can say dat. What you tryin' to cop?"

"What you got?" the male customer countered.

"What I got," Mike-Mike repeated in a deadpan tone. "Look, we gettin' off on da wrong foot already, 'cause you answerin' a question wit' a question. You came up here to cop somethin', right? So, I need to know what you tryin' to get, so hopefully I can get whatever it is you need, and we can go 'bout our separate ways," he said, growing a bit agitated.

"My bad moe, I ain't tryna get off on da wrong foot, I just wanna do some business, but umh..." he hesitated. "I'm workin' wit' seventeen," he announced.

He felt around in his pockets as if he were about to pull his money out. Just as Mike-Mike got a strange feeling, the dude pulled out a Glock .40 and aimed it at Mike-Mike's head.

Mike-Mike threw his hands up with disappointment as if the barrel of the gun was blinding his vision. "Slim, it ain't even got..." was all he managed to get out before the barrel of the gun came crashing down the side of his face.

"Shut ya bitch ass up! I didn't ask you to say nothin'! Sucka ass uptown nigga!"

Mike-Mike was on one knee holding the side of his head while the male aggressor dialed a number on his cell phone with his free hand.

"I got'im," he conveyed. "Stand outside the truck and watch out while I bring this fool out," he directed. He focused his attention back on Mike-Mike. "Now stand ya bitch ass up, and if you try anything funny I promise you won't live to regret it! Now c'mon!" he commanded, grabbing Mike-Mike by the arm and walking him out the building.

Mike-Mike immediately tried to glance around, hoping to find Slick or anybody else that was in the neighborhood for help. All of a sudden, it seemed as though no one was around except the vehicles that rode up and down Georgia Avenue. The male trailed close behind Mike-Mike's side as if they were together chatting, trying to avoid looking conspicuous, but anyone who was entangled in street life would've easily picked up on the act.

Mike-Mike was playing mental ping-pong, trying to figure-out a way to escape his attacker. Suddenly, his thoughts landed on the one mistake his aggressor had made, which was not searching him before abducting him. As the pair reached the curb, he was quickly trying to figure out a way to reach for his pistol without being obvious. As soon as the two stepped into the street to cross over Georgia Avenue, Slick emerged right on time from the darkness of the graveyard directly behind the two male individuals that stood outside the truck waiting on their partner and captive to cross over. The two male occupants were blinded by the danger that stood behind them.

When Mike-Mike and his aggressor crossed, the male that held on to Mike-Mike glanced in the direction of his two associates and instantly noticed the silhouette behind them aiming a pistol. He quickly tried to call out to them, but it was too late because Slick wasted no time placing bullets into the back of both their skulls. The sudden distraction of witnessing his two men shot gave Mike-Mike the time needed to reach for his own weapon. In a matter of seconds, he had his own pistol aimed at the rear right-side of his robber's face, pulling the trigger. The blast from his gun caused a portion of the front left-side of his abductor's face to separate from the rest of its surface.

"Who da bitch now!" Mike-Mike fumed, looking at his victim's corpse laying on the ground as Slick rushed to his side.

"We gotta get out of here!" Slick barked, snatching Mike-Mike by the arm and leading him through the pitch-black passageway between the buildings.

CHAPTER 22

For the next few days, the police swarmed the area trying to gather information on the three recent homicides. They were questioning everyone in the vicinity, but unfortunately for them, no one was cooperating. Though Mike-Mike and Slick weren't on the radar, they still kept a low profile, especially after the incident made headlines. Money was still circulating under the circumstances, but their present focus was to seek some hardware just in case the associates of the deceased tried to retaliate.

Mike-Mike's first option was to reach out to Zoe for assistance, and he immediately came through for them. Zoe told Mike-Mike he needed to take a ride with him and to make sure that he came alone.

Once Mike-Mike got off the phone from speaking with Zoe, he gathered his things to go meet up with him. Grabbing some money from his bedroom and then retrieving his Helly Hanson jacket from out the closet, he headed for the door with Slick trailing behind.

"Wait here til I get back," Mike-Mike told him.

"Fo' what!" Slick replied in a slightly raised tone.

"'Cause he told me to come alone."

"What, slim got a problem wit' me or somethin'. You need to start lettin' him know I'm ya right-hand, not ya stunt-devil! We s'pose to be hand to hand, arm to arm, side by side, ya feel me?"

"Of course, I feel ya," Mike-Mike concurred, avoiding Slick's gaze. "But it ain't dat serious, 'cause whoever he's takin' me to meet probably don't want no crowd," he explained, trying to reason with him.

"Yeah, whatever! Just let dat nigga know we partners not oppositions."

"I got ya slim. Just let me handle this, a'ight?"

"You do dat. Just hit me when you get back. I'll be over one of my shorty's houses."

"Cool and be careful."

"I'm straight, you be careful," Slick shot back, grabbing his things to leave also.

The two said a few more words before walking out the door behind one another and going their separate ways.

CHAPTER 23

When Mike-Mike met up with Zoe near the Langdon Recreation Center in Northeast, Zoe was sitting in a Chevy Astro van waiting on Mike-Mike to get in so that they could go see the gun connect who stayed in Baltimore, Maryland. The Astro van was equipped with a stash spot large enough to transport a substantial number of weapons or anything else he chose to conceal.

"Wassup?" Mike-Mike spoke, hopping in the van.

"I can't complain," Zoe responded. "How 'bout yourself?" he inquired, shaking his hand.

"Maintainin'."

"That's good. Make sure you buckle up," Zoe cautioned, before pulling off.

About thirty minutes into the drive Zoe inquired about the sudden urgency for the hardware.

"Is everything cool on your end, you ain't in no trouble, are you?"

"Huh...oh, naw," Mike-Mike replied, getting caught off guard. "You just never know, dat's all."

Zoe didn't respond because he assumed that Mike-Mike didn't want to speak on it, but he was aware of the murders in Mike-Mike's neighborhood from catching it on the news. Though he wanted to speak more on the situation, figuring that he could probably assist in the matter, he respected Mike-Mike's silence on the subject. Sensing his discomfort, he changed the topic.

"Listen-up, 'cause this guy that we meetin' up with is a military vet. He's going to be very specific about every detail of the guns, so just allow him to do all the talking, then pick out whatever it is that you want afterward," Zoe explained.

"I got you."

"Other than that, how are things moving with that demonstration?"

"Things been moving smoothly fo' da most part. Way better than I expected. I already ran through a few of them things."

"That's good," Zoe smiled. "I guess you didn't make me look bad after all, huh?" he joked.

"I told you I wouldn't, plus you gave me dat Benz...shid a nigga can't do nothin' but move up," he said with excitement. "Mannnn, I just wanna say I appreciate everything you done for me, it really means a lot."

"What's the use of having everything and not being able to share? Plus, your loyalty and determination got you where you are today."

"Dat's wassup, 'cause I'm fo'ever loyal," Mike-Mike vowed. "Not to jump off da subject, but I wanna holler at you 'bout somethin'."

"What's on your mind?"

"It's 'bout my man Slick."

"What about 'im?"

"He feels a certain kinda way when he can't be present when we handlin' business."

Zoe hesitated before answering, choosing his words wisely so that he wouldn't sound inconsiderate. "I know that's your man, but his feelings are not my concern. I'm not gon' to change how I conduct my business just because he feels a certain kind of way. To be honest with you, he shouldn't care how the business is being handled just as long as it gets done."

"I feel ya, but he is my partner," he tried to reason.

"Yeah just like Big Herm is mine, but do you see him with me when we conducting business? No. Want to know why, because I deal wit' you and he trusts me as a partner, no questions asked," he sternly expressed. Mike-Mike was thinking about what he said when Zoe interjected once again. "Now let me ask you something..."

"I'm listenin'."

"Why all of a sudden does he want to be present when we taking care of our business? He didn't have a problem before, so why now? Did you ask 'im that?"

"Never thought about it."

"Well maybe you two should have a talk, 'cause one thing for sure, and two things for certain, I'm not changing how I conduct my business and in this line of work, everything ain't for everybody," he said point blank.

Mike-Mike didn't respond because he knew that Zoe

had a point about switching the way he conducted his business on the account of someone's feelings. On the other hand, he understood Slick's viewpoint. When the time presented itself, he was going to have a one-on-one with his partner to try to clear up any unwelcoming emotions. Truthfully, as he thought about it, there wasn't any real reason for him to feel left out. Things were going smooth, and life couldn't have been better, besides the current situation, but once again, thanks to Zoe, things were sure to be more secure due to his connects.

"I have a serious question that I want to ask you," said Zoe, breaking Mike-Mike's train of thought.

"Wassup?"

Zoe took a deep breath before saying, "What would you do if you found out that someone you're close to hurt somebody that you love?"

"What kind of question is dat," Mike-Mike said in a faraway tone.

"Just answer the question," he replied, matching his tone.

"Dat's a difficult question to answer, but I guess it depends on da relationship between me and da person dat hurt someone I love. Hopefully, it never comes to dat, 'cause truthfully, I really don't know how I might react," he spoke sincerely, trying to figure out where that question came from.

After allowing the inquiry to circulate in his mind for a few more minutes, he decided to ask about the question but was interrupted by the ringing of Zoe's cell phone.

"What you have a G.P.S on me or something 'cause you called right on time. I'm turning off the exit as we speak," Zoe conveyed to the caller.

Shortly after, he hung up and was turning onto a narrow street where he found a parking space.

"We here and remember what we talked about when we go in there!" Zoe reminded as the two got out, heading towards the fenced and bricked in, three-level home.

Once they crossed the gate, the two walked around back so that they could enter through the back door. Zoe tapped on the door in a coded manner. Seconds later, the door opened up revealing a 6'5" muscular white male standing behind the door sporting a military cut with a huge grin on his face.

"Heyyy budyyy! Long time no see, how's it been?"

"Everything been good fo' the most part. How 'bout yourself?" Zoe replied, shaking the guy's hand.

"I can't complain. Surviving, you know. Who's the young fella?"

"Pete this Mike-Mike, and Mike-Mike this Pete," Zoe introduced the two before finally entering the house.

"Pleased to meet you. Any friend of Zoe's is a friend of mine. Welcome," he spoke, shaking Mike-Mike's hand with a firm grip.

"Likewise," Mike-Mike replied, pulling away from Pete's solid grip.

"Right this way," Pete invited, closing the door, then leading the way.

The room they entered was in the rear of the basement. Pete opened the bolted door, then stepped to the side to allow his guest access. *Damn,* thought Mike-Mike upon entering the weapon-filled room.

Inside the room were three Regale tables covered with a cache of arms. Sitting up against the wall were several shotguns and assault rifles. Mike-Mike in his young life had never witnessed such a numerous amount of weaponry at one time. The only time he had seen anything close to it was on T.V. Mike-Mike being the laid-back person that he was, disguised his excitement very well.

"So how can I be at y'all's service? Looking for anything particular?" Pete inquired, spreading his arms wide as if he was signifying that he had everything.

"See anything you want?" Zoe said to Mike-Mike.

Seeing so much to choose from, he just pointed at one of the Regale tables. Pete unhesitantly walked over to the table of his choice, then immediately picked up one of the handguns, describing its features.

"Well Bud, this right here is a Berretta PX4 Storm, which is a semiautomatic with a hell of a kick, but also easy to handle, accurate, and reliable. It comes with a durable light techno polymer frame, a standard Pica tinny rail, a three-dot sight system, a unique rotating barrel, and a locking system. This particular pistol comes in .40 S&W, and nine-millimeter," he precisely explained. Placing the gun back in its place he picked up another one, giving its details.

"This one right here is a Ruger SR9c compact, centerfire, nine-millimeter Luger. This particular firearm comes with an adjustable high-visibility three-dot sight system, a 1911 style ambidextrous manual safety, an internal trigger bar interlock, and a striker blocker. Plus, it only weighs 24.3 ounces. If you purchase this weapon here, I'll even throw in two extra ten plus one magazine cartridges, a finger grip extension floor plate, and a reversible back strap," he concluded, gently placing the gun back down on the table, picking up the next one to it. This time, though, he had a huge smile on his face, like a kid's first time at the amusement park.

"Now this one here is one of my favorites," he said in an all too easy tone. "I call this piece here…" he hesitated before continuing, "Mother Teresa, 'cause she's the winner of all peace prizes," he smiled lustfully. He suddenly held the revolver close to the side of his face as if he were taking a picture holding a trophy.

"It's only a five-shot Taurus cylinder revolver, but it always gets the job done. Trust me, I know," he spoke in nearly a whisper like he was talking to the revolver, then immediately went into the details of the powerful handgun.

"This beauty comes with a red optic fixed front sight. Plus, it's equipped with a reduced profile hammer. With this particular gun, I'll throw in a small grip for concealment, and a larger grip for range, but that's not all…" he sounded, taking a deep breath. "It not only fires .45 colt shells…" his words trailed off, "it also shoots 4-10-gauge shells, the two and a half-shot shells!" he boasted, kissing the side of the barrel.

Instead of placing Mother Teresa down, he tucked it in his waistband.

The describing of the arsenal of weapons went on for

nearly thirty minutes before he finally concluded his presentation or promoting of his storehouse of weaponry. When it was all said and done, he had anything one needed, from Glock seventeen's to A.R. fifteens. He even had laserlyte rear sight lasers with activating switches powered by 377 batteries that would indicate if the laser was constantly on or on pulse mode. Pete had so many different weapons to choose from that Mike-Mike was uncertain for a short moment, but he eventually picked out what he wanted, and he made it his business to purchase Mother Teressa just for himself. As they were leaving, Pete had a few words that he wanted to share with them.

"Listen up buds, I want y'all to always keep in mind that war may be fought with weapons, but they are won by man," he advised. "Just something to remember," he finalized, shaking their hands, then walking them out of the house.

CHAPTER 24

Slick wanted to refrain from being seen in the neighborhood, so he opted to lounge over at one of his female's houses until he heard back from Mike-Mike. He was trying to clear his head of the recent homicides that he and his partner had committed. Though they weren't suspects, he was still bothered by the fact that there was at least one person, which was Hubb, who could identify their presence at the crime scene. The exact person that brought the victims to them in the first place. *If it wasn't for his crackhead ass, none of this would have ever happened*, he thought.

Being that Hubb knew the danger he was in, Slick was hoping he wouldn't panic, pointing the finger just to secure himself from being prosecuted legally. Not wanting to take any chances, he made his mind up that Hubb had to be dealt with. It was apparent that if he ever pointed them out, it would be nothing for him to relocate, thinking nothing of his ill-doings. The only problem was for Slick to find him. He knew there was no way in hell Hubb would stay at his own place after what had gone down. After finalizing his thoughts, he pulled out a bag of weed and proceeded to twist himself a backwood while conversing with his lady friend who seemed to be tuned in to the television.

"What time ya folks come back in?" he inquired, as he finished rolling up his weed.

"Sometime after six," she replied, never taking her eyes off the T.V.

"You mind if I smoke in here?"

"No, just open the windows."

Regina was a cute redbone that stood five-foot-two, weighed around 135 lbs., with two gaps, one between her legs, and the other between her top front teeth. Both of them made her stand out for the better. Plus, her breasts were a mouth full, and her nipples seemed to always be erect. She kind of resembled the singer, Keyshia Cole, with jet black hair. She was definitely eye-catching, even in her tank top and tights she walked around the house in while sitting Indian style on her bed, exposing her cute pedicured toes. Slick couldn't help but stare at her lustfully, because of the way her nipples protruded through her tank top.

"Why ya nipples always stay hard?" he asked, getting off the bed to open the window.

"Because you make them like that," she flirted.

"Good answer...Damn good answer. I see you know how to shut a nigga up quick," he remarked, firing up the weed.

She just smiled at him as he clouded his mind with the high-grade marijuana. Once the effects started to take their course, he asked her if she wanted to take a hit. Regina accepted, even though she hardly ever smoked. She only took a few pulls before passing it back to him. Shortly after, she got up and walked into the bathroom to free herself from the taste and smell.

As she made her way to the bathroom, Slick admired how her tights fit her body like a pair of latex gloves, showing off every curve to perfection. By the time she came back, the weed was nearly gone. She sat behind Slick and began rubbing her hands through his braids.

"Whoever braided your hair did a good job," she complimented.

"Thanks. This female in my neighborhood hooked me up," he responded, turning around, staring at her and admiring her beauty.

"Why you staring at me like that?" she smirked, feeling the effects of the weed.

"Like what?"

"Like an animal that just saw its prey."

"Dat's because I have!" he roared, playfully springing on top of her, kissing and sucking on her neck.

The silliness only lasted about a minute before things started to get intense. He went from playfully sucking and kissing on her neck to eagerly massaging her breasts and then her ass. Regina instantly got turned on by his aggressiveness, which caused her to anxiously tug at his shirt freeing him from it before unbuckling his belt buckle to assist in freeing him of his jeans as well. When he was down to his boxers only, she wasted no time removing her own clothing.

As soon as they were only in their undergarments, they avidly went at it like a couple that hadn't seen one another in years. In a matter of seconds, they were in their birthday suits grabbing, pulling, and squeezing each other aggressively until Slick finally entered her swollen vagina missionary style. Regina moaned a sigh of satisfaction after feeling his manhood inside her. Slick gripped a handful of her hair, massaging her breasts with his free hand at the same time as he gyrated his hips in and out her gaping wet hole.

He was being a bit rough, but in her mind, the sex was feeling so good that she just allowed him to have his way with no complaints. As he got into a rhythm, he mounted her legs above her head and commenced to pounding her insides out like he was trying to use his penis to shake hands with her heart. Regina tried to lower her legs, but the way he had her pinned up there wasn't anything she could do. Luckily, he changed positions shortly after. Flipping her over and laying her on her stomach, he filled her insides as he simultaneously sucked on her earlobe and neck.

"Damn, you feel good!" Slick managed to blurt out while still penetrating her.

The effects of the weed mixed with her dripping wet vagina had him going into overdrive. Regina had her eyes closed enjoying the sexual onslaught he was putting on her.

"Ooh…Ooh…Oo Yess! Right there …I'm cum…innnn!" She yelped, causing him to dig in even more.

"Cum on this dick fo' daddy!" he encouraged.

Slick, immediately, pulled her up doggy style, drilling into her flesh as if he was a human jackhammer while smacking her ass and pulling her hair. He was pounding her so hard that she somehow ripped a hole in the pillowcase she was gripping as she euphorically climaxed. He wasn't quite finished because after she orgasmed, he mounted his hands on her hips, cocked his right leg up, and dug in her at a steady pace until he reached his semen eviction notice, emptying his full load of baby makers all over her backside.

"Ahhh yess!" Slick growned, releasing himself.

The sexual encounter was brief, but the intensity of it resembled a sex scene from the DMX movie, *Belly*.

The two collapsed onto the bed with a satisfying smirk on their faces. Moments after their sexual encounter Slick's phone lit-up breaking the silence. Retrieving his phone from the pocket of his jeans, he answered.

"Wassup?" he heaved, still somewhat out of breath.

"E'rything's good," conveyed, Mike-Mike. "I should be back shortly," he assured.

"A'ight, cool I'll meet you back at ya spot in a few."

"Dat's a bet, Why you breathin' into da phone like dat?"

"Dat's because I just had one helluva sexathon," Slick joked.

"Oh, yeah!"

"Sho-nuff!" he shot back. "But let me get off this phone so I can go get cleaned up and meet up wit' ya."

"You do dat, and one more thing."

"What's dat?"

"Let's do somethin' tonight like go somewhere, a club or Go-Go, so we can clear our heads," he suggested.

"Sounds good to me," Slick agreed. "I'll see you in a little bit."

"A'ight," replied Mike-Mike before hanging up.

Mike-Mike's intentions were not to only have a good time but to also try to defuse some of the resentment Slick held toward Zoe for not allowing him to be involved in the serious business when being conducted.

CHAPTER 25

Over in Northeast, DC, off Benning Road, was a tattoo parlor named Flawless that was owned by a man named Moe Kelly. His name rung bells in the streets mainly because of one of his old professions. He was an ex-boxer that had a low tolerance for anyone that stood in the way of him moving forward. Kelly was supposed to be the next elite fighter that came out of Washington, but like so many others, the streets grabbed hold of him, costing him his career. He'd developed a nose habit while on his mission to becoming a household name in the boxing world.

Though his habit thickened, he still conditioned himself on a regular basis as if he were training for the fight of his life. Because of his boxing reputation, people on the street didn't challenge him, which made it easy for him to exploit them. His favorite quote was, *Treat a man like a man and a Sucker like a Sucker*, and he stayed true to that saying. If you showed any weakness, he was going to definitely use that to his advantage.

One benefit of him preying on one's weakness led to him owning the very tattoo parlor he was sitting in at the moment with his partner who went by the name Rex. Rex was a known drug dealer that supplied a large quantity of the narcotics that flowed throughout the 21st section of Northeast, Washington, DC. Rex was of slim build, weighing roughly 172 lbs, standing 6 feet 2 inches, dark skinned with a bald head that was as smooth as marble.

Moe Kelly on the other hand, stood about 5 feet 9 inches tall, toting 215 lbs of mass and little body fat. He had the same complexion as his partner, wavy hair, and sported a neatly trimmed beard. The two of them were lounging in the shop when the door flung open. One of Moe Kelly's nephew's associates came storming in causing the pair to become defensive, reaching for their weapon.

"Snarz! What da fuck you doin' runnin' in here like someone chasing you or somethin'," Moe Kelly barked, brandishing a chrome .45 in his hand.

"Its ya nephew!" Snarz alerted him, holding his head down towards the floor.

"What about 'im!" frowned Moe Kelly, sensing the worst.

"He got killed," Snarz informed.

For a split second everything seemed to have stopped, until what he'd just heard registered.

"What!" Moe Kelly snapped in disbelief.

"Yeah slim, he got smashed up there off of Georgia Avenue by that Master Host hotel dat's close to Walter Reed hospital," he explained.

"What the fuck was he doin' up there in the first place!" he questioned, standing up, pacing back and forth.

"Him and da dudes he was wit' had to be up to something, 'cause every time they hook-up they be on all moves."

"So where the other dudes he was wit' at?"

"All three of em got smashed," he said, shaking his head.

Moe Kelly sat in silence for a few more seconds before glancing over at Rex, who already knew what time it was. "I'm tryin' to close casket whoever responsible, includin' their mother, father, sister, brother, or whoever else they close to!" he scolded coldly. After immediately closing the shop for the remainder of the day, Moe stormed out the shop with Rex, and Snarz trailing close behind.

CHAPTER 26

Mike-Mike finally made it back to his apartment safely after having to ride back on the highway, and maneuvering through the crevices of the buildings with a duffel bag full of weapons. Being cautious was an absolute must due to the amount of law enforcement scanning the area. Entering his apartment, he immediately went to place the duffel bag on top of his bed. With that done, he pulled out his cell phone to call Lil' Chico's mom Beverly to discuss some must need requirements for the near future. Just as he was finishing his brief discussion with Beverly, he heard a knock at his door.

"Who is it?"

"It's me," replied the familiar voice coming from the other side of his door.

Recognizing the voice, he quickly went to open it up, "Wassup? I thought you might've been Lil' Chico and 'em, until I heard ya voice," he proclaimed. "You got here quick," Mike- Mike remarked, stepping aside to allow Slick to enter.

"Why you say dat?"

"'Cause I called and told 'em to meet me over here, plus they was tryin' to cop some more work," he explained.

"What you bring back?" Slick inquired.

"Go look in da room on da bed."

As Slick walked toward the bedroom, Mike-Mike headed for the kitchen to get the work ready for when Lil' Chico and the other's arrived.

"Slim, you got some shit in here!" Slick exclaimed from the bedroom.

"Shid dat ain't shit, you should've seen what da dude had in his spot."

"Yeah well, I would've seen it if I went wit' you," Slick countered, coming from out the bedroom.

"You ain't gotta act like dat, plus I said somethin' to 'im 'bout dat situation."

"And what did he say?" he asked just as there was a knock at the door. Before Mike-Mike had a chance to respond, Slick dryly stated, "I'll get it," still wanting to know the answer to his question but figured he would wait until a better time to finish their conversation.

After looking through the peephole, he opened the door, "Whats good fellas?" Slick greeted his men as they entered the apartment.

As all seven of them piled up in the living room, Mike-Mike decided it was a good time to talk to them, making sure that they were on point just in case any kind of retribution came from the recent killings.

"Wassup wit' y'all," Mike-Mike spoke for the first time, "I want to holler at all y'all 'bout da incident dat happened a few days ago," he said rather frankly.

Sensing that he had everyone's attention, he continued, "I need fo' each of y'all to be on point, cause them bodies dat dropped da other day made da news. Which means dat not only are da police gon' to be pressin' this joint out but whoever fucks wit' them niggas dat got smashed might be on some bullshit too. With dat said, I wanna know who in here ain't strapped?"

"You already know… I keep's mine on me or close by," "Lil' Chico spoke up, pulling out a compact 380, placing it on the table.

"Shid me too," followed Lil' Kurt, revealing a beat-up looking High Point 9mm and placing his on the table as well.

"I keep dat tre pound on me at all times," Tre stressed cocky, whipping out a newly looking chrome 357 Smith & Wesson, placing it on his lap.

Lyran, Melvin, Nose, and Pete didn't have weapons or at least not on them.

"Wassup wit' y'all four, y'all don't have no hammas?" Slick inquired.

"I got one, I just don't have it on me," said Nose while the other three shook their heads no.

"A'ight look, don't even trip, 'cause I went out my way to fortify our security," Mike-Mike said, then asked Slick to grab the duffel bag from the room.

When Slick returned with the bag, everyone's eyes were glued to the bag he placed in the middle of the floor. After engaging in a few more words of being mindful of how serious the situation was, Mike-Mike gave Slick a nod to open the bag up. Slick immediately unzipped the duffel bag, unveiling its contents, causing everybody's body language to shift after viewing the hardware.

"Damn! Where y'all get all of those hammas from?" Lil' Chico sounded.

"Where they came from don't matter, just know dat we're straight from here on out if we ever need more," Mike-Mike said with conviction.

"Shid, dat's wassup."

"One more thing, my reason fo' bringin' the situation to y'all's attention is because a lot of good men got fucked around cause one of there homies got into some shit and left their men in da blind. I don't want dat to happen to us," Mike-Mike expressed, noticing his men nodding their heads in agreement.

"I respect dat," said Nose, walking over to give him some dap.

"Good, 'cause I wouldn't have said anything if I didn't fuck wit' y'all," he announced. "But anyway, Tre dat Tre-Five you got is straight. Lil' Kurt dat raggedy azz High Point you got has to go, cause it looks like da clip don't even stay in it. Lil' Chico dat 380 cool, but you better off with somethin' like this," he said with a lilt in his voice.

Mike-Mike reached into the bag, pulling out a .40 S&W Beretta Px4 Storm, popping in an extended clip then handing it over to Chico with a slight grin on his face.

"Damn, this joint real nice, plus it got da beam on it," he grinned, holding it up and examining it.

Next, Mike-Mike reached back into the bag pulling out a Ruger SR9c 9mm, then passed it over to Lil' Kurt. "Here, this fo' you, and hand me dat beat-up ass High-Point before you mess 'round and get ya'self killed wit' dat joint."

Lil' Kurt gladly handed over his old looking pistol before accepting the brand new 9mm that Mike-Mike gave him. When it was all said and done, everyone had a pistol with the exception of Melvin who declined to accept one, claiming that his folks would be the ones to kill him if they were to find a gun in their house.

"You sure?" asked Mike-Mike.

"Positive," Melvin assured him.

"A'ight cool, dat's on you, so now dat we got dat taken care of, let's get down to business, how much work y'all tryin' to get?"

They all commenced to pulling out small wads of cash, conveying to Mike-Mike what it was that they needed, but for some odd reason, Melvin's money wasn't anywhere close to the others. That was strange though, due to the constant sales that were flowing throughout the neighborhood. After grabbing their money, then giving them what their money called for, plus a little extra, he went on to ask Melvin why his stack was so small.

"I still got some left from last time," Melvin responded, avoiding his gaze.

"You know no matter what I got ya back, so if there's anything dat's goin' on wit' you, don't hesitate to let me know," Mike-Mike expressed.

"I got you, but everything cool for da most part," he said in a distant tone.

Mike-Mike not convinced that Melvin was telling the truth, just glared at him for a few more seconds before leaving the matter alone for the moment. "A'ight everybody else good?" he inquired directing his attention to the others.

Once they all agreed that they were good, he told them that he and Slick would get up with them later, 'cause they had some business to handle. They quickly got up and dapped one another up before heading for the door. As they were leaving, Mike-Mike told Lil' Chico to hold up for a minute because he wanted to ask him something.

"Wassup wit' Melvin?"

"What you mean?"

"Why he da only one whose money funny?"

"Shid, I don't know, it shouldn't be no reason, especially how this shit movin', it's basically sellin' itself, but you know slim. He probably slow walkin' his shit, if not then he must've somehow messed his bread-up and too embarrassed to say anythin'."

"Maybe so, but holler at 'im and see what's up wit' 'im when you get a chance and make sure he a'ight. 'Cause if he messed up his bread some kinda way, I don't have a problem throwin' 'im somethin' to get 'im back on his feet."

"I got you, I'll holla at 'im and see what's up then."

"Dat's a bet," said Mike-Mike, dapping him up before he got ready to leave.

"I'll get wit' y'all later on," said Lil' Chico, leaving out the door.

With Chico gone, Mike-Mike turned toward Slick and

asked him was he ready to do some shopping, so they could hit the club later that night.

"Hell yeah, I'm ready! Where you tryin' to go?"

"It don't matter, but lets at least stop by Neiman Marcus, 'cause I'm tryin' to bump into this thick ass white chick dat works there," smiled Mike-Mike.

"A white broad huh?" questioned Slick, looking at his partner sideways.

"Yeah, shawty jive bad, trust me you'll see if she's there. You ever seen dat T.V. show da Parkers?"

"Yeah, da one Brandy and Monique used to play in."

"Exactly! Shawty's shaped and looks just like da broad Six dat used to play on dat show," he depicted.

"Yeah, I hear you, I think you sicin' it now, cause Six was phat as shit!"

"I know," Mike-Mike said, rubbing his chin, staring into space as if he were imagining her being naked. "Yeah, let's get outta here, plus we need to stop on Kennedy Street, so we can cop some more of dat loud from Jamaican E," he said in a hushed tone. He grabbed the remainder of the guns in the duffel bag, putting them away in his bedroom before leaving out of the apartment with Slick trailing behind.

CHAPTER 27

Positioned in the Motel Six parking lot, across the street from Aspen Court's Apartment complex inside a Chevy *Impala* were Moe Kelly, Rex, and Snarz. After Snarz relayed the unfortunate news about Moe Kelly's nephew, the three of them immediately went to try to find out who was responsible for his nephew's demise. As they were conversing in the vehicle, Snarz noticed a group of teenagers who emerged from the rear of the buildings.

"You see them youngins comin' from out the back?" Snarz pointed.

"Yeah, I see'em, and stop pointin' fo' somebody see you!" Moe Kelly barked at Snarz.

"My bad, I didn't think anybody could see us behind this tint," he tried to reason.

"Nigga, da front windshield don't have no tint on it, fool!"

"Look, one of 'em walking off by himself," Rex interjected.

"Hell yeah," Moe Kelly stressed, putting out his cigarette. "Let's see which way he goes," he stated starting the Chevy up while keeping his eyes glued on the teenager that was walking alone.

As the teenager went to cross Georgia Avenue, a quick thought popped into Rex's head. "If youngin' cross over and walk down dat street, we could cut'im off at da end of da alley," he suggested, and just as he expected, the young teen was sure enough walking in that direction.

"Hurry up, so we don't lose 'im!" sounded Rex, reaching under his seat. He pulled out twin 30 round clip Heckler & Koch MPSK and handed one to Snarz, "you ever used one of these before," he asked Snarz.

"Naw, but all guns shoot da same," he replied, examining the fully automatic weapon.

"Well, take da safety off then," Rex said sarcastically.

"Shid, dat's easy," he relayed with confidence, pushing one of the buttons on the side and causing the whole clip to fall from beneath it.

"Stupid azz nigga give me this fo' you shoot one of us in the back," commanded Rex irately, snatching the gun back from him. "The safety right here, fool!" he drilled, popping the clip back into its place. "And make sure you click this button down once fo' semi, and twice fo' fully," he demonstrated, handing the weapon back to him.

"This ain't da time fo' class, cause da nigga right here," Moe Kelly warned as they quickly directed their attention to the teen that was approaching.

On cue, the teen reached the alleyway entrance to the hotel as Moe Kelly was pulling up. Without a second guess, when the teen got within a few feet of the vehicle, the doors flung open with Rex and Snarz aiming their fully automatic weapons in his direction.

The teen's eyes widened in alarm upon seeing the automatic weapons pointed toward him.

"Don't fuckin' move!" fumed Rex with grave deliberation.

Feeling vulnerable and relatively helpless, he threw his hands up in defeat as Rex and Snarz cautiously got out of the *Impala* to seize him. Once they grabbed him, they tossed him in the backseat, pushing him to the middle before pulling off.

"Go! Go! Go!" shouted Rex as soon as he got completely back into the vehicle.

"What I do!" the teen shrieked, his heart pounding with fear.

"Shut your scared azz up, nigga!" Moe Kelly snapped coldly, grinding out his words through clenched teeth.

The young male was petrified because he didn't have a clue as to why he was being kidnapped. Rex immediately commenced searching the teen just to make sure there were no unexpected surprises. Once he finished rummaging through his pockets and was convinced that the young male didn't have anything harmful on him, he began inspecting the few items he did have. There was a phone, a small amount of money and a bag of coke that for some strange reason stood out to him.

"Ay Moe, check this out," said Rex, handing over the block of yay.

As soon as Moe Kelly zoomed in on the familiar deep

pink tint, he immediately removed the block from the plastic and brought it up to his nose. The distinctive aroma, which was their signature blend, instantly struck his nostrils, causing his mind to change course. The identifiable color and smell had his train of thought playing mental ping-pong. He knew for a fact that the coke he held in his hand was from one of the bricks that were in the Yukon the night it was stolen.

"Look youngin', I'ma ask you a couple of quick questions, and I strongly advise you to be truthful wit' me or my men goin' to make you wish you had. Do we understand each other?" Moe Kelly spoke with brutal detachment. The teen nervously said that he understood as he fidgeted in his seat. "Good, 'cause da first thing dat I want to know is who's responsible for them recent three bodies dat happened in front of dat cemetery?"

"Bodies! I don't know what you talkin' 'bout," the teen responded, his eyes taking on a haunted look.

"So, you tellin' me, three bodies drop in ya backyard, and you don't know nothin' about it, huh?" he shot back sarcastically, giving him a scorching look through the rearview mirror.

"Man, I swear, I don't know who's responsible fo' them bodies! Whoever done it, probably too scared to talk about it 'cause dat shit made da news," he cried out in a voice raw with terror.

"See youngin'…" he paused briefly, "I don't know who you lil niggas' think y'all foolin', but you do know dat you fucked up, right!"

"Huh!" the kid replied, his lips twitching.

"First you say you don't know nothin' 'bout da bodies, then you turn around and say whoever done it probably too scared to talk about it 'cause it made da news. You sayin' dat leads me to believe dat you do know about da bodies and you tryin' to respect da code of silence. I respect dat, but trust me, now ain't da time to play tough guy, so I'ma ask you again," Moe hesitated before asking, "Who had somethin' to do wit' them three bodies dat dropped da other day over by dat cemetery?" he inquired, as his eyes narrowed with contempt.

"I swear to you dat I don't know who's responsible fo' them three bodies."

"Oh, yeah!" Moe Kelly replied, nodding his head toward Rex through the rearview mirror.

Without a second thought, Rex aimed his gun towards the teen's knee, then pulled the trigger.

"Awwwww!" the young man cried out from the excruciating pain that shot through him.

"Just a second ago you didn't have nothin' to say, but now you can't keep ya mouth shut," Moe Kelly smiled wickedly.

"Hopefully, dat'll jog ya memory."

"Stop cryin', nigga!" Rex interjected. "Fo' I give you somethin' to really cry 'bout," he added.

"I promise you I don't know. I don't know!" his voice degenerated to a childish whimper. He bent over, covering his knee as if his hands could stop the bleeding.

"Maybe da lil' nigga don't know nothin'," Snarz jumped in, feeling a slight bit of sympathy for the teen.

"Snarz, shut da fuck up, a'ight!" Moe Kelly huffed with

156

a flash of irritation crossing his face. Then he went back to questioning the young male. "Well, since you seem to not know anything about da bodies, let me ask you this. Where da fuck you get this yay from?"

"What!"

"You heard what da fuck I said, now answer my fuckin' question!"

"My man gave it to me," he winced.

"Know what, I'm tired of playin' wit' this lil' nigga!" sounded Rex. "Pull this muthafucka over, 'cause I got somethin' inside da truck dat'll definitely make this youngin' talk," he demanded.

Shortly after, Moe Kelly pulled over to the side. Rex quickly hopped out to grab something from the trunk. When Rex got out, the petrified teen wanted to make a quick move of desperation to hopefully save his life, even though he knew his wounded leg wouldn't allow him to make any sudden moves. Just as fast as the thought entered his mind, it vanished, because within a matter of seconds Rex was getting back into the vehicle. He was flashing a mini handsaw with blades on it that looked like shark teeth. The teen swallowed a lump in his throat upon seeing the razor-sharp handsaw in his hand.

"I like, I like," said Moe Kelly giving his approval, driving off, and getting right back to the matter at hand.

CHAPTER 28

"Mmh…Mmh, that entree was delicious. I never tried the Cajun Louisiana Bake before," smiled Mike-Mike's mother Gloria.

"I'm happy you enjoyed it," replied Anthony as the two left the Cheese Cake Factory, located off of Wisconsin Avenue.

"And to top it off with that Mango Cheesecake was the best," she smiled while her eyes sparkled with joy. As they walked she leaned over toward him, kissing him on his lips as they approached their vehicle.

Being a well-bred man, Anthony opened the passenger door first and made sure that she was secured before walking around to the driver's side to get in. Being the woman that she was, Gloria already had the driver's door opened by the time he reached it. He got in with a huge smile plastered across his face.

"What you smiling for?" she asked.

"What just happened was something I seen in a movie one time, that's all," he replied.

"Such as?"

"Such as me opening the door and waiting to see if you'd open the driver's door for me," he explained.

"So that was some kind of test?"

"No not at all, but if it was, you would've passed it," he explained.

"I wonder how many other tests you done put me through?"

"None baby, plus, the only tests I'm giving out is oral examinations," he casually stated, leaning over, giving her a passionate kiss, leaving her in a mild trance.

When their lips departed, he looked directly into her eyes, expressing his love for her. "I envisioned eternal life with you the first time I laid eyes on you. Nothing means more to me than to make you happy and being able to keep that beautiful smile on your face. I'm truly blessed to have someone such as you as my better-half," he caringly expressed, which caused her face to beam with happiness prior to him starting the car, readying himself to pull out of the parking garage.

She was so attuned to the heartfelt words that seemed to glide smoothly from his lips that she didn't realize that a tear had fallen from its confinement. Well, not until it landed on her hand resting on the center console. Caught off guard, she quickly went to grab a napkin from her purse to wipe her eyes.

Simultaneous to Anthony pulling out of the garage on Western Avenue, his eyes landed on the one individual that could surely ruin their perfect evening. As Gloria was about to look back up from wiping her eyes, Anthony leaned over for another kiss, but this time connecting a bit longer than the first one. By the time their lips separated, the person that sat in the vehicle at the traffic light right across from them in plain view was gone.

CHAPTER 29

Mike-Mike and Slick finally made it to Mazza Gallerie before parking in the garage and then walking into the mall, heading toward Neiman Marcus.

"Time to get fly, nigga!" Slick said, energized, giving his partner their signature handshake.

"Let's do it then," Mike-Mike smiled.

"I'm showin' my ass off tonight."

"Shid, you ain't da only one," agreed Mike-Mike as the pair strolled into the mall.

Almost immediately after entering Neiman Marcus, Mike-Mike spotted the one person he was hoping to bump into at the store. Ms. Widger was conversing with another female sales rep when the two entered the store.

"There she go, right there," Mike-Mike whispered, singling her out without pointing.

"Who Six?" Slick replied, trying to zoom in on who Mike- Mike was referring to.

"Yeah over there in dat white dress."

Slick quickly followed the direction of his partner's wistful eyes before landing on a beautiful Caucasian female that stood a short distance away.

"Damn, she bad!" he complimented.

"I told ya."

"And her co-worker ain't lookin' too bad either. Let's go over there," Slick suggested.

"No need to rush, 'cause they ain't goin' nowhere," said Mike-Mike.

"I thought dat was ya main reason fo' comin' here in da first place."

"It was, but she tried to act like I was out of her league, or too young fo' her at first, so I'm not tryin' to rush over there lookin' like some thirsty teen, ya feel me. Trust me, I'll get her," he confirmed with confidence, leading his partner in the opposite direction toward the men's section.

Shortly after browsing through the items, Mike-Mike spotted an eye-catching Gucci leather shoulder biker jacket that he couldn't resist.

"This joint official!" he boasted, lifting the jacket up.

"Dat joint hittin'!" Slick agreed. "Dat's you all da way."

"Now all I got to do is find a fit to go..." Mike-Mike's words trailed off as he turned around and saw Ms. Widger standing a few feet away. "Oh, how you doin'," he asked, acknowledging her as his eyebrows shot up in surprise.

"Well, how are you doin', Mr. I have to go find my parents because I can't afford any of this," she smiled, showing off her shiny white teeth while mocking him from their first encounter.

"Oh, I see you got jokes, huh!"

"No, not really, you just never told me your name," she informed him.

Damn! How did I forget that, he thought before telling her his name, "My name's Michael, but my friends call me Mike-Mike."

"Well, Mike-Mike, now that we been formally introduced is there anything that I can help you with since this particular store seems to have your interest?"

"How could it not, when this store has so much to offer?" he shot back, giving her an intriguing look.

"Well, I can tell you have good taste," she indirectly countered, reaching for the Gucci jacket he was holding on to. Although, Mike-Mike quickly caught on to what she was doing.

"Since it's understood dat I have good taste, why don't you give me an opportunity to show you my likings?"

"I see that you are a very persistent individual," she replied, disregarding his request, but her body language answered it for him.

"I only act this way when there's something or someone dat's unavoidable," he responded as Slick cleared his throat, interrupting their brief acquaintanceship.

"Excuse me fo' being rude, but it's a must dat I get introduced to da woman dat seems to have my brother's undivided attention," he politely stated, extending his hand for a greeting.

"Ms. Widger," she grinned, returning the friendly gesture.

"My name Slick, and it's a pleasure to meet you."

"Likewise," she nodded, turning her attention back to Mike-Mike. "Umh, will that be all for today?" she asked, referring to the Gucci jacket he was holding on to.

"Not at all. Hopefully, you can assist us in pickin' out a few items."

"We're not going to go through what we went through the last time are we?"

"I promise we won't," he assured her.

"Well then, right this way," she instructed, leading the way to another section of the store. "These are some of our newest fashions," she advised, gesturing her hands, showcasing the attire.

"I like this," Mike-Mike proclaimed. "You know what you know, huh?"

"I'm good at what I do."

"And dat is?" he inquired, wanting her to be more detailed.

"Being a stylist."

"Okay then, Ms. Stylist, say I was going on a first-time date to an elegant restaurant, what would you have me wear?"

"Since you've already picked out that Gucci jacket, I would probably put you in something like this Gucci slim woven shirt," she suggested, taking the shirt off the rack and placing it up to his body to see how it looked. "Or maybe something simpler like this GG-Sketch shirt over here," she said, placing the Gucci woven shirt back on the rack. From there they followed her over to another rack where she picked up the GG-Sketch shirt, duplicating what she had done with the first one.

"With this particular shirt, you can simply tuck it in while displaying a nice Gucci belt over a pair of faded blue jeans and complete the attire with a comfortable pair of

Gucci canvas leather sneakers that we have over there on the shelf," she concluded, awaiting his response.

"I like it. Let me get all of it, includin' da shoes, even though I haven't seen 'em, but I trust ya taste. I have one more request before we finish."

"I'm listening."

"I have a date accompanying me to this very nice restaurant. I'd like fo' you to pick out an eye-catchin' outfit fo' someone dat's about your height, and size?" Mike-Mike asked, noticing Slick had stepped off and was staring toward a mannequin a few feet away.

"I can show you if you don't mind walking over to the women's section," Ms. Widger informed him with a bit of jealousy written on her face.

"Not at all," he responded, smiling inside after witnessing her displeased facial expression. He knew he had her after seeing that.

"Follow me," she instructed, turning to lead the way, strutting off as if she owned the place.

Once they arrived in the women's section, she unhesitantly reached for a gorgeous Massoni body dress. "This dress says a lot without having to speak," she stated, removing the dress from its current location, placing it up to her own body to showcase it.

"Dat's real nice," he expressed. "Would you wear dat?"

"Of course, I wouldn't have picked it out if I wouldn't have worn it myself," she assured him.

"I tell you what, why don't you ring my items up, includin' dat dress, and write down ya info and be sure to have dat dress on when I pick you up to take you out to this fancy restaurant dat I have in mind."

"This is a two-thousand-dollar dress," she advised.

"I ask fo' ya info not da price of da dress," he reciprocated.

She never responded to his comment, she simply headed to the counter with the dress in tow. On the way to the register, Mike-Mike noticed Slick glued to the same mannequin, and told, Ms. Widger to stop there first, before going to the register.

"Wassup baby boy, you been glued to this mannequin fo' a minute," said Mike-Mike.

"Slim this it right here!" Slick responded, animatedly. "I got to have this whole outfit, shoes and all!" he said rubbing his hands together.

"Dat joint is like dat," Mike-Mike's agreed. "What's da hold-up, why didn't you get it?"

"Cause I only see it on display," he replied, turning toward Ms. Widger, asking her for assistance.

"I'm sorry, but that outfit is a sample that was sent from the manufacturer and won't be in our inventory until next week," she conveyed, noticing his facial expression go from animated to irate instantly.

Slick immediately walked over to the mannequin, checking out the sizes on it, then strolled back over to Ms. Widger and said, "da good thing is, me and dat mannequin just so happen to wear da same size. So, either y'all goin' to sale me da clothes off da mannequin's back or I'ma have to buy the whole mannequin wit' da clothes on 'im," he stated with an uncompromising glare in his eyes.

She looked over at Mike-Mike to see if his partner was

serious and when Mike-Mike shrugged his shoulders, indicating that he wasn't joking, she decided to appease his eagerness. She called upon the same female employee that she was conversing with when the two entered the store to remove the items off the mannequin and bring them to the counter.

"Now dat's what I'm talkin' bout! I like her already," Slick proclaimed, smiling.

"Slim you crazy, ya know dat," laughed Mike-Mike as the three of them walked to the counter to ring everything up.

Slick used the opportunity to initiate a conversation with the young African American woman who looked to be in her early twenties. After she placed the items on top of the counter, Slick stopped her before she walked off and whispered something to her, causing her to blush. Mike-Mike focused his attention back on Ms. Widger while she totaled their purchases.

"It comes to nine-thousand two-hundred, and thirty-five dollars," she announced.

Mike-Mike glanced at Slick, so he could take care of his part of the bill but was unable to get his attention. So, once he realized Slick and the female employee were engaged in an in-depth conversation, he decided to just pay the bill himself. Ms. Widger was somewhat stunned to see someone so young able to pay for such expensive items without worry. Not to mention topping it off with the two-thousand-dollar dress he purchased her.

"Put your dress in a separate bag, and hold on to it until we get together," he instructed her before she handed his bags over with her info. "You'll be hearing from me soon," Mike-Mike winked and then casually walked off.

"I'ma give you a call later on," Slick was telling the female as Mike-Mike was walking up.

"Shorty a'ight," Mike-Mike said, handing Slick his bags after they finished conversing as she'd strutted off.

"I see you paid fo' everything, huh?"

"Yeah, but I want my bread back fo' your stuff, 'cause this shit came up to damn near ninety-three hunid."

"Damn, what you buy?"

"You'll probably look at me crazy if I told you, but I'll fill you in once we get in da car," Mike-Mike replied as they headed out the store.

CHAPTER 30

"What was so important that I had to excuse myself from my woman to rush over here?" the man inquired as he entered Flawless Tattoo Parlor.

Upon entering, he noticed Moe Kelly and Rex engaged in conversation, while Snarz and another random young man competed in a game of Madden 13.

"Malice, what's good wit' cha? Glad you could make it," Moe Kelly greeted. "Got something in the back fo' you," he stated in a smooth laid-back manner, getting up and leading the way into the back. He walked kind of sluggish though as if he'd just had some serious nose candy.

"Who the fuck is that?" he fumed, giving Moe Kelly a scorching look once the two reached the back. Seeing someone tied up with a dark colored pillowcase over his head caused him to become vexed.

"We may have found out who was responsible fo' stealing our truck," he replied with a sweet grin on his face.

"How so?"

Moe Kelly filled him in on how everything came about,

starting with his nephew being killed to how they snatched the teen, stumbling across the work and ultimately ending up there.

"So, did he give you enough info on the two youngins that possibly had something to do with the truck being stolen with the shipment in it?" Malice questioned, stone-faced.

"I believe so."

"So why he here and they not?"

"We on top of it," Moe assured him.

"Don't call me 'til you have the youngins that are responsible," he stated in a grim tone.

"I got ya."

"And who's them two youngins out there playin' on that Xbox?"

"Da lil' chubby one is my nephew's man who put us up on game wit' everything dat transpired and da reason this whole situation came about, but da other youngin is just another nigga from da neighborhood," Moe Kelly explained.

"So, let me get this straight," he began. "You had me come over here after y'all snatched a nigga up and got some random fool loungin' around to be a witness!" He shook his head, giving him a crazed look. He was disappointed at his associate's lack of adroitness. "You need to tighten the hell up, 'cause you fallin' off. In this world you'll only be remembered for two things, the problems you create and the problems you solve. As of now, it seems as though all you have done is created a problem that I have to solve," he advised smirking. Malice swiftly pulled out a 9mn Beretta with a silencer attached to it, pointed it at the teen's head and pulled the trigger twice. "Clean this mess up," he ordered, tucking his pistol away, heading back out to the front where everybody was lounging.

He breezed past Rex, giving him a head nod as he approached the door to leave. Once he reached the door, he suddenly turned around, aiming his gun toward the teens playing on the Xbox before deciding to eject a bullet into the head of the young random teen from the neighborhood. The force behind the bullet caused his head to thrust forward from his seat, splattering his blood on the T.V. screen. Snarz quickly jumped from the sight of his man sprawled out in front of him. He immediately broke out into a sweat as his heart threatened to leap from his chest.

"What! You got a problem!" Malice barked, now pointing his weapon at Snarz's head, causing him to shake uncontrollably. "You better be lucky that you were vouched for or else you would've been lying next to your lil' friend," he warned, tucking his gun away, flipping the open sign to close, then casually walking out.

CHAPTER 31

"It's party time!" shouted Slick, stepping out of Mike-Mike's Lexus *GS*.

"Most definitely," Mike-Mike added, arming his alarm system before the two walked off, heading toward Club Ibiza.

The night breeze was warm. A gush of heated air massaged their faces as they blended in with the large crowd.

"Man, this line is wrapped around da corner!" Slick complained. Ain't no way we standin' in this long ass line. Especially, when we could probably cut da heads off everyone standin' in line and replace 'em all with Benjamin Franklin faces," he boasted.

"You right about dat," Mike-Mike agreed, giving Slick a quick smirk. "C'mon," he told him, stepping out of line and heading to the front.

The pair were turning a lot of heads on their way to the front. As they passed everyone, they seemed to draw the attention of the different groups of females standing in line.

Slick put a little extra lean in his walk after sensing all the eyes zooming in on them. With his arm in a sling, he was feeling like Scarface after his assassination attempt. Mike-Mike, on the other hand, felt the attention but didn't seem to pay it any mind as they approached the beginning of the line where the bouncers were positioned.

"Ay, big man, how much is it gon' cost to skip this long ass line?" asked Slick, thinking no matter the cost they could cover it.

"Sorry, my man, but if it were any other night y'all could've paid ya way through but tonight only the names on my list are allowed through these ropes," the bouncer stated, holding the list up.

"So, you tellin' us no matter da price we can't get in?"

"Not through here, but you can by standing in that line," he said, pointing them in the direction they should go.

Slick was feeling somewhat embarrassed after noticing a few onlookers in line snickering at seeing them get shot-down by the bouncer. Slick was about to pull enough money out of his pocket to pay the bouncer's next year's salary when all of a sudden, all the snickering stopped and every pair of eyes in line seemed to shoot past them. Following their wandering eyes, Mike-Mike immediately turned around to see what everyone was staring at.

When he turned, he noticed two Rolls Royce *Phantoms* pulling up in front of the club. The *Phantom* in front was an all white hard-top coupe and the house on wheels that trailed close behind was an all blue, Platinum colored convertible *Drophead Coupe'*. Both vehicles had two of the most beautiful women that graced the earth driving them. The woman that drove the all white hard-top coupe looked as if she were a piece of fine art that not even the world's greatest designer would've been able to duplicate. The woman that drove the convertible *Drophead Coupe* resembled the gorgeous Sudanese African that went by the name Umma from the book, *Midnight* by Sista Soulja.

On cue, both women emerged from the driver's side, showcasing bodies that could've been illegal to advertise. The woman in the white coupe wore an emerald green silk blouse, which clung to her breasts like plastic wrap, with a pair of black slacks that hugged her round ass suggestively. Now the woman in the convertible promoted a royal blue dress that gripped to her body like a second skin. Her mid-section was clinched with a wide black leather belt that made her waist look even smaller. Their captivating looks, and curvaceous bodies were followed as the two simultaneously walked around to the passenger side, opening the doors for their passengers.

A smile crept across Mike-Mike's face as the two familiar faces exited the vehicles. Occupying the all white hard top coupe was Big Herm flossing a brown Louis Vutton crocodile leather topcoat with the mink-fur trim, same color as the car, a thin Tom Ford collarless shirt, same color as his driver's blouse, tucked in his blinged-out LV belt. He also sported a pair of Louis Vuitton pants with the matching quarter-top crocodile boots to go with his topcoat. He stepped out smoothly but landed in a puddle of water.

"Baby, your boots!" his guest proclaimed, barely avoiding the splashing water.

"It's nothin' baby, they crocs, they belong in the water," he reminded, seemingly unfazed by the small puddle his boots were resting in before glancing at his Mont Blanc watch.

Zoe, on the other hand, poured out in a splash of ocean blue, neatly designed into a predominate midnight black and micro checkered blocks of grey Salvatore Ferragamo silk jacket, a thin form-fitting blue Zilli shirt that was tucked inside of his belt, also by Ferragamo and some slim-fitted jeans. He glided across the pavement in a pair of Ferragamo slip-ons.

Sneaking a peek at his non-diamond twenty-thousand-dollar Herms steel alligator watch, he glanced over at Big Herm, signaling that he was ready to enter the club. Both women politely shut their doors, then latched on to Zoe and Big Herm with a firm grip. As he walked to the front of the line, he immediately spotted Mike-Mike and his cohort standing next to the bouncer as they approached.

"Mike-Mike, what's good bruh?" he greeted as he embraced him, then acknowledged Slick with a head nod.

"Shid, we tryin' to duck this long ass line," he countered.

"That shouldn't be a problem," he responded. "I got you," he assured him, directing his attention to the bouncer that had just shot the two down, and told him that they were with him.

"I didn't know, Mr. Zomil, they never conveyed that to me. If so I would've made sure to let'em through," the bouncer responded apologetically, jittery as he unhooked the ropes to allow the group through.

"We understand, no need to explain, just let us through," Big Herm acknowledged as the bouncer stepped to the side, allowing them access.

Once the group entered, they headed to an elevator that led them to the V.I.P. section. Once the elevator doors opened, they were greeted by loud music and an Alicia Keys look-a-like, but she was tall and lean with a nice set of breasts. She wore a form fitted black dress that squeezed her slim hips and dipped low in the front revealing just enough cleavage to arouse any man. After she greeted everyone, she escorted them to their section.

"Damn!" Slick murmured, admiring the well-proportioned curves of the woman's body.

Their area had blood red velour couches with low rounded glass tables and 42-inch plasma screens all around showing different music videos. All of the waitresses wore similar attire, all black body dresses, just different cuts to them. Zoe casually whispered something to the woman, causing her to blush before walking off in the opposite direction.

"Slim, on everything I love, this club is off da chain!" Slick boasted. "Now where's da bar, so a nigga can do him?"

Hearing his partner's request, Mike-Mike walked over to Zoe to inquire about the bar since it was their first time in the club. Once Mike-Mike asked him about the bar, Zoe smiled back at him before excusing himself from his blue gem.

"What you smilin' fo'?" inquired Mike-Mike.

"'Cause this must be your first time in V.I.P.," he grinned.

"How you figure dat?"

"'Cause you would've known that in V.I.P. the bottles have legs baby boy, which means you don't have to go get'em, they'll come to you," he explained. "What you think that fine ass waitress was for, besides, keep your money cause in the next ten minutes our tables goin' to be filled with plenty of bottles," he assured him. "But since you in the mood to get somethin', how 'bout you and your man catch the escalator down to the lower level and bring some of them fine young ladies to the table to join us," Zoe, suggested.

"You serious?"

"Dead ass serious."

"Say no more, I'll be back in a few," Mike-Mike smiled, dapping Zoe up, then walking off.

CHAPTER 32

"Hubb, let me get another hit before you smoke it all!" begged the female fiend who Hubb had been laying low with since the incident between Mike-Mike and Slick.

"Bitch! If you don't shut da hell-up wit' all dat naggin'!" Hubb shot back, snatching his arm away, placing the glass pipe back up to his lips.

"You got the nerve to be calling somebody a bitch!" she fired back, rolling her neck with each syllable. "With your ungrateful ass! You're the one who's hiding from them young boys, 'cause you scared they going to do something to your ass!" she reminded. "Now give me my stuff!" she bellowed, reaching for the glass pipe, causing it to accidentally fall from Hubb's grip, shattering on the hardwood floor of her apartment.

"You geekin' bitch!" Hubb barked, shoving her halfway across the living room floor.

"Muthafucka!" she snapped in disbelief. "I know you didn't just put your hands on me!" she exclaimed jumping up and charging toward him, throwing wild windmill like punches.

Hubb was basically blocking her blows until he got fed up and struck her across her face, knocking her back down. "See what you made me do!" he scolded.

She grabbed her face, shocked that he actually put his hands on her, disregarding the fact that he was standing over her, cursing her out. Her shock caused her to block out any choice words spilling from his mouth, because all she could think of at the moment was a way to pay him back for putting his hands on her. Hubb messed up by doing two things, one, telling her his business and the other was putting his hands on her because women are like sieves, they can't hold water. Especially the vulnerable and broken-hearted ones who are willing to do what it takes to prove a point or get even.

CHAPTER 33

"You of all people should know I don't like playin' the club scene," Rex told Moe Kelly over the club's loud music as they stood by the bar.

"I feel ya, but I needed to get out to clear my head 'bout a few things," replied Moe Kelly, downing another double shot of Remy Martin V.S.O.P.

"I don't know why I let y'all talk me into this shit, 'cause we be doin' too much dirt in these streets to be partyin' and shit. Ya feel me?" Rex asked.

"I feel ya, but don't too many niggas get a chance to retaliate for the kinda things we done. We don't let niggas live to do so," he boasted, reaching into his top jacket pocket, pulling out a small baggie containing his drug of choice.

He discreetly used his long pinky nail to scoop out enough substance to take himself a sniff. After doing so, he immediately held his nose, tilting his head back to get a drain.

"How you plan on clearing your mind when you steady cloudin' it wit' that bullshit?"

"Come on Rex don't start that," he said, lifting his head back up.

"Don't start what?"

"You know I don't blow no bullshit."

"What!" declared Rex shaking his head.

He thought Moe Kelly was going to tell him to not blow his high, but instead, he responded with the wildest shit. Rex had to grin because he knew anything was liable to come out of his partner's mouth at any given time. One thing for sure was whether he blew or not that was his ace. They both had each other's backs no matter if one blew, snorted, shot up, or smoked.

"What's up wit' the extra baggage you totin' around?" Rex inquired about Snarz who was there with them.

"You of all people should know he's already seen too much to be left alone, besides its time fo' him to get his hands dirty. Just to even things out a bit, ya dig," he replied, reaching for a female's hand that was walking pass.

"Don't put your hands on me!" the female grimaced, snatching her hand away.

"Damn O.T, you disrespectful as shit! Can't you see da lady wit' someone? You need to get ya'self a better pair of frames if you can't see what's in front of you!" interjected the young male that was walking with the female before stepping off with five more females trailing behind him.

To say that Moe Kelly was insulted by the young man's blatant lack of respect was an understatement. Stunned, it took him a few more seconds to register what had just happened.

"I know this lil nigga didn't just…" his words trailed off

because of Rex grabbing his shoulder after he charged in the young male's direction.

"Don't move on impulse," Rex informed him. "Let's see where he goes. Plus, you said it was time to get your extra baggage's hand's dirty, right?" he winked.

"Sho-nuff," Moe Kelly replied, giving Rex a nefarious grin.

"Well now's the time," he suggested, tapping Snarz on his shoulder so they could keep eyes on the young man that Moe Kelly wanted to get at for his lack of respect.

CHAPTER 34

Upon entering the V.I.P., Slick realized that Mike-Mike had beat him to the punch because he already had a group of females at one of their tables. Approaching, he noticed that the tables were filled with enough drinks for everyone to indulge. Mike-Mike and the women's voices were both lowered and raised occupying the area like the music that was sounding through the speakers.

"How y'all ladies doin'? My name Slick," he introduced himself once he reached the table.

"Ladies please have a seat," said Mike-Mike, getting up from the couch to be heard over the music. "We are quite aware dat neither group knows one another, but we are here fo' one thing and one thing only, and dat's to have a good time. So please get acquainted, comfortable, and enjoy, plus there's plenty of drinks fo' everyone," he added. "And by da way, my name's Mike- Mike," he concluded, sitting back down next to the young lady he chose to wrap-up for the night.

The female that was occupying most of his time was

Makiya, the same female he'd met at the carwash recently. She was the reason it didn't take him long to gather up his group of ladies because shortly after he and Slick headed in different directions, he walked pass Makiya, almost stepping on her foot. When he went to excuse himself, he instantly recognized who she was.

"Makiya!" He called out to her giving her the once-over.

"Mike-Mike, how you doin'?" she replied, giving him that bright smile he noticed the first time they met.

"I'm doin' better now dat I ran into you, literally," he stated, looking down at her exposed feet, admiring what he saw.

The straps of her shoes exposed her pedicured toes, wrapped around her slim ankles and climbed up her toned calves past her knees and were tied on each side of her well-oiled thighs.

"You would've called if that was the case."

"Believe me I had every intention to, it's just dat a lot's been goin' on da past few days," he countered, loving how her skin was shining under the lights as if it had a coat of olive oil over it.

"I know how it can be at times. Hopefully, everything works out for the better."

"I'll be a'ight," he confirmed. "So, who you here wit'?" he inquired, changing the subject.

"A few of my girlfriends, who I can't seem to find at the moment."

"Well why don't I help you find 'em, then maybe y'all can join me in V. I.P.," he suggested.

"I must warn you It's quite a few of us," she conveyed,

giving him the heads up.

"It's cool, da more da better," he told her, keeping his tone polite as the pair headed off to locate her buddies so that they could go lounge in the V.I.P. area, where they were congregated.

CHAPTER 35

"Now you see why I said don't move on impulse," stated Rex. "Look what we ran into," he exclaimed as the trio observed the scenery from a distance, zooming into the V.I.P. area.

Moe Kelly felt his anger clawing its way to the top as he studied all the faces that were in attendance, fraternizing. His dark face twisted into a mask of disgust after noticing someone that he used to deal with on a personal level conversing with the same young male that had disrespected him. He watched attentively as the group seemed to be having an in-depth conversation.

"There go Big Herm over there standing off to the right," directed Rex without pointing.

"Yeah, I see 'im," he assured. "I wonder what they doin' hangin' wit' them youngins."

"Your guess is just as good as mine," replied Rex.

"Know what, it don't really matter. Ay Snarz, come here fo' a sec," Moe Kelly said with authority.

"Wassup?" asked Snarz, walking over to where Moe Kelly stood.

"You see that lil' nigga standin' over there wit' that sling on his arm?"

"I see'im, why what's up?"

"I need you to handle somethin' fo' me, and if you do, I'ma make sure I make you an offer you can't refuse," he assured him.

"What ya need me to do?" questioned Snarz.

"Wait outside for 'im, and under no circumstances does he leave here alive," he gravely relayed.

"I got you," he responded, matching his tone.

When Moe Kelly glared into his eyes, surprisingly he saw no fear and quickly thought about keeping him around for the long haul if he followed through with the order.

CHAPTER 36

Around 1:30 a.m., Lil' Chico and Tre were the last two on the block collecting sells. Ever since the old heads of the block stepped off, they were the last two standing.

"See, I'm 'bout this paper," Lil' Chico bragged. "Dat's why I'm da first on da block and the last to leave," he stated, counting his late-night earnings before securing it back into his cargo pants.

"You ain't da only one," added Tre. "But this shit ain't movin' quick enough fo' me," he complained.

"I don't see how not, especially with da prices we gettin' this shit fo' and on top of dat, da shit butter," Lil' Chico reminded, pulling out a bag of loud, readying himself to twist up a jay.

"I hear ya, but fuck all dat, I'm tryin' to have my own, so I can sell weight fo' da low, ya feel me."

"Gotta crawl before you walk, playboy."

"Only infants, and da cripple crawl and I'm neither."

"So, what's stoppin' you. Get ya own if dat's how you feel, I ain't tryin' to fix nothin' dat's not broke. I'm cool wit' gettin' this shit cheap. Man, I could break it down and make some big azz boulders and crush da block," Lil' Chico responded as he finished rolling his backwood and then pulling out his lighter to put some fire to it.

"Ain't nothin' stoppin' me, I'ma get it, trust-n-believe dat," he expressed, looking toward the sky as sudden thoughts rambled through his head. "Where Mike-Mike and Slick been since we last saw them earlier?" he inquired as Lil' Chico passed him the backwood.

"I think them niggas went to a club, 'cause they were talkin 'bout goin' shoppin', then partyin'."

"Nephew, one of y'all got two fo' thirty-five?" interjected a male fiend as he walked up.

"Slim, I'ma go 'head and get dat since you stayin' out here, 'cause I think I'm 'bout to call it a night," stated Tre, passing the backwood back to Lil' Chico so he could go make the sale.

"Go head, I'll see you tomorrow," replied Lil' Chico, giving him some dap before he left.

"See you tomorrow," he countered, then directed his attention at the fiend. "Ay Unc, meet me behind da buildin' over there," he directed with a head nod.

Not two minutes after Tre stepped off to handle his business, a female fiend walked up, "Wassup, Auntie?" asked Lil' Chico, blowing out a cloud of smoke.

"I'm not looking for anything, I was hoping to run into Mikey, Mike-Mike or something to that nature," she said.

"And who are you?"

"My name's Lisa, and I have some information on where Hubb may be."

"He's not out here, but if you have a contact number I'll

make sure dat he gets it," assured Lil' Chico.

"I already wrote it down," she informed handing him a piece of folded paper. "Thank you," she said as she turned to leave.

"'Scuse me, if you don't mind me askin', what happen to ya face?" he frowned after noticing the swelling on the right side of her face.

"It's funny you asked, 'cause that's the main reason I'm here, but I'd rather not go into details about it."

"I respect dat. You be careful."

"I will," she replied, giving a less than assuring smile before she walked off.

Unbeknownst to her, Hubb was watching her the entire time. He was hoping to sneak into his apartment, so he could grab a few things when he spotted Lisa. Knowing that his neighborhood wasn't an area she frequented, he knew what she was up to. Furious, he decided to postpone sneaking into the apartment and follow her.

CHAPTER 37

A few hours later, the club was finally letting out. The crowd was pouring out in groups. Some hung around to mingle while others rushed to their vehicles to escape the morning breeze. Inebriated, Mike-Mike and Slick stumbled out with their arms wrapped around the females that were occupying their time for the night.

"It's chilly out here," said Makiya, rubbing her arms.

"I got you, baby girl," Mike-Mike responded, taking off his Gucci jacket and wrapping it around her.

"That's better, thank you."

"Any time," he conveyed as her girlfriends were walking up.

"Makiya, you going to be okay?" questioned one of her girlfriends with a drunken slur.

"Yeah, I'm good, girl," she assured her.

"You better take good care of her, 'cause I don't want to have to come looking for you, you hear me," she joked.

"Trust me, she's in good hands," Mike-Mike replied. "Y'all just make sure you all make it home safely."

"We will and have fun," she smirked as she and the others all gave Makiya a hug before they paraded off.

"Let me see da keys, so I can go grab da car, cause shorty cold and I don't have a coat to give her," Slick said.

"Dat's a bet, 'cause I'm tryin' to holler at Zoe right quick anyway," Mike-Mike said, handing his car keys over.

"I'll be right back," he told Mike-Mike and his date, trotting off, allowing the cool air to smack him in his face, lessening his drunken mindset.

As he headed for the car, he had a set of piercing eyes on his trail. Oblivious to the danger that was lurking near him, he kept his focus on retrieving the Lexus, so his partner and their guest wouldn't be waiting long in the cool air. Especially, after coming from the sweltering club. His quick pace was putting some distance between him and his much bigger and slower aggressor, until the car keys slipped from his grip.

"Damn!" Slick uttered, looking down to locate where the keys had fallen on the dark street. Seconds later, he found them kissing the curb before continuing on. Finally, seeing the Lexus in his view, he slowed his pace, giving Snarz the time that he needed to close the distance between the two from the opposite side of the street. Snarz's eyes had no life, no warmth, only color as the darkness masked his killer's ambition and crooked thoughts.

For a two-hundred pounder, plus, he walked as light as a ninja while removing his 45-caliber handgun from his person, determined to prove himself.

***

"I truly appreciate everything you done tonight," Mike-Mike said to Zoe.

"It's all luv I'm just glad you enjoyed yourself," said Zoe.

"I definitely did, plus, I'm glad dat we got a chance to clear da air on dat situation," Mike-Mike admitted.

"Yeah' 'cause in this game, one should never change the way he conducts his business just to please the next person's conscious," replied Zoe.,

"I agree."

"Where your partner at anyway?" inquired Zoe, glancing around, noticing that Slick was nowhere to be found.

"He went to get da car, he should be pulling up in a min…" his words trailed off after hearing a loud roar from a gunshot, causing everyone within' earshot to briefly take cover.

"Get in the car," Zoe instructed his lady friend.

Big Herm, who was already seated in his Double R, quickly hopped out, gun tucked near his hip while checking on his comrade.

"What you waitin' on, let's roll out for these fools start actin' stupid!" stressed Big Herm.

"I'm comin'," he assured him. "You need a ride to your car?" Zoe asked Mike-Mike, noticing that his female guests were latched on to his wrist like a pair of handcuffs.

"Umh….," he hesitated, glancing at the two women, seeing the anxiety in their eyes. Knowing they were ready to vacate the area as fast as possible, he decided to take Zoe up on his offer. Just as soon as that thought entered his mind Slick was bending the corner.

"Naw, I'm cool 'cause he's comin' now," he said breathing a sigh of relief.

"Good, hit me tomorrow and let me know you a'ight," said Zoe, hopping in the driver's seat of his Phantom. He and Big Herm both pulled off leaving a cloud of black smoke in their trails.

Mike-Mike immediately ushered the women to his Lexus when Slick drove up. He allowed Slick's date to hop in the front-seat while he and his date both jumped in the back. "Slim, fo' a second I thought you got lost," uttered Mike-Mike before Slick pulled off.

Slick never responded, he simply shook his head and kept driving. Sensing something was wrong, Mike-Mike told him where to go and then sat back and chilled until the two were by themselves to talk. His gut feeling was telling him that the gunshot everyone heard was the reason for Slick's insoluble disposition.

***

Moe Kelly had a satisfying smirk on his face after he heard that gunshot, thinking that Snarz had done as he was told. Although, that look of satisfaction quickly faded when he saw a white Lexus pull up, and the group their intended target was with, hopped in.

"What da...!" he declared, sitting straight up in the driver's seat, zooming in from a short distance.

"I told you that nigga couldn't do it," Rex said.

"I'ma smash dat nigga!" boomed Moe Kelly, angry at the fact that Snarz didn't follow through with the hit.

He started his vehicle to search for Snarz, but Rex stopped him.

"Hold-up fo' a sec. Check out the car," he prompted.

"What about it?"

"White Lexus, VA plates," he reminded. "Sound familiar?"

Hell yeah! Dat youngin' we snatched did say somethin' 'bout a white Lexus wit' Virginia tags, Moe Kelly briefly thought to himself as he remembered.

"You thinkin' what I'm thinkin', 'cause I'm puttin' two and two together and it's definitely addin' up to four," Rex stated with accurate assumption. "We might've stumbled across the solution to our problem."

"No bullshit! We gon' get to the bottom of it real soon, but first things first. I'ma deal wit' this nigga Snarz, 'cause he's a definite liability," Moe Kelly proclaimed, pulling off to find Snarz, feeling like he'd already seen too much.

CHAPTER 38

Shortly after 3:00 in the morning, the couple was just getting into a comfortable sleep when the ringing of a cell phone awoke them. Cuddled up, the male occupant unwrapped his arm from around his better half so that he could answer his phone.

"Hello?" he answered, sitting straight up in the bed.

After briefly listening to what the caller was conveying to him, he inadvertently blurted-out, "WHAT!" startling his wife-to-be.

"Baby is everything alright?" she questioned in a concerned manner.

"Yes, baby," he replied calmly. "Everything's fine," he smiled the way a man with problems or concerns on his mind might smile to block a child's innocent view of the world. "Go back to sleep," he said to her, kissing her on her forehead. Though his face looked as if he didn't have a care in the world, his insides were burning from the information he'd just received.

Trusting his word, she rolled back over and allowed him

to finish his conversation. To keep from alarming her, he began to speak in codes, instructing the caller to handle a certain situation while he paid the H.N.I.C a visit to see what he could find out.

CHAPTER 39

Mike-Mike wanted to find out what was on his partner's mind since he didn't say two words the whole ride. Upon arriving at the Hyatt Regency Hotel, Mike-Mike and Slick purchased two rooms. They sent their guest to the rooms, telling them they would join them shortly.

"Talk to me, slim, what's botherin' you?" questioned Mike-Mike once the two were alone.

Slick stood there momentarily as his mind shifted as if it were a Rubik's Cube trying to get back to its original form. "Man, some nigga just had my life in his hands," Slick said slightly annoyed.

"What you talkin' 'bout?" frowned Mike-Mike.

"When I was 'bout to open da car door, I seen a nigga creepin' up on me through da window. By da time I noticed him, slim already had da joint to my head," he explained.

"What!" Mike-Mike snapped, causing his lip to curl in disgust.

"Yeah, bruh," Slick shook his head. "I saw my life flash in front of me. I wouldn't be here now if, fo' whatever reason, dat fool wouldn't have had a change of heart."

"So, where da gun-shot come from?"

"Dat came from slim. I thought da fool was tryin' to rob me at first, until he let off a shot in da air, tellin' me to get da fuck on before he changed his mind. Shid, he didn't have to tell me twice," he added, forcing a smile.

"I bet he didn't, but this ain't no laughin' matter. We need to figure out what dat shit was all about."

"I'm already hip," he agreed. "Da only thing I could think of was da dude I said somethin' to in da club, but dat shit wasn't really 'bout nothin'."

"What you say to da dude?"

"Shit, fo' real. Da nigga grabbed my shorty's hand, and I said some slick shit to 'im, then stepped off," he explained.

"You think it was da same dude?"

"Not sure, I never got a good look. I only saw his reflection through da car window," Slick explained.

"We gotta be more on point, so we don't fall victim. This shit could've ended fo' da worst, ya feel me."

"Hell yeah, dat incident woke a nigga up. I'm not givin' another muthafucka a chance to take mine again, and dat's a promise!" he voiced as his face contorted with every word he spoke, causing him to look like a different person. Slick was already a powder keg, and that incident basically lit the fuse.

"Dat goes fo' da both of us," countered Mike-Mike, matching his tone. "But let's not beat ourselves in da head over somethin' dat did not happen. It's a learning experience," he spoke embracing his partner.

"You right," he agreed. "This shit comes wit' da

territory," Slick reasoned.

"True dat, but at da same time we can't let this situation blow over, cause whatever it was about could still surface again if we don't figure out what caused it. But let's worry about it at a better time cause right now we both have two bad azz females in our rooms waitin' on us and a nigga jive twisted. So, let's go up there and allow them to help us fo'get about all this bullshit," he suggested.

"What we waitin' on then," Slick replied as they headed upstairs to their rooms.

No sooner than Mike-Mike broke the threshold, Makiya's scent perfumed the air. Though the lights were dim, he noticed her clothes neatly folded over the back of one of the chairs. Hearing the shower running, he began to remove his top layer of clothing as he stepped further into the room. Looking around, he admired the layout of the spacious, well-ornamented room, especially the numerous mirrors that gave it a more alluring feel.

I'm about to start working out, he thought as he stood in his tank top, glancing into one of the wall mirrors. Moments later, the shower turned off, and Makiya emerged from the bathroom wearing only a towel wrapped around her. Seeing her standing there with a smile on her face sparked a flame. It was an untamed feeling that quickly caused exotic thoughts to attack his mental state as she glided over toward him.

Her wide hips swung left then right, crossing over one another. He was in a mild trance, watching her full breasts bounce up and down as if they were grooving to their own beat. Mike-Mike had never tasted pussy before, but her looks were so appealing to his bodily senses, that he was contemplating breaking in his virgin tongue. Once she got close enough that only their body heat separated the two, she asked him did he like what he saw, releasing the towel with one slight pull, causing it to fall to the ground like a fallen flag.

She stood there, exposing her ripe cinnamon breasts and brown, silver dollar nipples. He noticed that her body didn't have any stretch marks, nor a scar on it. He glanced in the mirror, seeing one of the most shapely, curvaceous asses he'd ever seen in person. That did it because he couldn't take it no more.

Mike-Mike immediately commenced to sucking on her neck and passion marking her body, like an animal marks its territory. He gently lifted her by her plump ass, laid her on the bed, then removed the remainder of his clothing quicker than Superman changed in a booth. He was so erect that the skin on his penis felt as though it wanted to burst. She gently pushed him back as she laid back on the bed, spreading her legs like a V, massaging her vaginal area with her thumb and forefinger.

Admiring what he saw, while inhaling her sweet essence, he thought to himself, fuck it, there's a first time for everything. Without a second thought, he headed down south toward her water gate. He flicked his tongue, teasing the tip of her clitoris, licking it until the tiny piece of pink flesh swole to nearly double its size. The way he had her moaning, and squirming, she would've never thought that it was his first time. Not regretting his decision, he continued licking and sucking until his face was covered with her love juices. Her enticing look and the way she was massaging her full breasts had him eager to enter her wet canal.

"Relax," he stated in a soft whisper, slowly ascending from her vagina so he could ease himself into her welcoming love tunnel.

Soft moans escaped her breath when he finally opened the door to her water park. Not wanting to rush he started off with slow, deep strokes. Her walls were massaging him, feeling like warm silk, causing him to get into a better groove. Once the tightness loosened around his shaft, he went from a Kenny Latimore melody to a Beastie Boys tune, digging deeper, and deeper into her womb. With the thought of having her curvaceous backside in the air, he pulled out, turned her around, then positioned her face down and her ass up. Her butt jiggled with each movement when he got off the bed to pull her closer to him. Her voluptuous backside was picture perfect and he was more than ready to dive deep back into her gushing vagina.

As she rested there in a ramp position, he gripped the crevice of her hips with his left hand and then held on to his shaft firmly with his right. He teased her pussy with the tip of his penis, causing her to beg for him to put it all the way in. Granting her request, he thrust himself into her juice box. He had her mind in a frenzy from the way he was drilling her and then pulling out and teasing her with the tip of his penis, over and over, back and forth. Their sexual encounter not only had them sweaty but the wall too. Mike-

Mike threw one of his legs onto the bed so that he could dig deeper. She was taking his pounding like a champ, he quickly wondered if she could take it in her rear. With that thought, he stuck his thumb in her ass, and to his surprise, she didn't object. He worked his thumb in there until it felt loose, then replaced his thumb with the tip of his penis slowly working his dick into her rear end.

"Ooooh!" she moaned, reaching to play with her clitoris as he worked his way deeper into her backside, "Sssss…ssss…sssss," she hissed with each slow stroke.

Getting sexed in her backside wasn't something that she was used to, but the fact he had her so horny, she allowed him to have his way with her.

While Mike-Mike was taking his time slow grinding in her, Slick was in the other room, in a zone, going at it sideways with his lady friend. He was drilling her from the back as his body was angled horizontally to her left near her ass. The position they were in looked as if they were a moving T. He was pounding her wildly as he tried to shake away his thoughts. His near-death incident kept replaying in his head like the loop of a bad movie. His lady friend was damn near trying to crawl away from his pleasurable punishment, but his firm grip wouldn't allow her to go far.

All that could be heard throughout the hotel room was his bloated scrotum repeatedly slapping against her ass. All of a sudden, he rolled her over on her stomach, pumping and grinding repeatedly until their bodies couldn't take the pureness of it anymore. Slick released a load of built up pressure. As he strained to release himself, his partner was in the next room having the best orgasm that he'd ever experienced in his teenage years.

CHAPTER 40

The following morning Zoe was at his body shop making sure that his employees were working diligently so that his recent orders could be fulfilled promptly. He was very hands on when it came down to his business because he understood that to build a successful empire he had to get down and dirty himself. His consistency and return policy that stated, there were options in place within the first two years if anything were to go wrong with a vehicle he provided had his business continuously booming as time went by.

It was a win-win situation for the buyers since they were able to put full coverage insurance on their vehicles. Once it was insured, if they chose to, they could total the vehicle off as a loss and receive the vehicle's blue book value. In return, they could triple the amount they purchased the vehicle for. Word of mouth had orders coming in from up and down the east coast and slowly stretching over to the Midwest. Business was booming, money was flowing like wine from a vineyard and he and Big Herm were there to drink it all up. While continuing to supervise his shop, a certain mood changer entered, causing him to stare at the male individual who stood at the entrance. Zoe casually got up and headed over to speak with his unexpected guest.

"Surprise, surprise," Zoe stated, giving a feigned smile. "What can I help you with?" he inquired, now standing within arms reach.

"You say that like I'm not welcomed," countered the unexpected guest.

"Why wouldn't you be welcomed?"

"Don't know, you tell me?"

"Tell you what," he frowned. "You showed up at my place of business, so it's only right for me to ask, how can I help you," Zoe stated stoned-faced.

"So that's how you greet an old partner and potential future customer," he grinned.

"A future customer, huh!" Zoe replied tediously, not believing a word that was spilling from his guest's mouth.

"Of course, why else would I be here? I was lookin' to purchase a vehicle, a truck actually," he proclaimed, glancing around the shop from where he stood.

Zoe stared at him strangely before responding to his request, "Year, make, and model?"

I'm not lookin' fo' anything extravagant, just something simple like a…umm… he paused briefly. "Newer model Chevy *Yukon*," he requested.

"That's all?"

"Yeah, but make sure it's green and add one of those built-in stashes that could hold about, let's see…" his words trailed off as if he was in deep thought, "'Bout thirty bricks. You think you could handle that fo' me?" he inquired, studying Zoe's reaction for signs of guilt.

"How soon do you need it?" Zoe replied, keeping his poker face intact the entire time.

"I need it like yesterday, but when you call fo' me to pick up the truck, make sure the empty compartment is filled wit' the thirty bricks you stole from me!" he sternly instructed.

"That I stole," Zoe said, pointing at himself. "Man, I don't know whatchu talkin' 'bout," Zoe replied vacantly.

"Maybe you do, or maybe you don't, but let me make somethin' clear to you," he said, removing his Chrome Heart frames, shooting Zoe a scorching look. "Zoe, you know me, and you know I always stand on what I say," the man sharply uttered as his eyes blazed murderously.

"If I find out fo' sure that you had anything to do with my truck being stolen, which isn't hard to believe considerin' the kind of business you in," he spoke, moving in a bit closer, consider this empire you built under new management," he barked his warning in an authoritative tone. Placing his frames back on, he stepped away and headed out the shop before Zoe ever had a chance to respond.

CHAPTER 41

Mike-Mike might've only slept two hours after his hedonistic encounter before another frightening nightmare jolted him awake. Him and sleep didn't always see eye to eye since the nightmares began in the first place. Popping up sweaty, he glanced over at Makiya who was still sleeping peacefully and was relieved that he hadn't awakened her out of her peaceful sleep. He got out of bed, walked over to the window and saw that the sun had risen high in the smog-filled sky. Daydreaming for a moment, he decided to call and break the news to Slick about finally breaking his tongues virginity. When he retrieved his phone, he saw that he had eight urgent missed calls, all from Monique.

Sensing something was wrong, he quickly called her first. She immediately picked up and relayed the pressing message to him, which instantly caused Mike-Mike to become furious.

"Don't move til I get there!" he demanded, hanging up before quickly waking Makiya.

He told her to get dressed while simultaneously calling Slick to inform him of the news he'd just received. Fifteen minutes later, the four of them were hurrying out of the hotel. He dropped the women off first since they didn't stay too far away from where they were and then sped up 14th Street toward his apartment. Shortly after, he parked on Aspen Street, hopped out, then hurriedly walked to his building. As soon as the two bent the corner, Monique was standing on the steps.

"My spot messed up?" he asked anxiously as he approached her, speeding into the building.

"I never went all the way in, I just peeked in," she responded, trailing behind him and Slick.

When he got to his door, out of instinct he pulled out Mother Teresa, which caused Slick to follow suit, whipping out his pistol as well. Upon entering, Mother Teresa led the way as his eyes quickly scanned the area. He whispered for Monique to stay put while he and Slick walked inside. Slick headed for the kitchen, and Mike-Mike went toward the bedroom.

Feeling secure that no one other than them was in there at the time, he tucked his gun away and began searching to figure out what was missing. After a brief inspection, he noticed that thirty-five hundred dollars that he left on top of his television was missing and the duffle bag with the remainder of the guns was gone also, but everything else seemed to be intact. He told Monique to come in after he left his bedroom

"What's missin'?" inquired Slick, coming out of the kitchen.

Mike-Mike told him what was stolen while making a call on his phone.

"Who you callin'?" asked Monique.

"A locksmith to come fix this shit right quick."

As soon as he handled his business with the locksmith, he got right back to the matter at hand.

"Call the crew and tell'em to meet up at Fort Stevens Park, A.S.A.P.!" Mike-Mike ordered slamming his fist into his open hand.

"Fo' what?" asked Slick.

"Cause haven't nobody else been in here outside the crew!" he stated coldly.

"You think one of 'em done this?"

"If not, then who?"

"I hope you wrong, but if not, you already know what time it is," Slick said, giving predatory expressions.

"No question," Mike-Mike added, then turned toward Monique, asking her if she minded staying until the locksmith showed. He informed her that he and Slick needed to go meet up with the rest of the crew.

"I don't mind, but don't forget that I have to pick up some things for my son's birthday party," she reminded. "I was hoping you could take me since I don't have a car."

"I didn't forget. Matter-of-fact I got somethin' fo' ya," he conveyed, reaching into his pocket, pulling out a wad of cash. He peeled off a few bills passing it to her along with the keys to his Lexus with the chain and scroll connected to it that Anthony had given him.

"I told ya I gotchu, just pay fo' da locksmith and everything else you can keep fo' ya'self."

"Are you serious!" She excitedly asked.

"Dead azz," he replied stone-faced.

"Oh my God, thanks!" She responded vigorously giving him a tight squeeze as she tried to shield her sea of emotion.

Out of nowhere, she leaned in kissing him for the first time ever. The kiss they shared was somewhat awkward, but it still set off a lustful spark between them as if two electric voltages were touching. Momentarily lost for words, he broke the silence by telling her he'd meet her later to get the new set of keys the locksmith would leave with her after he changed the locks.

"Okay," she nodded.

"Bet," he concluded before telling Slick they were leaving to meet up with the crew at Fort Stevens Park.

CHAPTER 42

"That was Malice," Moe Kelly told Rex, after ending his call.

"What he say?" Rex questioned, driving westbound on Benning Road.

"He said he paid Zoe a visit this morning."

"And?"

"And nothin' really, just a minor conversation between the two. He said Zoe had his poker face on the whole time, so he couldn't really tell if he actually knew anything or not," he explained.

"That nigga Zoe ain't no fool, he's a calculated thinker. He knows how to move amongst the wolves. He's never goin' to expose his full hand, you should know that. He's the type to keep bluffin' for a minute, then when you think that his mind set, he'll get you for everything," Rex enunciated, depicting his statement.

"Yeah, I'm hip, but ain't no duckin' this one. He gon' get what's comin' to him, especially after we snatch up one of these fools if not both. Trust me, his whole hand's gon' be exposed," he voiced mischievously looking at his partner.

Rex returned the nefarious glare, then something from the corner of his eye got his attention, causing him to make a U- turn at the next intersection.

"Where you goin'?" Asked Moe Kelly.

"I'm tryin' to see somethin'," he replied, making another U-turn. He headed back in the same direction he'd just come from and then made an immediate right turn in the middle of the block. "I knew I recognized that walk. Look at ya man," he pointed.

Moe Kelly immediately spotted Snarz slow walking when he turned to see what Rex was talking about. "Look what we have here. It seems we always find what we lookin' fo' when we stop lookin'," he commented. "Let me out right here while you cut 'im off' at the end of the block," he directed, hopping out, walking fast to catch up with Snarz. Snarz wasn't paying any attention to his surroundings as Rex drove right past him.

Once he reached the corner, Rex was there blocking his path, "What's up, fatboy!" Rex uttered, causing Snarz's heart to instantly beat like a drum in his ear as he turned to run, but bumped right into Moe Kelly.

"What happened last night?" bellowed Moe Kelly ferociously. Snarz's lips started to tremble as fear glazed his eyes.

Feeling like there wasn't anything left to do, he unexpectedly punched Moe Kelly in his face, staggering him before taking off and running through the cut of the apartment buildings on his left. Moe Kelly quickly recovered, then took off after him. Rex sped off, so he could try and cut Snarz off before he made it to the rear of the buildings where there was an exit.

Maybe it was fear, but for a two-hundred-plus pounder, Snarz was moving pretty fast until his lack of conditioning got the best of him. Shortly after, his legs started to feel like dead weight, causing him to slow to a moderate pace. Sweating profusely and tired, he decided to pull out the same .45 caliber gun that Moe Kelly had given him the previous night. He was so focused on finding out where Moe Kelly was coming from, he didn't notice Rex creeping up until he felt a hard blow to his head.

"Ughhh!" he shouted, falling to the ground holding his head, as if his hands could stop the severe pain he was in.

"Give me that muthafuckin' pistol, nigga!" Rex stammered with rage, snatching the gun from Snarz's grip, right as Moe Kelly was running up.

"See what you did Fatboy!" said Moe Kelly, holding his lip. "Nigga, you busted my lip and now you gon' pay!" he snapped, heaving slightly from chasing after Snarz.

"Look what the fool had on 'im," Rex stated, showcasing the gun in his hand.

"Oh yeah, I know this fool didn't still have the gun on 'im like he was goin' to use it," he grimaced. "Let me see that," he said, reaching for the pistol. "Let me show 'im how to use it."

"Please, Moe, man don't do this, just give me another chance to make it up to you!" Snarz pleaded, tears filling his eyes, knowing that he was about to face the consequences of his actions.

"Maybe in another lifetime, fatboy!" Moe Kelly said coldly, placing the large caliber gun under Snarz's chin. He jerked the trigger once, causing brain fragments to shoot up through the top of his skull. The force from the blast sent vibrations through Moe Kelly's hand. "C'mon let's get outta here fo' someone sees us!" he directed as he and Rex fled the scene, leaving Snarz there to be picked up by the coroner.

CHAPTER 43

Everyone finally met up at Fort Stevens Park. Noticing that Melvin was the only one missing, Mike-Mike immediately inquired about his where-a-bouts, "Any of y'all seen or talked to Melvin?" he asked, addressing no one in particular.

"I haven't seen or heard from 'im since we left ya spot yesterday," Lil' Chico spoke up as the other's simply shook their heads no.

"Try to reach 'im right quick," he told Lil' Chico.

"I got ya," he replied, pulling out his cell phone to make the call, but was sent straight to voicemail. "I got da voicemail."

Mike-Mike and Slick looked at one another, both of their thoughts on the same page. In their minds, all signs were pointing toward Melvin. Not only was he not answering his phone, but he was the only one who didn't have any re-up money the day prior.

"What's this all about, anyway?" Lil' Chico inquired, sensing an eerie vibe.

"This was about to be a seven men entering and six men

leavin' type of meetin', but it was obvious who was gon' be da one not leavin'," said Mike-Mike.

"What dat s'posed to mean!" retorted Nose, frowning his face up.

"It means someone broke into my man's shit last night, and ain't nobody been in da spot but da homies!" Slick remarked defensively, speaking up for the first time.

"Exactly, and we don't need no weak link in this circle," Mike-Mike added.

"Sorry to hear that and I can assure you dat I had nothin' to do wit' it. Man, regardless of da situation, I ain't just gon' sit and play pussy if a nigga tries to slump me, no matter who it is," Nose stressed.

"One thing fo' sure; if you had anythin' to do wit' it you was gettin' dealt wit'!" Slick shot back, getting in Nose's face.

"And I bet I wasn't goin' out without a fight!" he countered, holding his ground.

"So what ya tryin' to say, dat it can't happen!" Slick barked, gripping the handle of his pistol that was stationed on his hip.

"I said what I said!" Nose stated coldly, reaching for his own pistol.

"Hold-up y'all two!" Mike-Mike interjected, stepping between them. "Both of y'all pipe down, cause it's quite obvious who da weak link is. So, it ain't no need fo' this right here."

Though the weight from their pistols was heavy, their thoughts were heavier and even more deadly. They stood and stared daggers into each other's skulls, as neither one was willing to back down.

"Look, Nose, I feel where you comin' from, but at da same time in order fo' us to continue to get this money, we gotta drop da dead weight before it drowns us," said Mike-Mike.

"I feel you, Bruh, trust me, but there's no reasonin' when it comes to my life, I value mines, ya feel me," he avowed, never losing eye contact with Slick, who still had fire in his eyes.

"Yeah, I feel ya, but now all I need to know is dat y'all two a'ight," he said, looking back-n-forth between the pair.

"Yeah, I'm cool, if he's cool," Nose responded.

Mike-Mike looked at his partner for confirmation before releasing his hand from his chest.

"I'm cool," Slick grimaced, releasing his grip from the handle of his gun, straightening his clothes.

Upon hearing the particulars of the meeting, Lil' Chico cut his eyes at Tre, who didn't seem too surprised by the sudden news, but he brushed off his speculative thoughts due to Melvin's actions.

Once Mike-Mike was sure the two were okay he turned to the others and said, "We all know dat a thief is worse than a murderer and dat dey both just can't be trusted, period!" he stated as his eyes took on a strange mixture of anger and sadness, because of one of his close comrade's crossing him after he'd done nothing but try to help them come up. "But ya know what," he remarked, pausing briefly and shaking his head side to side. "It's sad to say, but don't none of this shit surprise me, 'cause its always someone in ya circle dat be on some cruddy shit!" he huffed, his face hot and pinched with resentment. "I just don't see how a muthafucka could scheme and plot on da same people dat's tryin' to help them out. It's all good though, 'cause niggas like dat don't last long and I can assure dat!" he spoke with grave deliberations.

The impact of his statement hit some of them like a head-on collision. As for some of the others, his words simply bounced off them like a sound wave ricocheting off the walls.

"Trust me, Bruh, I feel where you comin' from, but I can honestly say dat you don't never have to worry 'bout me being on some sheisty shit, and I expect da same in return," Lil' Chico spoke up.

"Dat goes fo' me too," followed Lil' Kurt.

"Like I said before, I ain't on them type of times," Nose added. "I'm not trying to be rude but let me put a bug in ya ear before I leave," he asked, pulling Mike-Mike to the side away from the others.

"Wassup?" asked Mike-Mike.

"Look, Bruh, I know shit looks suspect on Melvin's part, but I've known slim damn near my whole life and he ain't never done no wild shit like dat. I'm sayin' dat to say, you might wanna take a deeper look into the situation before assumin' what looks like the obvious," he suggested.

"People change wit' time, Nose," he countered.

"Yeah, maturity comes wit' that too, but if you right and I'm wrong, by all means, handle ya business, cause I can't stand a snake my damn self," he said rather frankly.

"I'll see wassup," Mike-Mike hesitated before answering.

"On dat note, I'm out, I got shit to do. Oh, tell ya, partner, to get off my line 'cause I'm not da enemy," he concluded dapping Mike-Mike up before walking off, leaving him there to give some thought to what they'd just discussed.

After giving some serious consideration to what Nose said, Mike-Mike went back to join the others, so he could wrap up the meeting. Before him and Slick departed, he told Pete and Lyran to try and locate Melvin and get back with him when they did. He then communicated to the rest of the crew that he would catch up with them later on.

CHAPTER 44

Big Herm rushed to the shop to talk to Zoe after hearing about the unexpected visit. The two were in Zoe's private office discussing the situation.

"So, he just showed up questioning you about the shipment being stolen?"

"Basically, plus he included a few threats," he grinned. "It wouldn't have been him if he hadn't," he said as the pair briefly sat in silence, each haunted by their own thoughts.

When the fog in their minds finally cleared, Big Herm picked back up where they left off.

"I wonder where the info surfaced from? It wasn't no way for 'im to point the finger back at you, unless someone from our camp said somethin'," he alluded.

"Maybe, but if you ask me I just think he's fishin'."

"If he's fishin', then he damn sure have a hook, he just hasn't reeled it in yet."

"Well we just have to pop the line or make sure it ain't nothin' but trash and seaweed on the hook if he does," Zoe countered, his network of thoughts kicking in.

"I'm wit' you, but where do we start?"

"It's only a few links on this chain, so I figure we just unhook 'em all," he said, reclining in his chair, interlocking his fingers, as he waited on his partner's response.

"So, you ready to clean house?"

"It's better to be safe than sorry. We got too much invested to jeopardize it. Besides, its the reason I had his trump card in my pocket all along for times like this," he stated unremorseful of his decision.

"Then it's law, what's understood don't need to be explained," Big Herm agreed, understanding his partner's viewpoint. "So when does the eviction begin?"

"Soon, real soon," he assured him with a wicked grin.

CHAPTER 45

Mike-Mike's mother was in her bedroom watching Lifetime when Anthony waltzed through the door, calling out to her.

"In the bedroom!" Gloria sounded, announcing her whereabouts.

He casually headed to the room with a smile on his face and one arm around his back. She immediately noticed his delightful demeanor when he entered the bedroom.

"Someone seems to be in a good mood today," she commented.

"I'm in a good mood every day that we together," he proclaimed, bringing his arm from around his back, revealing a dozen red roses.

"They're beautiful!" she responded excitedly, getting out of bed to give him a hug and a kiss. "What's the occasion?" she smiled.

"Why it have to be an occasion?"

"'Cause I know you," she blushed.

"Okay you got me, but don't think there's an occasion every time I bring you something, 'cause that's not the case."

"Okay," she agreed.

"But I was thinking ..." he said between kisses, "that we ..." kiss, "take us ..." another kiss, "a nice week-long vacation," kiss...kiss, he suggested, waiting on her response.

"When and where?" she shot back.

"Let's leave next week. We can go any place you pick and choose," he offered.

"I would love to, but it's too unexpected."

"Why?" he questioned as the wrinkles in his forehead became apparent from possibly being let down.

"Because of my job and my son that's out there doing God know's what," she informed.

"Do you trust me?"

"Of course, why you ask?"

"Then allow me to lead, and I promise to keep the water from your eyes and return a measure of joy into your heart," he spoke sincerely.

As the tears became cloudy in her eyes, he licked her face, wiping her tears away like a cat does when they clean their kittens.

Without a second thought, she gave in, "Okay," she agreed. "Let me notify my job and then clear my schedule," she announced.

"Thank you," he kissed her again. "You take care of that while I go tie up a few loose ends myself."

Gloria was his centerpiece and all his decisions were based around her. He wanted to always be by her side loving, providing, and protecting her. In order to do so, he had to come clean about something in the past. A part of him wanted to leave well enough alone, but another side of him thought it was just best for him to come clean. Even though he knew that the secret he held could very well be the deciding factor over their future.

CHAPTER 46

Several hours had passed since Monique met up with Mike-Mike to give him his apartment keys. Plus, a spare to her spot so he could move the remainder of the bricks to a safer location. Lost in Memory Lane, she couldn't stop thinking about their brief but passionate encounter. The kiss the two shared made the flower in her bloom. Though it was short and quick, it felt so right that it was at that moment she knew he was the one. He had every quality a woman could ask for in a man, yet she felt as though she was venturing into the darkness if she approached him about furthering their friendship because of his hard-to-read demeanor.

Not sure of how he felt, she opted to play things by ear so that she wouldn't risk ruining their friendship. Her thoughts were jam packed like the downtown evening traffic as she pulled into a parking space at the Prince George's Mall. Her amorous feelings toward him had her feeling as nervous as a cat stuck in a tree. Killing the engine on the Lexus, she coolly stepped out with the confidence of a lioness, arched her back and left her plethora of thoughts in the car while she headed into the mall to purchase the remainder of the things she needed for her son's birthday party.

***

Meanwhile, while Monique was at the mall unloading her pockets, Mike-Mike was at her apartment loading the work to be moved elsewhere. Being in the presence of her home made him think about their brief intimate moment and the fact that she always made time for him even if it cut into her schedule. It was clear as a Steuben Crystal that she had strong feelings for him, but he wasn't quite sure of his feelings towards her. Their passionate chimera felt kind of awkward because of their close friendship, but he couldn't continue to deny the fact that their encounter felt as though they belonged. With so much on his plate at the moment, he stored his network of thoughts concerning the two intense encounters away while he focused back on the task at hand.

Glancing at his watch, he figured that he needed to hurry if he wanted to stash the work at its new undisclosed location. After securing everything, he made sure that he put everything back like it was, then headed out the door. On his way down the hallway steps, he phoned Slick to check on him since he hadn't heard from him since he dropped him off at his car after leaving the park earlier that day. Mike-Mike wanted to make sure there wasn't any lingering animosity between Nose and him since their heated exchange, but Slick never answered as he maneuvered through the buildings, treading towards his vehicle. On his way, he bumped into his neighbor Mr. Washington, who wanted to briefly speak with him, but Mike-Mike brushed him off due to the twenty or more years worth of drugs he was traveling with on his person. He promised Mr. Washington that he would stop by to talk with him as soon as he got back.

Unbeknownst to Mike-Mike, what Mr. Washington was trying to relay to him would've shed some light on who broke into his apartment the prior night. But as Mike-Mike sped off, a set of eyes watched on intensely, and the person they belonged to was willing to do what it took to keep his perfidy unknown.

CHAPTER 47

Hours later, the sun was setting, leaving faint streaks of red in the sky. The sinister perpetrator thought it was the perfect time for him to make his move, though he was racing against time like sand spilling through the narrow passage of an hourglass. As Mr. Washington sat in his favorite recliner watching a re-run of Good Times he heard a light tap at his door.

"That must be that boy," he said in nearly a whisper, getting up from his chair to answer the door. "Who is it?"

"Uh…" the voice hesitated, "it's me."

Disregarding the peephole, he answered the door, thinking it was Mike-Mike. "I thought that might've been you," he said, swinging the door open. Mr. Washington's eyes almost popped out of their sockets upon witnessing the silhouette that stood before him, eyes blazing murderously. He was frozen as if someone just pressed an invisible gun to his head. "You, not Michael!" he stuttered.

"I know," the individual grimaced, quickly forcing Mr. Washington to the wall, covering his mouth with his left hand, and utilizing his free hand to plunge a knife deep into his chest.

Mr. Washington instantly felt a stinging like pins and needles, only sharper, as if a low-level electric current was running through him. Blood immediately began to pour from the wound as he tried to yell for help and fight back, but his attacker's strength quickly emasculated him from doing so. The intruder showed no repentance as he pushed the knife deeper, and deeper. Shortly after, Mr. Washington stopped resisting and eventually blacked out. Heaving from a sign of exhaustion, the attacker pulled his blade from Mr. Washington's chest, then silently crept back out the building as if nothing had happened.

CHAPTER 48

Momentarily absent from the eyes of the public, a stream of violent crimes swept over the Nation's Capital like a plague. D.C. was quickly transforming into a city where dreams were lost as bodies began to pile up with more to follow. Living off the fruits of his labor, Ronald Hays was preparing himself for the Miami Heat versus San Antonio Spurs N.B.A. Finals. In the luxury of his newly purchased Columbia Heights home, he stockpiled his table with all the necessities as he waited for his guest to arrive. With his better half and their two kids out catching a movie at the Magic Johnson theatre, he had the four-bedroom, three-level, single-family home all to himself. Minutes before the game was supposed to start, he heard a knock at the door.

"There they go," he uttered, as he went to open the door, "just in time!" he smiled, allowing his guest to enter.

"This is nice!" said guest number one, giving Ronald some dap upon entering, followed by guest number two, acknowledging the home's elegant layout as well. "Yeah, real nice Ronald."

"Thanks, you two. Care for a beer?"

"Why not," said guest number one.

"I'll have one too," added guest number two.

"I'll be right back. Make ya'self at home," Ronald stated, walking off toward the kitchen as the guests headed for the living room.

"Let's make a toast," Ronald said after walking into the living room, handing his two guests their beers.

"What we toastin' to?" spoke guest number one.

"Let's toast to just being able to function in life. My reason for sayin' that is," he hesitated, "not even a full year ago I was on the verge of being homeless. I know that if it wasn't for y'all two good men, I wouldn't have any of this," he vented, his eyes brimming with joy.

"Well, I'm glad you appreciate what we done. At the same time, you work hard for what you got, so you have to thank ya'self first and foremost," guest number one spoke up.

"I do work hard, don't I?" he smiled.

"Don't flatter ya'self, drink up," guest number one countered as all three men clung glasses and took a sip of their Heinekens.

"So, who do you two predict to win the NBA Finals?" Ronald inquired.

"I think the team that's willing to sacrifice more will win. 'Cause one can't become champions unless the team is willing to do something they might hate in order to achieve something they love," said guest number one.

"I agree," added guest number two.

"That's real talk, but it don't really matter to me, but if I had to choose, I'd say the Spurs, especially after what happened in last year's finals. There's no way they should've lost last year's finals," Ronald replied.

"There's definitely a lot of built-up animosity from last year's game," said guest number two.

"You better know it," Ronald shot back.

"Speakin' of games, let me ask you a question," said guest number one, sipping his beer.

"Sure."

"If life were a game of chess, what piece would you consider ya'self to be?"

"That's easy, unlike you two kings, I wouldn't consider myself to be nothin' more than a pawn," Ronald answered.

"And why is that?"

"'Cause I really don't have no value," he proclaimed.

"But pawns have plenty of value. Think about it. What's the most important duty of the pawn?"

"I would have to say, their alacrity to sacrifice themselves to protect the king", Ronald stated.

"So, the king isn't wrong for sacrificing his pawns to avoid regicide?"

That question caused Ronald to look at his guests strangely for the first time. Now paying attention, he realized that they both had on gloves, and it wasn't even cold enough for them. He suddenly had a bad feeling as if something unpleasant was about to occur. "Did I do something wr..wro...wrong?" he stuttered.

"Not at all, but in order for the king to avoid getting

checkmated, he must eradicate a few valuable pieces," guest number one said, nodding his head at guest number two.

Guest number two, already knowing what time it was, immediately pulled out his .45 caliber handgun, aiming it toward Ronald's head.

The sight of the gun caused Ronald to suddenly become dizzy, light-headed like after an intense workout in the sweltering heat. Eyes clouding with tears, his last thoughts were of his wife and kids, but that quickly left his brain as a bullet exploded into it.

"Let's get out of here," directed guest number one.

As the pair left the house, beers in hand, a set of hawk eyes were glued to them while they got in their vehicle and pulled off.

CHAPTER 49

Hours had passed since Monique left Prince George's Mall. From there, she headed out Central Avenue to pay for the Moon Bouncer for her son's party and then drove out Virginia to Tyson's Corner, so she could get an outfit that she had on lay-a-way. With the extra money that Mike-Mike gave her, she was able to do so. Even after a busy day, she couldn't keep him off her mind. Although trying to figure him out was like trying to walk on water, she eventually psyched herself up enough to ask him out on their first date.

At a little after nine, she was finally leaving the mall. She decided to call her mother to check on her kids and to also inform her that everything was taken care of, including the Moon Bouncer. Speaking with her briefly, she ended the call, promising her son was going to have the best birthday party ever.

On her way to her vehicle, her thoughts went right back to Mike-Mike. She admired everything about him, his smile, voice, the way he rubbed his hands together when he talked and his sexy limp due to the tragic accident that claimed the life of his little sister. With that thought, she silently said a prayer for the both of them. After doing so, her scrambled thoughts began to catch traction when she noticed some guy smiling at her. Ignoring the stranger, she casually removed her keys from her purse so that she could place her bags in the trunk.

"Didn't expect to see you twice in one day," spoke the stranger.

"Excuse me, do I know you?" she inquired, placing the bags in the trunk.

"You don't remember me from Prince George's Mall earlier when I offered to help with all them bags you were carryin'," he reminded.

"Oh, of course, I'm sorry, it's been a long day," she apologized. "And now you out here also, what a coincidence," she stated, closing the trunk.

"Maybe so, but I believe there's a reason fo' everything," he countered.

"If so, then what's your reason?"

"What's my reason fo' being out here."

"That's what I asked."

"I had to rush out here to grab something I couldn't get from P.G. Mall earlier," he stated.

"All the way out here?"

"Unfortunately."

"Well I hope you found what you were looking for," she said, pressing the unlock button on her key ring.

"Actually, I just did," he stated coldly, his soft face hardening.

Noticing his facial expression change caused the small hairs on the back of her neck to stir. She quickly tried to get in her vehicle, but out of nowhere, a silhouette appeared from behind, grabbing her in a bear hug violently yanking her. The silhouette's rough hands pressed hard against her mouth before she could scream. Monique never had a chance as the two men overpowered her, kidnapping her with ease.

CHAPTER 50

Mike-Mike sensed an unpleasant vibe when he made it back to his neighborhood from stashing the work and taking care of a few other things. Once he approached Slick, Lil' Chico, Pete, and Lyran, he immediately asked what was up with all the sad faces.

"They found Melvin's body in Rock Creek Park," conveyed Slick.

"Yeah, he was found wit' two to da head," added Pete, glancing at Mike-Mike with suspicion.

"I don't know why you cutting ya eyes at me, 'cause I didn't do it!" Mike-Mike retorted defensively.

"That's not all," said Slick.

"What else is it?"

"Somebody put dat knife in ya neighbor Mr. Washington. I'on't know if he made it or not, but he was rushed to da hospital."

"You serious!" he snapped in disbelief. "Who da fuck would wanna stab an old ass man!"

"Who knows," Slick shrugged.

"He wanted to holler at me 'bout somethin' earlier, but I brushed 'im off rushin' to handle somethin'," he explained as his mind wandered off in deep thought. "I wonder what he was tryin' to tell me," he said to himself.

Curiosity started to get the best of him because his speculative thoughts went into overdrive. He now wondered was whatever Mr. Washington had to say to him somehow related to his stabbing.

"Oh, I fo'got to give ya this yesterday," Lil' Chico said, pulling out a piece of paper, passing it to him.

"What this?" Mike-Mike replied, unfolding the paper to view its content.

"Some lady named Lisa came by yesterday and gave me that, she claimed to know where Hubbs been or somethin' to dat nature. I meant to give it to you earlier when we was at da park, but it slipped my mind."

"Good lookin'," replied Mike-Mike, flashing the piece of paper to Slick who was aware of the situation.

As he tucked the paper away, Tre, Lil' Kurt, and Nose were bending the corner, approaching the group.

"Here y'all go," Tre announced. "What's up wit' y'all?" he greeted, dapping everybody up.

"Bad news as usual," relayed Pete.

"Like what?"

"Fo' starters, somebody put dat knife in old man Mr. Washington."

"And," Tre responded nonchalantly.

"What cha mean and!" Mike-Mike fired back. "This joint gon' be extra hot now dat some fool done stabbed an old person 'round here!"

"I feel ya, but I don't feel no sympathy fo' dat nosey ass old man!" Tre said with conviction, causing Mike-Mike to simply shake his head.

"Dat's not all," Pete interjected.

Tre never responded, he just looked at Pete with a vacant look. Seeing the mournful look in his eyes, he sensed something even worse was about to come out of his mouth.

"Melvin's body was found in Rock Creek Park this afternoon," he commiserated.

"What!" Fumed Nose, directing his attention at Mike-Mike and Slick.

Catching the awkward stares, Mike-Mike was about to defend himself when out of nowhere Nose unexpectedly struck him in his face. "I know you had somethin' to do wit' dat shit!" he barked, rushing overtop of him, preparing to strike again. As his hand cocked back, Slick's pistol was already out, pointing in Nose's face, halting him as his arm was in striking motion.

"I wish you would!" Slick warned, stone-faced, as the look in his eyes showed that his threat wasn't an idle one.

"So, it's like dat huh!" Nose asked in a grim tone, at the sight of the gun in his face.

Mike-Mike quickly reached up, grabbing Slick's arm before the situation escalated, knowing Nose was only venting from the personal relationship he had with Melvin.

"Look, I can see why you might assume dat I had somethin' to do wit' it, but I promise you on my lil' sister grave, I didn't play a part in dat shit. Dat's my word as a man," Mike-Mike assured him, spitting out blood, then picking himself up off the ground.

"I would've said dat too," countered Nose, looking back-n-forth between the two with venomous eyes.

"Nose, I'm tellin' you, it wasn't me," Mike-Mike pleaded, trying to reach out to him.

"Don't put ya hands on me!" he said point blank, then looked at Slick who still had his gun in hand. "You plan on using dat?" he questioned Slick.

Mike-Mike quickly nodded for Slick to put the gun away. "Naw, ain't no need fo' it," Slick replied, tucking the pistol away.

"Good, 'cause I'm out!" Nose scoffed, storming off, leaving them standing there to marinate in their own thoughts.

"We might have to watch dat nigga," Slick whispered feverishly.

"Let me go holler at him," Kurt chimed in, rushing off to catch up with Nose, hoping the spur-of-the-moment incident didn't spark anything within the circle.

"He'll be a'ight once he cools off," said Lil' Chico.

"Yeah, I hope so fo' his sake," Slick uttered.

"Leave dat shit alone. He just ventin' because of how close him and Melvin was," stated Mike-Mike.

"Well, regardless he shouldn't be puttin' his hands on nobody unless he wants some work," Slick coldly stated.

"Just like you shouldn't have pulled dat gun out," he shot back. "He still a part of this circle. Leave dat gunplay fo' them other niggas."

"Yeah whatever," Slick replied, brushing off Mike-Mike's last comment. "I need a drink, I'm 'bout to hit da liquor store."

"Shid I'm ridin' wit' you," said Lil' Chico.

"Me too," added Pete, followed by Lyran and Tre.

"Y'all go 'head. I'll catch-up wit'chu later," said Mike-Mike.

"You sure you ain't tryin' to roll?" asked Slick.

"Nah I'm good, plus I'ma go clean myself up."

"Yeah, you do dat, 'cause he jive caught you wit' a good one," Slick joked.

Mike-Mike smiled back, telling them that he would see them tomorrow, then dapped them up before going his separate way.

***

"Ay Nose!" Kurt called out. "Hold-up!"

When Nose stopped and turned to face him, he displayed a sinister look, resembling the devil himself. Kurt had never seen such a wicked look plastered across his homie's face before, and from the looks of him, he knew that his comrade was full of enmity. Recognizing his mental attitude, he quickly tried to find the right words to say, hoping they would calm his nerves after his brief altercation.

"I know you heated about what happened, Slick was wrong fo' pullin' dat hamma out, but slim on some real shit, you know he didn't mean to do dat," he tried to reason.

"He's old enough to know dat every decision he makes has consequences to 'em. I'm not da one who pulled da gun out," he countered defensively. "Man, and if it's one thing dat I learned in these streets..." he hesitated, "its to never pull out a gun unless you plan to use it," he coldly stated as he turned to walk off, not giving Kurt a chance to respond.

CHAPTER 51

Mike-Mike stood in front of his bathroom mirror, dabbing at his open wound, reflecting on all the events that led up to this point. His mood was closer to depressed and deeply disturbed after assessing his situation. The chain of events had his thoughts piled up like a stack of groceries.

He came to the realization that the fast life was causing everyone around him to act in a reckless manner, including himself. Though financially he was comfortable, all the money he'd received in that short period of time didn't amount to the torment he put his mother through by leaving home for the sake of the streets. On top of everything, the covetous, recreant ways of his so-called friends gave him a sudden feeling of doubt, fear, and uneasiness.

Sprung by a conglomerate of baleful thoughts, he knew more sooner than later he'd need to pump his brakes or the fast life was going to forcefully drive him into a steel wall. Not wanting to crash, it was time for him to start making more calculated choices, starting with finding out the outcome of Mr. Washington's condition, hoping that he had pulled through. Right after he finished cleaning himself up, he went to retrieve his phone, so he could make the necessary calls to track down Mr. Washington's whereabouts. Equipped with his name and round about age, it didn't take long to locate him.

Peeking at his watch seeing that it was almost ten o'clock, he quickly grabbed his keys and headed out the door. Twenty minutes later, he was rushing through the double doors of Howard University Hospital. Once he reached the receptionist desk, he right away requested the location of the EMERGENCY ROOM. After claiming to be the grieving nephew he was allowed a ten-minute visit. The first thing Mike-Mike noticed once he entered was how tired, pale, and drained Mr. Washington appeared as if he'd just given blood.

"How you feelin' Mr. Washington?" he commiserated as he closed the gap between them.

"Tired and sore but I'll live," he responded in a deadpan tone before shifting his body toward Mike-Mike.

"Try not to move too much," he conveyed, reaching out to help him position himself.

"I'm okay, it'll take more than a simple knife to take this old man out," he joked, trying to sound upbeat.

"I hear ya. I'm just glad dat ya still here wit' us."

"Yeah, well thank God for Life Alert because I probably wouldn't be," he moaned from the pain. "Whoever invented it was a genius," he chuckled slyly, causing Mike-Mike to share a laugh with him.

"Mr. Washington, I know dat this might not be a good time to ask you this, but my time here is limited, and I need to know somethin'," he hesitated.

"What is it?"

"I need to know is what happened to you have anything to do wit' what you had to tell me earlier?"

The question caused Mr. Washington's stomach to contract into a tight ball. The murderous expression that exuded from the young male that attempted to take his life was embedded in his mind.

The recollecting of the incident caused him to hesitate before speaking, "It had everything to do with what happened to me," he disclosed.

"What was it about?"

"It was about your apartment being broke in to. Your so-called friend must've somehow found out that I seen what he done."

"You saw who broke into my spot!?" he exclaimed as the sudden news caused his face to contort fiercely.

"Yeah, I saw him and that's what I was trying to tell you."

"My fault Mr. Washington, but dat wasn't a good time fo' me," he said shaking his head. "Now I feel like this is all my fault. If I would've just taken da time to hear you out, I probably could have prevented this from happenin' to you."

"You can't fault yourself because of someone else's greed. You can't expect loyalty from people who would do anything for money. You just have to be more aware of your surroundings, 'cause it's obvious he isn't your friend."

"Yeah, I know," he agreed. "Since dat's understood I need to know who it was," he said point blank.

With the exception of his name, Mr. Washington began depicting an unclouded picture of the disloyal teen as if he was standing directly in front of him. Mike-Mike knew exactly who Mr. Washington was speaking of from his detailed description. As the discovery sank into the crevices of his brain, he became more and more heated.

"Do anyone else know 'bout this?"

"I might be a nosey old man, but I don't run my mouth," he vowed. "I never told on anyone in my entire life."

"Good, keep it dat way and keep this between us," he countered as the doctor came in indicating that their time was up. "I was just gettin' ready to leave doc," Mike-Mike stated as he got himself ready to leave.

"We have to run some test to make sure there's no internal bleeding and some detectives are on their way to speak with you," the Doctor informed Mr. Washington.

"Dat's my cue," Mike-Mike whispered to Mr. Washington.

"You go on," instructed Mr. Washington, "I got them don't worry," he winked.

"Get you some rest, Uncle, and I'll be back to check on ya," he replied before heading for the door. "Thanks, Doc," he said leaving out before the detectives arrived.

CHAPTER 52

The Benz *Coupe's* leather seats were glued to Mike-Mike's back as he punched the vehicle with a high-torque snarl up Georgia Avenue. His network of thoughts caused him to become furious as he buried the pin of the Benz's speedometer, disregarding all traffic laws as he flew past a police squad car. Witnessing the law-breaking driver of the luxury coupe zooming by, the police cruiser right away tried to go into pursuit.

Once the red and blue cherry's flashed, Mike-Mike expertly downshifted his gears, made a sharp right turn onto New Hampshire Avenue and swiftly smacked the clutch back up to third, fourth and then fifth distancing himself from the officer before the chase even began. Soon after, he was entering his neighborhood. Driving North on Georgia Avenue he glanced to his left and spotted some of his homies in the fissures of the buildings.

He found a parking spot on the back street and hopped out with a murderous mentality. Approaching the apartments from off Aspen Street, the group's drunken speech became clearer. Angry about the information he'd received from Mr. Washington, he was on the verge of committing mischief off impulse. Armed with a homicidal mind state and something more threatening on his person, a fatalistic situation was nearing.

As he pulled out his five-shot *Taurus* and proceeded to advance forward his cell phone faintly started its familiar subliminal hum. The selected ringtone halted him in his approach. The fact that Monique was calling him at that hour was out of the ordinary and that fact alone had urged him to answer the call.

"I swear it must be some kind of sign fo' you to be callin' me at this time," he answered, never taking his eyes off his mark.

"Well, hopefully the sign reads fo' you to follow my exact instructions or else you might not see ya lil' lady friend again!" threatened the unknown caller on the other end of the line.

"Who da hell is this!?" he uttered with brutal detachment.

"Don't worry 'bout who I am, what I want is what's important...."

"Fuck you want from me!" Mike-Mike interjected.

"What I want is fo' you to return somethin' that you stole from me."

"Stole!" he cut in.

"Yeah, stole!" the caller barked. "That truck you stole wit' the goods in it," he reminded. "Ring a bell?"

"Man, I 'on't know what you talkin' 'bout," he dissimulated.

"So, you don't know what I'm talkin' 'bout, huh?" he asked in a deadly tone. "Well I tell you what, you have exactly seventy-two hours to figure it out or else your lil' lady friend here gon' be found in an unknown park like your so-called man that told us everything we needed to know," the stranger spoke in a voice that was as cold as crucifixion, ending the call before Mike-Mike got a chance to respond.

"Hello! Hello! Fuck!" he fumed, almost dropping the phone as a surge of cold sizzled down his spine and the back of his legs.

He immediately felt as if someone had shoved a blade deep in his heart, leaving him momentarily speechless. He could feel the pit of emptiness expanding in his stomach as his heart ached stupendously for Monique. He tucked Mother Teresa away as he took several deep breaths to gain his composer.

The loss of his baby sister had caused him to have a guarded attitude for the women he was connected to. The fact that Monique always seemed to be there when he needed her, she was without question one of those women. The tables were turned and now she needed him more than ever, because her life depended on it. At that very moment, something clicked inside him and his safety was no longer an issue. All that mattered at that moment was getting her back safely by any means necessary.

CHAPTER 53

Monique's unforeseen abduction had her mind in a fog as if she was dumped dead center in a pitch-black maze. Though she was disoriented and afraid, the conversation she'd just overheard shed some light on a dark situation. She immediately became vex after finding out that she was kidnapped because of Mike-Mike's street dealings. *So, all that stuff he had in my place must've belonged to these people,* she thought. Why would he put me in this predicament after all I done for him? A conglomerate of negative thoughts zipped through her mind, and at that very moment, the likelihood of seeing her kids again became distinctly possible.

Just being in the same room with her abductors had her more nervous than a deer running from a pack of starving lions, but she somehow managed to keep calm under pressure. She still couldn't figure out how she got entangled in the situation. Just as the thought crossed her mind, her kidnapper's conversation became clear as day, answering her question as if they were mind readers.

"Yeah if it wasn't for that youngin' we snatched the other day, we wouldn't have got hip to that white Lexus," said Moe Kelly loud enough for Monique to overhear.

That damn car, she thought. *So, they were following the car and I just so happened to be driving it or was that the reason he gave me the car because he knew they were aware of it. He had to know,* she summarized. *These probably the same people that broke into his apartment looking for that stuff,* she theorized as her breaths quickened from thoughts of Mike-Mike placing her in a vulnerable situation.

Seventy-two hours, seventy-two, kept flashing through her mind repeatedly like a re-run. *My son's birthday party is in exactly three days,* she reminded herself before silently saying a must needed prayer to herself. After saying a quick prayer, she could only hope that she could escape the madness and reunite with her loved ones. The kidnapper's conversation once again became crystal clear. What she heard only made matters worse.

"Even if they come through we still can't let her go cause she's seen our faces," Rex stated.

"I never planned to," confirmed Moe Kelly.

The news was striking like hammer blows and all of her hopes flew out the window like someone smoking from inside of a moving vehicle. All she could do was hope that her prayers be answered by the man upstairs.

CHAPTER 54

In the wee hours of the morning, Malice received a surprising text message. Though he was relaxing in the comfort of his home, the pressing message snapped him out of his comfort zone. He quickly got out of bed, heading into the living room out of ear utterance of his significant other who was resting beside him. Without delay, he returned the call the second he entered the living room.

"I figured you'd call as soon as you saw that text message," claimed Moe Kelly when he answered.

"You figured right," Malice replied in nearly a whisper, "Now who's this girl again?" he inquired, trying to obtain some clarity.

"She's our link to the chain that got stolen," he informed. "Plus, I already spoke wit' the jeweler and told 'im he had seventy-two hours to straighten that situation out," he explicated in a coded manner.

"So basically, our gut feelin' was dead-on 'bout ol' boy, huh?"

"No question! She might be the link to the chain but our

man's the medallion that holds all the weight."

"When you on top of your game you ain't to be messed wit', you hear me," he heartened. "That's why I be needin' you clear headed," Malice added.

"I feel where you comin' from but that nose candy don't change who I am, it just makes me more aggressive towards niggas or fuck the dog shit out them bitches," Moe Kelly said point blank.

"Yeah well, tomorrow mornin' I'll definitely be payin' slim a visit," Malice countered, disregarding Moe Kelly's last statement.

"You need me to roll wit' you?"

"Naw, I'm straight, plus, you need to keep a close eye on that link."

"Rex could do that. That shit ain't 'bout nothin."

"I can handle it, plus you already know I move better alone."

"A'ight cool, just hit me if you need us."

"Fo' sure," stated Malice ending the call as an evil expression covered his face.

Validating what he already suspected caused his nefarious thoughts to take over. Being a man of his word, he knew that tomorrow's visit wasn't going to be a pleasant one, but it was definitely a visit he was looking forward to.

CHAPTER 55

Mike-Mike immediately texted Slick to come by as soon as possible once he made it back to his apartment. The instant Slick received the urgent message he headed in the direction of Mike-Mike's apartment without informing the group as to why he was rushing off. Though he was inebriated, he made it to Mike-Mike's spot as fast as one's legs could carry one who was drunk.

As soon as Mike-Mike open his door, Slick instantly noticed the stressful look that was plastered across his face. The expression he displayed was as if a loved one was being washed away by the ocean's current and there wasn't anything he could have done to prevent it.

"Is e'rything a'ight?" questioned Slick while entering the apartment.

"Man, somebody snatched Monique!" he quickly shot back, his eyes wide in alarm.

"Who got Monique!?" he frowned, slurring his words.

"I 'on't know exactly who, but someone called me from her phone, talkin' 'bout they got her and that I got seventy-two hours to give back da bricks we took!" Mike-Mike conveyed.

"You serious!?" Slick countered sounding a lot more sober.

"Dead azz," he assured, "and dat's not it," he added.

"What else is it?"

"Whoever they are, they're da same ones dat smashed Melvin," he confirmed.

"How ya figure dat?" he frowned.

"'Cause he told me if I ain't come-up wit' it, she gon' be found in some unknown park just like your man dat told 'im," he explained.

"So dat explains what happened to Melvin," replied Slick, rubbing his chin.

"Yeah," agreed Mike-Mike.

"This shit don't look good. Ain't no way we could come up wit' somethin' we only had half of."

"I'm already hip and dat's why I need to go holler at Zoe first thing in da mornin'."

"Yeah, dat might be your best bet cause we damn sure can't go searchin' fo' someone dat's basically a ghost to us."

"I know," he concurred, stress lines forming on his forehead. "Shit!" he blurted out realizing that he was in a no- win situation.

"I feel ya, bruh, but we gotta figure out somethin' and quick 'cause seventy-two hours ain't dat much time," relayed Slick, patting Mike-Mike on his back.

"I know this isn't a good time to bring this up but..." Mike-Mike hesitated.

"But what?"

"I also found out who broke in my shit."

"No bullshit!" Slick said in astonishment as his face glazed with shock.

"Yeah, and you were just wit'im."

"Who?" he inquired, eager to know.

After taking a brief moment to collect his thoughts, he began explicating how he came across the friend/enemy of the group. The more he explained, the more Slick felt his insides heating up, similar to what liquor felt like when it entered his system.

"Dat's crazy!'' Slick shook his head in disgust. "Dat's da shit I be talkin' 'bout right there. You can't even trust ya so-called men!" he lashed out in frustration. "I'ma handle dat nigga myself," he vowed.

"Naw, I got 'im right after we deal wit' this Monique situation first. Don't wanna get sidetracked 'cause she needs us more than anything right about now," Mike-Mike verbalized as he slumped into his couch.

Silence filled the air as the pair's thoughts began to flicker on what was going on. Analyzing their circumstance, Slick broke the quietness by trying to connect the dots.

"A'ight look, it's obvious dat whoever da dude is dat called you got on ya line through Monique, right?"

"Yeah," agreed Mike-Mike.

"So, how did they get on her line through Melvin?" he threw out there as a question and not a fact.

"Good question, but it don't make any sense 'cause why would he send 'em her way and not straight to us?"

"Fo' da same reason they doin' now. Using her as bait," Slick suggested.

"It's possible, but my gut's tellin' me it's somethin' else," Mike-Mike stated lifting up off the couch, pacing back-n-forth, wrecking his brain trying to find the solution to the problem.

"A'ight, let's use da what if method. What if they got to me through Mo-Mo and they got to her through Melvin? Now da question is; how, did they get hip to Melvin," he self-contradicted, causing them both to go into deep thought.

After careful thinking, it was as if the same answer slapped them in the face at the same time, 'cause both of them looked at one another and blurted out, "Hubb!"

"Dat might be it! He probably put 'im on our line through them just to save his own ass," Slick summed up. "But if dat's da case, how da fuck do we s'pose to find Hubb's crackhead azz?"

"Dat's another problem," Mike-Mike replied. Soon after a sudden thought came out of nowhere like a sudden breeze. "I got it!" Mike-Mike exclaimed, heading toward his bedroom.

"Where you goin'?" Slick inquired.

In a matter of seconds, Mike-Mike was walking back out. "Remember da piece of paper dat Lil' Chico gave me wit' dat woman's phone number and address on it," he reminded, showing him the folded paper.

"Damn, I almost fo'got all about dat. What you want me to try to catch up wit' her in da mornin' while you go holler at Zoe?"

"Shid, every second count right now. I'm 'bout to call her now," he said point blank. Mike-Mike pulled out his cell phone and dialed her number hoping to get an answer, but it went straight to voicemail. "Damn, it went to her voicemail," he rattled.

"Try again," Slick suggested.

Without hesitation, Mike-Mike tried again and again but got the same results. "Fuck it, I'm goin' over there!" he stressed.

"It's two o'clock in da mornin'," Slick pointed out.

"And?" he asked unconcerned.

"You sure you wanna go over there this time of mornin'?"

"Time waits fo' no one, and this might be our best chance of catchin' her," Mike-Mike urged.

"Fuck it then, c'mon."

"Just let me grab my jacket," replied Mike-Mike, stepping off to retrieve it before coming right back, rushing out his apartment door with Slick trailing close behind.

CHAPTER 56

No words were spoken as Mike-Mike drove to their destination. Stopping at a traffic light, he briefly closed his eyes and cleared his mind of everything but the task at hand while taking several slow, deep breaths like a comedian does before a live performance. Driving off, he reminded himself to not replace logic with emotion and to stay calm, so he could assess the situation more clearly. Shortly after, they were entering Lisa's neighborhood.

"Turn right there," Slick directed. "Her apartment should be comin' up," he advised, glancing at the piece of paper.

When Mike-Mike slowed to make the turn, he felt his adrenaline surge and his heart begun to beat almost unpleasantly in time with the car's indicator.

"There it go," Slick announced pointing toward the building that sat to his left in the middle of the block.

"Let me find somewhere to park on da next street over just in case her window faces da street."

Once he found a spot to park, the pair got out and

quickly scanned the area like Hawks perched on top of a utility pole. With the mindset of there's a strong possibility of a set of wandering eyes when you least expect them, the two walked attentively and as casually as possible heading toward her building.

"Apartment 202," Slick uttered, reaching the building.

Once inside the building, they hiked the flight of stairs that led to her door. Without delay, Mike-Mike put his ear to the door listening for signs of movement, but the sound that came from inside the apartment was as silent as a grave. He made one last attempt to call her phone before deciding to knock on her door. After getting the same result, he lightly tapped on her door.

"Man, she can't hear dat," Slick whispered. "Knock on it," he said in a quietly raised voice.

But out of nowhere Mike-Mike grabbed the knob and turned it not actually believing it to be unlocked, but to his surprise it opened. "Oh shit!" he mumbled, slightly pushing the door open, peaking his head inside.

"Bruh, hold-up!" Slick muttered, halting Mike-Mike in his approach while pulling out his P90 Ruger with a clip hanging out of it that could be used as a kickstand. "Let ya pistol lead da way, fo' you get ya face blown-off," he warned.

Without hesitation, Mike-Mike whipped out Mother Teresa, sticking her out in front of him as he cautiously followed behind her when he stepped in. The apartment was damn near pitch dark like two closed eyelids, but within a matter of seconds, their eyes adjusted. After adapting to the darkness, they proceeded further into the apartment. As the pair moved forward, the squeaking of the hardwood floor caused them both to pause instantly in their movement. Hoping they hadn't alert anyone, they stood frozen solid, like a pair of ice sickles praying that Mother Teresa and Slick's P90 Rugers wouldn't have to come alive and wake-up the neighbors. Once they were content that no one was warned, they continued.

When they passed the living room a flicker of light came from the kitchen window, giving them a faint but better view of the rest of the apartment. That slight glimmer of light allowed them to look further past the narrow hallway they stood in and see that it was a two-bedroom apartment. Mutely inching closer toward the back, Mike-Mike whispered for Slick to check the room on the right while he searched the room that was straight ahead.

With nothing else to be said, the pair veered off entering the separate rooms. Upon entering, both of their heartbeats begun to race a bit from the anticipation of possibly walking into a hazardous situation. With their pistols in hand they cautiously scanned the room hoping to find Lisa, but after a thorough search, the two came back out signifying that it was empty. Glancing at the bathroom that sat with the door wide-open, Mike-Mike silently stepped over clicking on the switch to see that it was also vacant.

"Empty," stated Mike-Mike turning the light back off.

"So, what now?" Slick inquired.

"Don't know," he shrugged uncertain of their next move. "I'm just gon' wait til da mornin' to holler at Zoe," he advised. "C'mon let's get outta here," he stated, tucking his pistol away proceeding to exit. Within a matter of seconds, the front door squealed open.

"Oh, shit!" uttered Mike-Mike, grabbing Slick, tucking themselves behind the wall of the room that Slick was just in.

In no time, some noise came from the kitchen as if someone was rummaging through the refrigerator. The unknown had their hearts beating like drums, mouths' dry, and butterflies in their stomachs. Not wanting to scare or cause harm to someone's home they invaded just to question, Mike-Mike considered his next move. Deciding to step out and announce his presence as the silhouette passed by to enter the bedroom, Mike-Mike called out to her in a quiet raised voice.

"Lisa don't be scared, we not goin' to..." was all he managed to say before quickly realizing the person that was standing before him in fascinating horror was no one other than Hubb himself. Before Hubb could react, Mike-Mike had him pinned against the wall covering his mouth to keep Hubb from raising his voice and yelling out in fear. Instead of causing a scene, Hubb simply stood there shocked in stunned silence.

"Just da man we're lookin' fo' and your crackhead azz walked straight to us," Mike-Mike grimaced, grinding out his words through clenched teeth while Slick had the barrel of his Ruger pressed against Hubb's temple. "So, this is where you been hidin' at huh?"

Hubb was so nervous and high that he was shaking like a bobblehead in a moving vehicle. "Whatchu thought, we wasn't gon' see each other again, 'cause ya crack head azz damn sure tried us not once but twice," Mike-Mike fumed. "And now this time you done fucked around and got Monique snatched-up!"

"What!" Hubb mouthed, confused.

"You heard what da fuck I said. Monique's missin' because of your dumb azz."

"Monique missin'," he reiterated, shocked. "Man, you have to believe me, I didn't have anything to do with what happened to her or them dudes tryin' to rob you. I was just as surprised as you two," he pleaded.

"You expect us to believe dat shit!" Slick interjected pressing his pistol harder into Hubb's temple. "Then why you hidin' out?!"

"'Cause I'm no fool and from da outside lookin' in, I looked guilty, so I hid out outta fear not regret."

"Man, fuck all dat! I ain't tryin' to hear dat shit!" Slick roared, snatching Hubb into the room that he had searched, slinging him onto the floor face up with the barrel now pointed between his eyes.

"Please don't do this! Why would I try to set y'all up? Y'all ain't never done anything to me!" he implored, lips twitching out of fear. "If anything, you two should know I definitely wouldn't harm Monique, knowing she's a single parent wit' two kids. Plus, I watched her grow-up!" he tried to induce, noticing the crazed look in Slick's eyes as he stood there gripping the handle in a threatening manner.

"Fuck all dat cryin' shit, where them dudes be at you

brung to us?" Slick inquired, racking a bullet into the chamber.

"I think they from off Benning Road somewhere," Hubb whimpered, shaking like he was outside in freezing weather naked.

"Where at on Bennin' Road?" asked Mike-Mike.

"Around by 21st somewhere."

"You sure?"

"Kinda, but I am sure that da dude I brung to meet you have a big-time drug dealer uncle that own a Tattoo Shop on 19th and Benning Road," he advised.

"An uncle dat's a big-time drug dealer," frowned a skeptical Mike-Mike. "Dat shit didn't draw a red flag when he told you he wanted to come around da way to buy some work after already knowing dat his folks should have da shit!"

"Yeah at first, but after he told me his people took a major loss, I pretty much figured they needed it. I didn't mean no harm. I thought I was helping both of y'all out by bringing you two some business and gettin' them some product."

"You said his folks took a major loss?"

"Yeah, word on da street is it was large too," he informed.

"Hubb, how da hell you know all of this?"

"Man, I'm a licensed crackhead, I travel da hoods more than tourists travel da world! You'll be s'prised at all da shit I've seen and heard." He paused briefly before saying, "wait a minute," he said suspiciously, glancing back and forth between the two of them. "Now, I see what's goin' on," he stated as if he'd just discovered the last missing piece to an unsolved mystery.

"What da fuck is you talkin' 'bout?" asked Slick, lowering his pistol out of Hubb's face.

"A gain for a loss," he enunciated.

"What!" exclaimed Mike-Mike.

"A gain for a loss," Hubb reiterated. "Y'all gained from they loss," he summarized. "No wonder they tried to rob you," he said looking at Mike-Mike. "They must've figured y'all had somethin' to do wit' his people's stuff being ripped off, especially after poppin' up with them can't resist prices 'round da same time they got hit."

"You got all da answers, huh?"

"I wouldn't say that, just common sense," Hubb replied.

"Well, since you seem to have this all figured out, let's see if you can fix it."

"Fix what? '

"Whatchu mean fix what!" Mike Mike grimaced. "This problem you created. You brung unwelcomed visitors to our hood and because of dat Melvin's dead and Monique got snatched up."

"Y'all created that problem when you two started sellin' ounces for damn near half the price it was worth. DC ain't but so big. You should've known it wasn't gon' take long for word to spread around," Hubb countered, making them aware of their slip up.

"You made your point, but da fact of da matter is we need you to help us find slim's folks so we can hopefully find Monique before it's too late, and we have less than seventy-two hours to get it done."

"What y'all want me to do?" he said apprehensively.

"You could start by showin' us where this Tattoo Shop is."

"How 'bout I just tell y'all where it is. That dude a kill me if he sees me after what happened to his nephew."

"Look! Fuck what they gon' do to you. You better be more worried 'bout what we gon' do if you don't," Slick threatened.

"If that's all I have to do to make things better, I'm in."

"Good. Now c'mon," stated Slick, picking Hubb up from the floor.

As the trio headed to the door, Mike-Mike was hoping that they were one step closer to achieving a means to end a depressing situation.

CHAPTER 57

When they got close to the Tattoo Parlor, the trio parked a block away zooming in on the shop looking for any suspicious activity. Getting heavy-eyed after sitting for nearly an hour without any suspicious movement, Mike-Mike decided to wrap things up.

"We gon' slide back through later," said Mike-Mike glancing at his timepiece, "I'm tryin' to be at Zoe's shop when it opens," he informed them.

"Dat's a bet, 'cause I'm getting sleepy as shit from just sittin' here anyway," Slick replied, starting the car up.

Soon after, they were dropping Hubb back off and then drove over to Zoe's body shop.

"We still got 'bout forty more minutes 'til da shop opens," stated Mike-Mike as they blended with the vehicles that were outside the shop. Once parked, the two reclined their seats and got comfortable until Zoe showed. Before you knew it, the pair had dozed off, until the closing of a car door awoke them out of their catnap.

"Damn, we must've dozed off," Mike-Mike said as he jumped up, focusing on the male occupant that was entering the shop. "You saw who dat was?"

"Hell yeah," Slick replied, lifting his seat up. "Wonder what he's doin' here first thing in da mornin'", his eye's narrowing in suspicion.

"I'on't know but I'm 'bout to find-out," Mike-Mike stated, avidly stepping out the vehicle anxious to discover why the familiar face was walking into Zoe's shop, which seemed odd.

"I'm comin' wit' you!" Slick insisted.

"Hold fast. I need fo' you to stay here and watch out just in case someone else shows up. Plus, I'm not goin' in, I'ma walk 'round da side and peep through da office window."

"You sure?"

"Positive. Just give me five minutes."

"A'ight dat's a bet," he agreed before Mike-Mike treaded off.

***

Zoe was in his office sorting through some papers when his door swung open. His eyebrows ascended in surprise when a male individual stood venomously in the doorway brandishing a weapon.

"What's wit' the gun?" questioned Zoe, tossing the stack of papers onto his desk.

"What I tell you I was goin' to do if I found out you had anything to do wit' my stuff being stolen," he growled, lips pursed with suppressed fury.

"What you find out?"

"More than enough to prove my theory," he shot back,

inching closer. "Especially after Ronald who was probably the one person who knew about the whole situation ended up dead after you and your comrade came from payin' 'im a visit," he smirked.

"How would you know that?" replied Zoe, giving him a funny look.

"'Cause I just so happened to be stoppin' by as y'all were leavin'," he informed.

"Is that so?" he grinned. "You seem to have it all figured out, but you know what?" Zoe asked, rubbing his chin in a laid-back manner.

"Say what you gotta say!" he shot back.

"Something told me you were gon' show up more sooner than later."

"Why, because of guilt?"

"Naw, 'cause you too predictable."

"In that case, you already know what's expected and should've prepared fo' the inevitable."

"Well it's funny that you say that 'cause I would've been a fool not to," he countered as the restroom door swung open with Big Herm standing behind it aiming two twin, extended-clipped Glock twenty-ones straight toward Malice's chest. "Now that the tables are turned I have a confession to make, but before I get to that let me say this," he paused briefly gathering his thoughts. "The most expensive thing in the world is trust, it can take years to earn, and just a matter of seconds to lose," he quoted staring at Malice with contempt. "All of that went out the window along wit' any respect that I had fo' you when you decided to leave me six and a half years ago," he confirmed.

"So that's what this is all about? You still salty about somethin' that happened over six years ago!" he fumed. "Only women hold grudges that long!"

"Man, only a fool wit' no morals or principles a plow into two innocent teenagers killing one and severely injuring the other, and then just pull-off leavin' his so-called partner on the scene!" countered Zoe, pointing his finger like a parent does to their child when they're in trouble.

"Don't act like you don't know why I didn't stay! We had enough drugs to put us both away fo' a long time! Only a fool would've stayed. You made your choice and I made mine," Malice remarked, standing firm, holding his ground.

"You absolutely right, and you know what's crazy 'bout all of this. Not only did I take your shipment, but karma is a muthafucka. 'Cause the same person who luckily survived that accident you caused back then is the exact individual I sent to snatch the truck!" Zoe confessed.

"Yeah, whatever!" Malice retorted defensively, not believing what Zoe was conveying to him, 'cause if it was true then he already knew who he was speaking of. "You tryin' to mess wit' my head, huh?"

"It's too late in the game to be foolin' wit' your head, plus too much been exposed."

Malice's arm commenced to slowly drop as the information he'd just received showed deterioration in his thinking, followed by a scene that occurred a short time ago. The time he spotted his future son-n-law behind the wheel of an expensive coupe the evening he drove out of the Cheese Cake Factory parking garage with his better half, gave him reason to believe Zoe's statement. An erring quietness lingered throughout the room trailed by his eyes fading to a blackness that mirrored the unavoidable retribution that he was about to deliver.

"Well since we comin' clean about everything, I have something I wanna confess myself," Malice admitted in a grim tone, placing his weapon on the ground as if he surrendered.

"I'm listenin'," Zoe responded with a grin, respecting the fact that Malice gave in.

"That same night, six and a half years ago when I lost you as a partner, I gained another in your place," he smirked.

"Oh yeah, and who might that be?" he replied unmoved.

"Your supposed to been right-hand," he coldly stated.

"Yeah, I hear you," he shrugged, brushing off his assertion. "My s'pose to been right-hand," Zoe asked laughing it off. "You hear this shit," he said to Big Herm. "Man, shoot this fool," he ordered, but when Big Herm didn't react, his eyes turned into slits as the implication became crystal in his mind that the double-cross was in effect.

"Big Herm," Malice nodded, causing him to go from aiming at his chest to pointing both Glocks directly toward Zoe's thorax.

The look that Zoe showcased was as if he was hooked to

an I.V. and all the blood was being drained from his body. Looking pale and defeated from his most trusted associate turning on him, he acted off emotions by reaching for his pistol that was located on his waistline.

Before Zoe even got close to removing his weapon, Big Herm applied pressure to the trigger sending two slugs into his torso, cracking his chest plate. The force of the blast sent Zoe backwards into the wall, covering the hole as if he could stop the bleeding. As he was fighting to catch his breath, Malice scooped his own pistol up from the ground, walked over and stood over Zoe and placed his gun to his forehead.

"Guess that wasn't so predictable, huh? One thing I learned is that life is like an elevator, on your way to the top sometimes you have to stop and drop people off and you just got dropped off," he stated acidly. Seconds later, two more dynamite detonating booms sounded out as he grouped two .44 Bulldog rounds into his forehead. By the time the echo from the gun blast faded, a slight noise was heard from over by the window, causing the two to snap their necks in that direction.

"What was that!" barked Malice as the pair rushed toward the window but didn't see anything. "Out front!" he ordered, storming to the entrance.

Furious that someone might've witnessed the killing, the pair was eager to track down the onlooker. When they finally made it outside of the shop all they saw was the tail end of a vehicle accelerating over the hill, vanishing before they got a chance to get a good look at it. "Damn!" fumed Malice, shaking his head disappointedly. "Let's get outta here," he instructed, immediately leaving the scene.

CHAPTER 58

"What da hell happened?" questioned Slick as Mike-Mike zipped in and out of traffic, turning a death ear to his inquisitions.

Mike-Mike was so sickened by what he'd just stumbled upon and seen with his own eyes that he basically blanked out. Gaped in stunned silence, Slick had to yell out to him to get his attention, "Mike-Mike!" he roared, finally snapping him out of his hypnotic state.

Mike-Mike didn't speak, he simply glanced over at him, vacuously.

"Bruh, slow this muthafucka down fo' you kill us or get us bagged and tell me what da hell happened back there!" Slick demanded point blank.

Letting up off the accelerator, Mike-Mike slowly began to zone back into reality. A short distance later, he pulled along side the road, trying to gather his conflicted thoughts. His insides were boiling like a steaming tea kettle and Slick knew that whatever had him that heated had to have been very disturbing.

"Slim, listen to me, I need you to get it together and let me know what happened 'cause time is tickin' on this Monique situation," he advised.

Hearing Monique's name forced him to shake off the muddle that was distracting his better judgment. Taking a few deep breaths, he looked over at Slick with unsettling, pain-filled eyes before finally speaking, "Zoe's dead," he commiserated.

"What!" he frowned. "How!" Slick asked shaking his head. "I mean," he paused taking a deep breath. "This can't be happening," he expressed, grabbing his temple as if he could stop his disturbing thoughts from penetrating through his mind. "Was ya folks behind it?" Slick questioned.

"Yeah and no," he said in a faraway tone.

"What dat s'pose to mean, I'm confused," Slick remarked, sounding mysterious.

"It means he's not da only one who shot 'im," Mike-Mike tried to clarify.

"Somebody else was already in there?"

"Yeah," shaking his head.

"Who?" Slick shot back with questioning eyes.

Leaning back in his seat like he was mentally exhausted, Mike-Mike revealed Big Herm's name and waited for his partner's reaction. Hearing Big Herm's name was shocking but not surprising. Slick had always felt some form of negative energy when they were around one another. Even at the club, Big Herm, kind of stayed to the side, away from the group, he thought. "To be honest, dat shit don't surprise me one bit, especially after you used to always tell me how you used to catch dat clown staring or cutting his eyes at you. All those were signs."

"Yeah, you right," he agreed. "But dat's not it," he enlightened Slick.

"What else is it?"

"I found out who was responsible fo' hittin' me and my baby sister da day she got killed," he disclosed with a solemn face.

The unforeseen news caused Slick to become lightheaded as if fatigued from an overexerted, sweltering workout. He couldn't believe what he was hearing and was apprehensive about asking who was accountable for his partners lifelong emotional scar. The touchy subject had taken its toll on his sidekick's mind and it was clearly evident by the look that was plastered on his face.

Though years of the unknown was revealed, the pair was on borrowed time and needed to quickly come up with a strategy to get Monique back alive and well or there was gonna be, yet another female swiped out of his life. The thought was overwhelming but being despondent was the last thing they needed at that moment. Looking back over at his crony he finally decided to ask who was at fault for his baby sister's demise.

"Was it Big Herm?" Slick questioned in a hushed tone.

Eyes now bloodshot red from all the built-up stress and strain that was rapidly weighing down on him, he glanced over and shook his head no. He immediately began to explain how everything unfolded from beginning to end leaving nothing untold. The mind-boggling incident left Slick at a loss for words.

"Dat's crazy," Slick said, as he shook his head. "On e'rything, bruh, I wouldn't have guessed in a million years that he was responsible for ya grief," he sympathized. "Now da question is, was he already aware dat ya family was da same people he caused years of suffering prior to him basically becoming part of da family," Slick theorized.

"Don't know, but I plan on finding out," he assured.

"I hate to think it, but da world's small, not dat small, he had to know. This ain't no coincidence," Slick stated unambiguously.

"I'm wit' you on dat," Mike-Mike agreed. "Ma Duke's gon' be crushed once she finds out 'bout this."

"Hell yeah. How you plan on tellin' her?" asked Slick.

"Don't know," he shrugged. "Fo' real I can't even think straight. It's just too much happenin' right now."

"I feel ya, bruh, but we gotta stay focused and figure out our next move, 'cause Zoe's out da picture as far as this Monique situation goes."

"I'm hip," Mike-Mike concurred, tilting his head down. "Fuck!" he shouted. "Ain't nothin' goin' right," he verbalized. "We have to come up wit' somethin' fast," he stated as he meticulously began to formulate a plan.

After a few minutes of trying to think of something that made sense, the only thing he came up with was false hope. "Know what, bruh, I'm just gon' give 'em what's left, and try to convince 'em to let me trade places wit' her," he summarized.

"Hell naw!" Slick disagreed. "Dat's out da question, plus I think I got a better idea."

"And what's dat?"

"You sure they didn't see ya through da window, right?"

"Positive."

"Well look, I was thinkin'…"

CHAPTER 59

Mike-Mike's pulse was racing rapidly as he and Slick sent out urgent text messages to every member in their circle. The text stated, to meet-up at the spot a.s.a.p. and to not come empty-handed. With qualms blanketing the situation, and barely any time to concoct a strategic plan, the duo was banking on Slick's last-minute suggestion.

Once the texts were forwarded, in next to no time, they were parking on Aspen St. bolting toward Mike-Mike's apartment. Soon after, members of their crew were filing in, exchanging questioning glances. Nose was the only *No show* after it was all said and done.

"Anyone heard from or seen Nose?" Mike-Mike inquired.

"It's still early, ain't no tellin' where he at," Lil' Kurt, replied.

"Yeah, you right," Mike-Mike agreed.

"Dat nigga probably didn't show cause he still salty 'bout yesterday," Slick spoke up.

"Maybe or maybe not, but what's this all about,

anyway?" asked Tre, quickly changing the subject, due to Nose not being there to defend himself.

"It's about Monique. Da same dudes dat smashed Melvin snatched her up," explained Mike-Mike.

"You serious!" frowned Pete. "Who da fuck is da nigga!" he bellowed.

"It's a long story, and right now isn't da time to explain, but I do know it's goin' to take all of us to try to get her back," he advised.

Monique was like a sister to everybody there, so after hearing about her abduction, they were willing to do whatever they could to assist without thinking twice about it.

"So, what's da plan?" Lil' Chico questioned, eyes giving off a strange mixture of anger and sadness.

"Just follow our lead, cause we 'bout to try somethin' dat could mess around and get real ugly," Mike-Mike said point blank. "But first we need to get us some vehicles before we make a move. Oh, and Slick, you may as well get on top of what we talked about on da way here," he instructed with a hidden message. "Then text me when you grab dat and wait fo' my call."

"I'm on top of it," countered Slick.

"Tre you ride with 'im and da rest of y'all ride wit' me. Everybody strapped?" No one responded, but the rigorous click-clacking resonances of pistols being loaded and readied answered his question. "Good then, let's be out," he exclaimed, feeling the adrenaline coursing through his arteries.

CHAPTER 60

When Malice and Big Herm stormed off from Zoe's body shop, the two headed in different directions. Concerned that someone witnessed the murder, Big Herm rushed to a separate location where Zoe stored important paperwork, with hopes of finding a list of all the employees who worked in his shop. If and when he found it, he was sure to pay each one a visit. Big Herm wasn't by far the scared type, but the faceless situation had him uneasy. Nearing his location, he pulled out his cell phone and dialed Malice's number.

"Did you find it?" answered Malice.

"Nah, I'm almost at the spot now," he confirmed, "but if this list isn't here everything could turn fo' the worst," replied Big Herm, showing signs of nervousness by excessively clearing his throat.

"You don't think I know that!" Malice retorted defensively, pulling up to his destination. "Look, make sure you find that list and right after I deal wit' this situation over here, we gon' get on top of that a.s.a.p.!" he assured, rubbing his temples as the recent event also had him on the edge.

"A'ight, I'ma hit you when I leave."

"You do dat," countered Malice, hanging up, then briefly leaning back in his seat, gathering his thoughts. After sitting back, mulling over everything for a few minutes, he threw his game face back on, then got out his vehicle, heading into another place of business that demanded his attention.

Not too long after they hung up, Big Herm finally reached the address that he was navigating to. Finding parking, he strolled into the building with one thing on his mind. Entering, he anxiously began to search the areas where he knew that Zoe stored his important papers. Nearly thirty minutes later, after looking high and low, he came up empty-handed.

"Damn!" he barked out of frustration. "It has to be in here somewhere," he said to himself, taking a breather.

While doing so, his eyes never stop scanning the area. His eagerness resulted in him overlooking what was right in front of him all along. Not wanting to be in the spot too long and risk the chance of being seen, he made his way toward the exit. On his way out, he stumbled across the employee's list that was stationed on a mesh triple tray paper wall mount by the door. Grabbing the list with a smile on his face, his phone lit up with an unfamiliar number. Normally, he didn't answer numbers he didn't know, but something urged him to.

"Yeah?" he answered, wondering who was on the other end, but quickly picked up on the caller's voice. "What's good wit' you?"

After engaging in a brief conversation and seeing a free opportunity to receiving a large lump-sum of money, he chose to meet up with the caller. "See you in twenty minutes," he concluded, ending the call. Tucking his phone away with a nefarious grin spread across his face, he realized within a matter of hours how things were starting to move upward for him with Zoe out of the picture. At least that's what he thought.

CHAPTER 61

The fact that stealing vehicles was Mike-Mike's first line of work, made it elementary for him to snatch two means of transportation. After their two vehicles of choice were taken, Mike-Mike immediately began to put Slick's plan into motion. Hoping that it developed accordingly, he pulled out his cell phone and dialed the required number to move forward with the scheme.

It didn't take long for the individual to pick up on the other end. Staying calm, cool, and collected, Mike-Mike tried his hand, surprisingly the person on the opposite end bought what he was selling and furthermore agreed to meet up.

"It's a go!" Mike-Mike conveyed to Lil' Chico who was laid back in the passenger seat.

He phoned Lil' Kurt who trailed close behind in another vehicle with Pete and Lyran to advise them of what to do when they arrived at there destination. With penetrating thoughts, he glanced at the time, then sped up so that he could get to the meeting spot first to scope out the area. However, the encounter went, either way, he knew that Mother Teresa was going to have the final say-so. Though he was determined to handle his business, the closer he got to the meeting place the more the butterflies formed in his stomach. Not the one to show his uneasiness, he threw on his poker face and continued.

***

As soon as Tre found out that Slick was going to pick up the remainder of the kilo's, his covetous way instantly kicked in. Seeing his opportunity to finally come up, he quickly formulated a plan of his own. Pulling out his iPhone, he sent out a text.

You up?

Minutes later, he received a reply, *Yeah, why wassup?*

Where you at?

Ridin' 'round tryin' to clear my head.

Guess who I'm ridin' wit'?

Who?

Ya man!

My man?

Yeah, ya man Slick.

Oh yeah! Dat nigga ain't no man of mine, plus I'ma make his eyes pop out his head when I run into him by himself.

Time waits fo' no one, if you tryin' to see this fool. I'm turning my location on, so you can track us.

Bet!

But you gotta move fast.
Say no more, O.M.W

Deleting the text messages, Tre turned toward Slick with a wicked grin on his face. "How far we gotta go?"

"Shid we almost there," Slick replied.

Tre simply leaned back in his seat, smiling inside like a kid when it's their first time at an amusement park. He didn't think twice about snaking out his man, all that was on his mind was getting them bricks in his possession. PERIOD!

CHAPTER 62

Nearing his location, Big Herm decided to give Malice a call to let him know that he'd found the list.

"Yeah?" Malice answered on the first ring. "I got it," he confirmed.

"Good."

"What's next?"

"I'm on my way over to Moe's spot, just meet me over there. Plus, I need to talk to you about somethin' anyway."

"A'ight cool, I'll be there soon, right after I meet these folks not too far from Moe's shop."

"I'll see you when you get there," replied Malice prior to hanging up.

Before long, Big Herm was pulling up to his meeting spot, which was in a lower level parking garage. Once he found parking, he briefly sat there, flashing a superior grin, knowing a free large sum of money was heading his way. Just when he was about to make the call to let the person he was meeting know that he was there, like clockwork, his phone lit-up with the number of the individual.

***

Malice couldn't get Zoe's confession out of his mind. Zoe basically in so many words informing him that his step-son was accountable for stealing the truck made things complicated for him. If what Zoe had said had any merit to it, then the female that his associates kidnapped must have some relations to Mike-Mike, which can cause all types of calamities. For one, Moe Kelly was very adamant about seeking vengeance on anyone who had any ties to his nephews killing. From the looks of things, Mike-Mike definitely had his hands in the situation.

"Damn!' he snapped in disbelief, knowing that his step-son was now a target.

For the moment, he just hoped that Zoe was messing with his head, and that's why he needed to talk with Big Herm, just to get some clarity. Pulling up to his location, he parked, then hopped out with scrambled thoughts. The last time he visited this very shop, he left behind two dead bodies, and from the looks of things this drop by wasn't going to be a pleasant one.

CHAPTER 63

Placing the needed call, Mike-Mike grabbed his backpack from the backseat, then proceeded to get out. "Slide over in the driver's seat," he instructed Lil' Chico.

"I got you," he replied.

Mike-Mike shut the door and headed over to handle his business. As he approached, he casually glanced around to see if anything seemed out of the norm. He put a little extra pep in his step once everything checked out good. When the male individual came in plain view, he forced a faint smile, then walked to the passenger side and hopped in.

"Wassup big homie?" Mike-Mike greeted, shutting the door behind himself.

"Busy as always," the guy smirked. "And you?"

"Running 'round tryin' to figure some things out," he enunciated.

"Such as?"

"It's just a lot dat's been goin' on, and I need to holler at Zoe a.s.a.p. but his phone keeps going to voicemail."

"Well ain't no tellin' what he's up to, but if I talk to 'im before you do, I'll make sure to let 'im know."

"A'ight cool, do dat fo' me," he remarked, handing the backpack over to him. "Make sure he get's dat and give 'im this message fo' me."

"What's this?" he inquired, receiving the backpack, preparing to open it. "And what's your message?

"Tell 'im a wise man once told me, dat da saddest thing about betrayal is dat it never comes from ya enemies," he stated coldly. He instantly turned an unfriendly eye on Big Herm for the first time while simultaneously revealing Mother Teresa, aiming her directly toward him.

Big Herm glanced into the backpack, noticing that it was nothing more than a bunch of trash. He immediately looked over at Mike-Mike who had a huge gun pointing at him. At that point, Big Herm's heart instantly begun racing as if two motorcycles were trying to cross the finish line.

"What's this all about?" he stuttered, not sure of the sudden encounter.

"News flash, I was da one at da shop this mornin'," he revealed. "I seen and heard everything."

Hearing those words spill from Mike-Mike's lips left him speechless as if karma had plucked his tongue straight out of his mouth.

"You know what," Mike-Mike briefly paused, "Zoe once asked me what I would do if I ever found out dat someone I was close to ever hurt someone I loved. At da time, I didnt have a direct answer, but now I do," he spoke in a sinister tone, "and dat's to eliminate everyone dat had any affiliation wit' da situation," he concluded.

"But I..." was all Big Herm managed to spit out, 'cause suddenly without warning, two explosive sounds came quickly one after the other, silencing Big Herms disloyalty.

Feeling no deep regret for his actions, Mike-Mike snatched the backpack back and reached over to grab Big Herm's cell phone off his lap before hopping back out, as if nothing happened. On cue, Lil' Chico pulled up, pushing the passenger door open for him to get in. Emerging from the garage, his men in another vehicle pulled off to trail behind after staying parked on the main street, just to keep an eye-out.

"Now what?" asked Lil' Chico not knowing which direction to go.

"Head over to dat location I was tellin' you about not too long ago, off of Benning Road," directed Mike-Mike, now searching through Big Herm's phone.

A sudden idea popped up after recognizing a number in his phone, but before acting on it, he decided to call Slick to make sure that everything was still going as predicted. Not getting an answer, he sent him a text. Trusting that everything was still on course, he settled to move forward with the expectations of him meeting back up with them shortly.

CHAPTER 64

Finally arriving at his stop, Slick glanced at the time, then at Tre before instructing him to come help remove the work from under the blocks of cement it was buried beneath. With the intentions of once and for all having the Kilo's in his possession, Tre anxiously stepped out of the car, waiting to follow. As Slick led the way, both of their minds were on two different agendas and neither was beneficial to the other. Still having his arm in a sling from his gunshot wound, when the pair reached the area, Slick pointed to the spot. "It's buried under there. Just move da cement blocks out da way and pull da bag out da hole."

"Why da fuck he stash da shit way out here!" Tre verbalized, not actually looking for an answer.

Eager to get the work in his hands, he walked over to the designated area, kneeled down and commenced to removing the blocks of cement to the side. Once he finished, he quickly noticed that there was no hole to stick his arm in. "Ain't no hole here!" he raised his voice out of frustration, turning halfway around toward Slick only to be met with a gun pointed at him.

"What's the ultimate price fo' betrayal?" Slick spoke in a hushed tone, inching closer.

"What!" Tre shot back, throwing his hands in the air.

"You heard exactly what I said!" he grimaced.

"Who betrayed who!?" he replied nervously.

"Who!" Slick chuckled. "Oh, you must've thought you got away wit' dat sneaky shit, huh! Just so ya know, Mr. Washington didn't die," he informed him. "You gotta be a fucked-up individual to stab an old ass man and on top of dat, you tried to crud out da one-person dat was helping us eat," he concluded.

Just when he was about to apply pressure to the trigger, he heard a familiar voice come from behind.

"Ya might wanna think twice about dat," curted the voice training his pistol on Slick's back.

A slight smile spread across Tre's face when he noticed Nose popping up on time.

Slick just squinted his eyes, wondering how Nose just appeared suddenly out of nowhere. Though Nose had the upper-hand on him, he never once took his eye's off of Tre who he knew was also armed with a weapon. Tre seeing the murder in Slick's eyes had enough street smarts to not even blink the wrong way.

"I guess this what it all comes down to, huh? Childhood friends takin' each other out," Slick said bluntly.

"It seemed to me dat you and ya partner started that trend wit' Melvin."

"I give ya my word, we didn't have no hands in what happened to Melvin," he assured, "but since you seem so sure about it do whachu gotta do," he surrendered, lowering his gun that had Tre in its sight. Turning to face Nose he said, "Just know I'm not da one you should be worried about, this snake ass nigga dat you call ya'self savin' is da one you need to be concerned about," Slick stressed as Tre stood up from the ground.

"Nose shoot dat nigga!" Tre huffed, reaching for his own pistol.

Looking Slick directly in his eyes, Nose spat on the ground then said in a raspy voice, "Every decision has consequences," before squeezing the trigger.

CHAPTER 65

Entering the shop, Malice was met by Rex who was watching something on television.

"Where Moe Kelly at?"

"He stepped out fo' a sec, but he should be back soon."

"Where the girl at?"

"In the back," he pointed.

"I'll be back," he said walking toward the back.

Once he reached the back he immediately spotted the frightened young female gagged, plus, bound hand and feet in the corner. She looked as if hope was a distant reality. Dry tears decorated her puffy face while fatigue outlined her appearance. Inching closer toward her, he kneeled in front of her using his index finger to lift her head up by her chin. "Do you know why you here?" he questioned, removing the gag from Monique's mouth.

"Please, I didn't do anything!" she cried out, eyes transfixed with horror.

"I know you scared, but you need to calm down and answer my quest…," his words trailed off after zooming in on a familiar item that she sported around her neck. "Where you get this from?" he inquired, referring to the chain that he now palmed in his hand.

"I got it from a friend of mine," she stuttered nervously.

"What's your friend's name?' he replied, palming the scripted scroll that read, *Knowledge will give you Power, but Character will give you Respect.*

"Mike-Mike," she responded.

Hearing that name and reading the scroll with the script that he personally had custom made, confirmed any questions that he had for Big Herm. It also validated every word that Zoe had spoken before his demise. Finding out that his step-son had a close connection to the young woman that sat bounded before him, withdrew any future punishment that he had planned for the female whose life was basically in the palm of his hand like the scroll she wore. Though he was cold hearted when it came to his street dealings, he couldn't find it in himself to cause harm to another female in his step-son's life.

***

Pulling up two cars deep to their destination, both vehicles found parking that was close enough to have a clear view of the Tattoo Shop, but with as much distance as necessary to not seem suspicious. From their positions, Mike-Mike could see that the shop gave the impression of being open but obviously wasn't due to the closed sign that hung from inside the window.

"Something definitely goin' on in there," Mike-Mike speculated, after zooming in on the shop.

"Let's hope fo' her sake, but my question is, out of all places, why here?" inquired Lil' Chico.

"Yo' guess is as good as mine, but if she's not in there, I bet somebody in there has a good idea where she is. We just have to get it out of 'em one way or another."

"Let's make it happen then. You know I'm wit' cha all da way," countered Lil' Chico with conviction.

"'Preciate ya bruh," dapping him up seconds before his phone lit up. He quickly answered after looking down at the number. "I assumed you got my text, 'cause you ain't pick up when I called."

"Yeah, I got it and I'm right here on Benning Road, passing Springarn High School, plus I got company," he informed.

"Company!" Mike-Mike shot back, you didn't get on top of that situation?"

"Yeah and no."

"I'm confused, 'cause if you did, then what company do you have?"

"Man look, you'll see when I meet up wit' you 'cause you already know I ain't tryin' to rap over this horn. Where you at anyway?"

"We parked on da corner of 18th and Benning Road," he relayed.

"A'ight, be there in a minute."

"Dat's a bet," Mike-Mike replied, hanging up wondering what could've transpired between Slick and Tre, and on top of that who was his passenger.

Before long, his curiosity was met when he noticed Slick and Nose walking toward the vehicle. Just before the two reached the car he noticed that Slick's attention was glued on someone that was steps away from entering the Tattoo Parlor.

"What, ya know slim or somethin'?"

"Not sure, but he looks reeaaal familiar," stressing his point while trying to remember where he knew the male individual from.

"Dat's da first person we seen go in there since we been here, and if you look closely, they got a closed sign on the door."

"Yeah, I see it, so you think she's in there?" asked Slick.

"We're 'bout to find out. How y'all two manage to hook up anyway?" glancing at Slick and Nose.

"Tre's snake ass texted me and told me he was ridin' wit' Slick, and if I wanted to get back at 'im fo' pulling his gun out on me, he was gon' turn on his phones locator so I could track them. After I thought about it, I knew it was more to it, so when I arrived at da spot, I sat and listened to their conversation and realized dat Tre was on some cruddy shit da whole time. Once I seen dat, I done what I thought was da best thing to do at da time, which was drop da dead weight," he explained nonchalantly.

"Well, he definitely got what he had comin' to 'im, and I'm just glad you made da right choice," he acknowledged. "So y'all good?"

"Are we good?" asked Nose, peeping over at Slick for a response.

Slick's mind was still trying to register the dude's face that entered the Tattoo shop when the question came his way. "Yeah, we good," he replied, followed by a pound of the fist.

"Dat's wassup and I think you just gave me an idea Nose," Mike-Mike stated, pulling out his cell phone. "I'm about to see if her phone's locator is on, since dat's da phone they used to call from.

"Hell yeah!" Lil' Chico agreed, a bit animated.

Seconds later, spark's flared in Mike-Mike's eyes. "Got it!" he exclaimed. flashing his phone screen so they all could see.

The red location indicator pinpointed her phones whereabouts, which was exactly where they had pinned their hopes, on the Tattoo Parlor.

"Bingo!" Nose said seconds before Slick blurted out that he'd remembered the dude's face.

"From where?" inquired Mike-Mike.

"Dat's da dude I was tellin' you I got into it wit' at da club," he said, directing his comment to Mike-Mike. "I swear, I think he had somethin' to do wit' what almost happened to me when da joint let out."

"You sure?" said Mike-Mike.

"Muthafuckin' right I'm sure! I'm tryin' to see dat nigga!" he fumed, catching everybody off guard by jumping out the vehicle heading in the direction of the Tattoo shop.

"Slick whachu doin!" Mike-Mike tried to call out to him, but Slick kept marching. "Shit! C'mon y'all," he ordered, then jumped out to try and catch up with Slick.

***

Releasing the chain from his grips, Malice commenced to unbinding Monique's hands and feet. After doing so, he put his forefinger up to his mouth, indicating for her to keep quiet. Due to her being tied up for so long, when he stood her up he had to hold on to her to keep her from falling. It didn't take long for her legs to gain enough circulation to move again. When they were able to, he took the first steps to ushering her towards the back door. As soon as they took two steps forward, the last thing that Malice wanted to happen, happened. The front door chimed, followed by Moe Kelly's voice. In next to no time, Rex was relaying to Moe Kelly that company was in the back.

Upon hearing that, Malice quickly guided Monique back to the chair, sitting her back down, then loosely binding her mouth and hands a split second before Moe Kelly walked in. Not having enough time to bind her feet, Malice stood in front of Monique to hopefully obstruct Moe Kelly's view.

"Glad you finally made it," Moe Kelly stated with an off-balance look painting his expression.

"Why your face all screwed up, you a'ight?" Malice shot back, disregarding Moe Kelly's statement.

"I'on't know, I ain't sure," he shrugged.

"What you mean by that?" questioned Malice, hands indiscreetly motioning closer in the direction of his firearm, just in case.

While Moe Kelly's mind was still trying to decipher the familiar face outside the shop, Malice was assuming that Moe Kelly somehow peeped Monique's unbound feet and was trying to figure out why. Sensing things were just about to turn for the worst, Malice was seconds away from pulling his pistol to gain control of the situation when Moe Kelly out of nowhere blurted, "Dat's who dat was!"

"What you talkin' 'bout?" Malice responded confused.

"Da youngin' I just saw across da street!" he made known.

"What youngin'?"

"From da club!" he remembered. "He's one of da same youngin's dat's su'pose to be bringin' us back da shit they stole."

"So, what you sayin' is that one of the youngins that took my truck is outside?"

"Dat's exactly what I'm sayin'," Mo Kelly assured seconds before hearing Rex relaying to someone that the shop was closed for the day. Overhearing his partner talking to somebody after what he just remembered quickly drew a red flag. "Shit, Rex!" he exclaimed. Facial expression changing from skeptical to dreadful, "Malice c'mon, I think we got company!" Mo Kelly announced, pulling out his .45 caliber, rushing back toward the front.

As soon as Moe Kelley stormed out the room Malice's mind shifted into overdrive. If what Moe Kelly just revealed was accurate, then there was a strong chance that his soon to be step-son could've been who he was talking about. If so, then there was no way possible he could allow himself to be seen inside the shop.

With that thought in mind and no time to waste, he made a last-minute attempt out of desperation to slip away unseen.

***

Mike-Mike hopped out from the driver's seat, followed by Lil' Chico and Nose. When the other three members in the other vehicle saw what was happening, they too swiftly jumped out and trailed behind. Mike-Mike was trying to catch up with Slick who was striding angrily toward the Tattoo shop. He finally reached him a short distance away from the parlor.

"Slick, hold up!?" he sounded, before grabbing his right shoulder and spinning him halfway around. "You can't do it like dat, bruh. Your actin' off emotions and you know we 'on't move like dat."

"I'm tryin' to catch this nigga, 'cause ain't no tellin' when da next time I'ma run into him again!" Slick shot back.

"I feel where ya comin' from, but you makin' this about you and right now isn't da time. This about Monique," Mike-Mike firmly stipulated.

After briefly giving thought to the matter and realizing that he was acting out of anger, he apologized. "You right, bruh, my bad."

Lookin' around, he instantly realized that people were

303

eyeballing them oddly. "C'mon let's get away from right here, 'cause folks jive lookin' at us crazy," stated Mike-Mike.

"Dat's a bet," agreed Slick as the two headed back toward the car.

Luckily, the rest of the group didn't seem suspicious, 'cause it really would've drawn a red flag to the onlookers. Glancing at his wristwatch and seeing that both hands were leveled on the twelve, Mike-Mike decided right then and there that they may as well make their move because time was flying by like a moving jet. With his mind made up, the second that Lil' Kurt, Lyran, and Pete came within' ear distance, he instructed them to head over to the shop to find out what was going on.

"A'ight, we got it," assured the trio before stepping off.

"You don't think we should go wit' 'em?" asked Lil' Chico.

"Nah, we drawin' unwanted attention to ourselves, plus, we can keep an eye on 'em from da car,"Mike-Mike added, continuing in the direction of their vehicle.

As they neared their car, out of the blue, a sequence of ear-splitting sounds caught everyone's attention, mounting them in place as if they were nails being drilled in the concrete. When they turned to see what was going on, the first thing that caught their eyes was Pete slammed up against a parked vehicle in front of the shop, holding his chest as if he'd been shot. Immediately after, Lil' Kurt was recklessly firing back into the shop's broken window, bringing pandemonium to the block.

"Shit, c'mon!" barked Mike-Mike, sprinting toward the commotion, followed by his crew. As they closed the gap, Pete was still clutching his chest, gun in hand, staggering in their direction. By the time they reached him, his jog had reduced to him dragging his feet, stumbling from side to side like a heavy drinker.

"One of y'all get 'im to da car!" yelled, Mike-Mike, as he pulled Pete from near a parked car. "Hold-on, bruh, we gon' get chu some help!" he assured, handing him over to Lil' Chico and Nose, who carried Pete off to the vehicle, so they could try to get him some help.

Mike-Mike and Slick continued toward the Tattoo Parlor.

With all the chaos, it was just a matter of time before the cops showed. They were so determined to aid and assist their two associates while trying to find Monique at the same time, that getting caught was the furthest thing from their minds. When they finally reached the shop, all they saw was a shop that was riddled with gunfire and a blood trail that started at the front door and led toward the rear of the shop.

The two carefully followed the trail of blood, until it led them to a rear hallway door that was slightly opened. Mike-Mike quickly placed his fingers to his lips, telling Slick to keep quiet, before proceeding through. After all that had just taken place, they made it a point to cautiously open the door, and were surprised that nothing was waiting for them on the other side. It was clear, with the exception of the same trail of blood that extended well beyond a wide open back door.

"Fuck!" cursed Mike-Mike out of frustration, feeling doubtful about Monique's return. Especially, after what had just transpired.

"Man, this shit is all bad," Slick stated, shaking his head. "We need to get outta here 'fore da police come. Plus, we need to find out where Lil' Kurt and Lyran at."

"I'ma try to call 'em," Mike-Mike replied, bowing his head in defeat. He rushed out the back door to avoid being seen by anymore eyewitnesses that were lingering in front of the shop.

Exiting through the back of the shop, they took off running through the alleyway that led to 18th Street. Just as Mike-Mike was reaching for his phone to call either Lil' Kurt or Lyran, his cell began its familiar humming noise, alerting him of a call. "This Lil' Kurt right here," he told Slick, reducing his pace. "Y'all a'ight? Where y'all at?" he quizzered, bombarding him with questions.

"We ran out da back door tryin' to catch them fools, but they somehow got away," Lil' Kurt responded on the other end.

"Where dat trail of blood come from?" Mike-Mike inquired.

"I think I hit one of 'em; matter of fact I know I did," he acknowledged.

"Was there any sign of Monique?"

"Not at all, bruh," he replied in a quiet but slightly

elevated voice. "Where y'all at so we can come get you and get from 'round here, cause we in da car?" he asked quickly changing the subject, knowing that Mike-Mike was bothered by not being able to locate Monique.

"We standing on 18th right now," he replied.

"Come to 18th and Benning Road 'cause we 'bout to pull up," he instructed.

"We'll be there in a sec," Mike-Mike assured, tucking his phone away while proceeding toward Benning Road. Both parties arrived simultaneously. Hearing the sirens in the distance, Mike-Mike and Slick quickly jumped in the backseat as Lil' Kurt sped off to get away before law enforcement showed.

Mike-Mike's frustration was plastered all over his face. His eyes were bloodshot red, and his movements were as if he might snap at any moment.

"Bruh, we gon' get her back," Lil' Kurt stated, trying to lighten a situation that was turning for the worst.

Mike-Mike never responded, he just kept staring out the window. He was deep in his own thoughts until his phone snapped him out of his mental hiatus. "Yeah?" he answered.

After only seconds into the conversation, he looked like he wanted to throw his phone out the window, but he just hung up. He just kept squeezing it until the veins in his hands surfaced from gripping it so tightly.

"What happen?" asked Slick.

"Pete didn't make it," he hesitated, causing a mixture of sadness and anger to cover their faces as the breaking news hit them hard.

"Fuck!" cursed Lil' Kurt, followed by Lyran banging his fist on the dashboard.

Slick simply shook his head with sadness depicting his expressions. While the weight of the news forced Mike-Mike's head to fall back on the headrest, everything was seemingly falling apart. Then without warning, he felt a vibration coming from the opposite pocket that he just placed his phone in. Reaching into it he pulled out Big Herm's phone that he'd forgotten due to all the chaos.

He glanced at the screen, so he could read the incoming text message and instantly recognized the sender's number as he began to read the message: *Change of plans, don't come to the Tatto shop it's officially shut down for good. Meet me at our other spot in thirty minutes. I'll be there right after I stop by my lady's house to grab a few things. Do not, under no circumstance, answer any calls from Moe Kelly. I'll explain everything once I meet up with you. Oh, by the way, I have the girl.*

Looking up with murderous eyes, he instructed Lil' Kurt to drop him off. He never informed the others of what he'd just read, cause to him, running into his mother's boyfriend was personal.

"Where at?" asked Lil' Kurt.

"Take me to my mother's house," he replied, his lip's pursed with suppressed fury.

Noticing his partner's demeanor, Slick told Mike-Mike that he was coming with him. Mike-Mike quickly declined by telling him that he had to handle something by himself.

CHAPTER 66

Moe Kelly overcame a lot of hurdles in his lifetime, but the recent barriers that surfaced were enough to leave him speechless. Having to bury his nephew in the next couple of days was one obstacle he didn't want to ever cross. Now, as he watched his partner in crime take his last breath, it was as if all his worst nightmares were suddenly comin' to haunt him. No whips or chains could've inflicted more pain than the mental torture he was enduring at that moment.

The sinister glare he displayed was murderous enough to make Charles Manson think twice about crossing his path. A quick death by all parties involved wasn't enough to appease his hunger. He wanted everyone to feel the same torment he felt, including Malice who literally backdoored them by physically walking out of one, basically leaving them for dead. The act caused his heart to rapidly palpitate like a beating drum, while the anger inside of him surged through his veins with venomous intentions. His mindset locked in the notion of sacrificing everything just to ensure that everyone that was at the helm of his suffering crumbled like the Twin Towers. Vengeance was his and he planned on seeking it in blood.

Epilogue

Losing yet another soldier, due to the lures of the streets, caused the group to ride in silence. Before long, Lil' Kurt was pulling up to the corner of Piney Branch and Whittier Place where Mike-Mike's mom resided.

"Bruh, you sure you don't want me to come wit' you?" questioned Slick, sensing that his sidekick was up to something.

"Nah, I'm straight. I'm just gonna check on Ma Dukes," he replied, avoiding eye contact.

"You sure?" Slick asked, once again, his eyes narrowing in suspicion.

"Positive. I'ma get back up wit' y'all in a few," he tried to say with conviction.

"What about Monique?" inquired Lil' Kurt.

"We still have some time if it isn't too late, after what just happened. So, after I leave from here, we're going' to get back on top of that," he responded, stepping out of the vehicle, ending the conversation.

He was hoping that his gut feeling was leading him in

the right direction, if so, then he might be able to save Monique himself. Once they pulled off, his face instantly hardened as he edged toward the alley that led to his mother's house. As soon as he made the right turn into the alleyway, his nostrils flared up upon seeing Malice's car already in the driveway.

With his right hand suddenly gripping the steel on his hip, he cautiously crept through the yard and up the stairs, entering the house through an already opened backdoor. His stomach contracted into a tight ball while he tip-toed through the kitchen. Hearing faint sounds seemingly coming from the bedroom, he removed Mother Teresa from his hip, allowing her to lead the way. Inching his way past the dining room into the fissure heading toward the bedroom, the veins in his neck stood out in livid ridges. The second he bent the corner, he saw Malice kneeling down with his back toward him stuffing a gym bag with various items.

"You planning on goin' somewhere?" Mike-Mike grimaced, catching Malice off-guard.

Stunned, Malice just stood there in silence as if he were a burglar that got caught red-handed. He slowly raised his hands in the air, cautiously peered out the corner of his eyes, observing Mike-Mike leveling a gun in his direction. At that very moment, the power in Malice's mind went out, plunging him into darkness, muting all surrounding sounds as guilt masked his appearance.

"How can you live wit' ya'self knowin' you caused all da pain to da same people dat showed you nothin' but luv from da beginnin'? We trusted you, and to think, we almost made you a part of our family," Mike-Mike scolded, gritting through clinched teeth.

He moved closer, pressing the cold steel to the back of Malice's head.

"I didn't mean for it to be like this," Malice commiserated, amplifying a hue of shame.

"I 'on't see how you could've expected anything different, Anthony!" he shot back defensively. "Or should I say Malice!" Mike-Mike added, proving his assertion, triggering Malice to gawk in disbelief upon hearing his alias, that he was also known by, called-out.

"I guess ya wonderin' how I stumbled on dat, huh? Just so ya know, I was da one at Zoe's shop dis mornin'," he revealed, tightening his grip.

That last statement struck Malice hard like a hammer blow to the head. Right then and there, he realized that no reasoning was valuable enough to defend his actions. How would he explain that after nearly four years of regret, he'd finally decided to take responsibility for his mistake? By confronting the grieving parent of the victim while being prepared to suffer whatever consequences that came his way. Mike-Mike wouldn't have had any understanding as far as when the time presented itself for Malice to come face to face with his mother. Nor, how out of the blue, an unspoken attraction took up the space between them, leading him into uncharted territory, ultimately prompting him to remaining silent.

"Where is she!" Mike-Mike demanded in a powerful and authoritative tone, interrupting Malice's deep thoughts.

"Where's who?" he replied, obviously not on the same page as Mike-Mike due to everything that was being brought to light.

"Don't act like ya don't know who I'm talkin' 'bout," he barked. Mike-Mike used his free hand to pull Big Herm's cell phone out of his pocket navigated straight to the text message, placing the phone right in front of Malice to see. "Dat is a text dat ya sent from your phone, right?" he asked, trying to take advantage of Malice's vulnerable disposition.

Malice's face glazed with shock upon viewing the text that he sent from his personal cell phone number that he knew without question Mike-Mike was familiar with.

"Now let's try dis again, where is she?" he asked, tucking the phone away. "And I ain't askin' you again. I put dat on my baby sister!" he threatened in a voice as cold as death.

Clearly in a no-win situation, because of the justifiable rage that Mike-Mike felt toward him, Malice simply looked up at Mike-Mike, long-faced, fixing his lips to say something. Suddenly, a voice came from out of nowhere, startling both of them.

"Michael Gardner! What in God's name are you doing!" shouted his mother.

"Ma!" Mike-Mike gasped in surprise, turning partially around to face her.

"Why is there a gun in my house and how come you pointing it at Anthony?" she clamored in exasperation.

"Ma, I swear it's not what you think," he conveyed, trying to keep her calm, redirecting his attention back to Malice.

"You wanna tell her, or should I?" Mike-Mike asked as he looked piercingly at Malice.

"Tell me what!" Her lips began to twitch from the unknown.

"Go 'head tell her…Tell…Tell her what I know!" he urged infuriated.

"Anthony, what is he talkin' about?"

"I'm sorry," he hesitated.

"Sorry for what?"

"I was going to tell you."

"What is it, 'cause you scaring me?" her voice degenerated into a childish whimper.

"Tell her!" Mike-Mike fumed becoming impatient.

Every time Malice commenced to speak, it seemed as though the words refused to come out. Though he had plans to tell her, he just didn't want her to find out in that manner. He'd already anticipated how he'd tell her during their vacation. Now that was no more, due to Mike-Mike forcing him to bring everything into the open.

Never had Malice felt so vulnerable and relatively helpless before, which led him to feel some kind of resentment toward Mike-Mike. Without notice, an incredible surge of anger surfaced, causing the muscles in his jaws to jerk. His anger resulted in the killer in him coming back into reality.

"I see he's not tryin' to tell you, so I guess I'ma have to," Mike-Mike said to his mother. He was tired of Malice prolonging it. Briefly taking his eyes off of Malice, he began to inform her himself. "Ma…" he began, pausing for a second as tears swelled up in his eyes. "Malice is da one…"

"Who!" She asked cutting him off, not aware of Anthony's street name.

"Dat's Anthony's alias, and like I was sayin' he's da one who…" he started to say, when out of nowhere, Malice angrily sprang toward him, taking hold of the arm that held the gun in it.

"You two stop it!" Mike-Mike's mom screamed as she watched with numb horror.

Normally Malice's strength would've been able to manhandle Mike-Mike, but the built-up anger inside of Mike-Mike wouldn't allow Malice to take advantage. The pair were touching and knocking over everything in the bedroom. As they tried to overpower one another for control of the gun, a gunshot went off. It halted and silenced every other sound and movement in the room as the random bullet found its mark.

The individual immediately felt themselves losing consciousness. Labored sounds came from their heaving chest as they pressed their hands against their torn flesh. Fighting to catch their breath, but no longer able to, 'caused the raw and emotional scene to take a quick turn and end with **A Gain For A Loss.**

TO BE CONTINUED…

A Conversation with the Author

Darrell Bracey, Jr.

What inspired you to begin writing? Did this occur before or after being sentenced to prison?

Prison was where I first developed the interest, which first sparked after reading a manuscript by an unpublished author by the name of Samual O'Atis out of Chicago, who was incarcerated. He kept urging me to read it, and to my surprise, once I perused the pages, I couldn't put it down. During such time, I ended up going to the *Hole* aka *Shu* in Fed. terms, with a group of D.C. homies and Samual O'Atis. He was housed in a cell directly under me, so I was able to talk with him through the vents of our cells. Bored with nothing else to do, I communicated to him that I wanted to start writing a book to occupy my time. He immediately encouraged me to do so and gave me some pointers on how to begin sequencing a story. From there, the author Darrell Bracey, Jr. pioneered, and like the saying goes, *the rest is history.*

How did you come up with your debut novel, *Concrete Jungle's* storyline?

Believe it or not, I freestyled the entire book, so when people ask me that question, I basically tell them that I went in the booth and Jay Z'd or Lil Wayne'd that thing. (LOL)

What are some of the setbacks you've experienced while writing in prison?

317

Distractions! There are always distractions in prison. Whether personal or otherwise, it's always exhausting when dealing with multiple personalities and circumstances that may hinder the creative process on a daily basis. One must learn how to block out certain things and continue striving toward their goals.

Do you plan to write other types of genres?

Most definitely. My plan is to venture off in the near future into something that I call, *Urban Thriller*. It's going to be as if a collaboration between James Patterson and myself came to fruition.

How do you promote the sales of your books while in prison?

Being as though I can't put the footwork in myself, I basically rely on social media and word of mouth. In addition, with my business associate, Byron *"B-Bo"* Dorsey, founder of Bloc Extension Publishing, makes things a lot smoother on the administrative side of it. He handles other promotional methods such as catalog placement, cross-promotions and postcards/flyers.

Are there any other writer's that you're able to bond with while incarcerated?

I built a bond with quite a few writers through my travels. Out of them all, I chose to do business with one in particular that goes by the name of Elijah Phillips. He's going to be the first writer under my imprint, *BOUT DAT LYFE PUBLICATIONS*, so be on the lookout.

What advice can you give other writers who are incarcerated and seeking to get in the business?

First and foremost, learn the business, learn how to read contracts, so you don't sign your hard work and dedication away like so many authors have, PERIOD!

What are your plans once you are released from prison?

My goals are monumental. I plan on working until I no longer have to introduce myself. I have dreams of seeing one of my projects on those huge billboards and in movie theaters. Trust me, I won't stop until it transitions into reality. I'm like a lion when it comes to achieving what I set-out to do. I don't just chase my goals, I HUNT 'EM DOWN!

Any final words?

I want to thank friends, family and my fans for supporting my craft. You all give me the inspiration to continue doling-out quality material. I'm very appreciative of your embracive sentiments. Until the next one, stay tuned.

Coming Soon

Bout Dat Lyfe Publications
&
Bloc Extension Publishing
-Presents-

Coming Soon...

Eyes of Betrayal: Divided Loyalties by Byron R. Dorsey
Concrete Jungle 2 by Darrell Bracey, Jr.
Press 4 Time: by Darrell Bracey, Jr.

Press 4 Time

A Sneek Peek

By: Darrell Bracey, Jr.

Prologue

1901 D Street, Southeast, Washington DC housed some of the worlds most notorious criminals. It was a jungle where real humans acted like wild animals. It wasn't a spot for wannabes and pretenders because someone was sure to spot that feature a mile away. Respect was earned, not given, and if you were a coward being left alone that was because you were being extorted, some man's punk or you were able to smuggle contraband into the facility. Another thing about DC jail was that anyone with a high-profile case stood out.

On this particular day, a certain individual that was listed as having the most recent high-profile case comparable to the Linwood Grey case was due in court. The District Court immates were moved from one holding cell to another before they were shackled together with metal chains, leg irons, and a device called the black box, which was almost impossible for even the craftiest convict to pick the lock. The armed U.S. Marshalls closely watched as dozens of inmates boarded the 15-passenger van. The inmates were giving each other some encouraging words, hoping to ease some of the built-up anxiety that comes with having to stand before the judge.

"Time to put y'alls' boxing gloves on men!" one of the prisoner's shouted as the van pulled off.

Once the van was checked at the security gate, and the Marshalls were given back their service weapons, they were allowed through. Soon after clearing the gate, the driver took 17th Street and Barney Circle. The misty morning weather was just as congested as the rush hour traffic, thought the driver, making a right turn blending in with traffic.

The inmates were glued to the windows checking out the view hoping to catch a glimpse of some females driving pass. A sense of edginess pervaded the van as they continued toward their destination where the uncertain awaited them. The scenery momentarily eased their minds, but at the same time caused disappointment from wishing they were the ones looking inside the van instead of out.

All twelve of the inmates seemed to be mentally roaming around when a loud roar caught all of their attention. Looking to see where the noise was coming from, they turned toward the sound and noticed several bikers rapidly approaching. When the bikers caught up with the van, all the inmates' mouths dropped after noticing they were all women. The tight leather suits that looked like a second layer of skin caused the prisoners, as well as the guards', mouths to water. As the group stared lustfully, the last thing anyone would've thought was taking place on the opposite side of the van. An additional biker with someone on the back rode unnoticed, due to the commotion on the other side. This allowed the rider on the back of the bike time to connect a lodestone incendiary device onto the van. Once attached, the biker took off, causing the rest of the pack to follow.

Once they sped off everybody except the high-profile inmate went into an uproar. With the outcome of his future heavy on his mind, he went unfazed by the female bikers in tights. He continued giving thought to the matter at hand when a burst of smoke caught his attention. Not alarming enough to cause a scene, but subtle enough to raise his curiosity. Leaning up in his seat to further inspect, he quickly realized that the fumes were coming from an apparatus stuck to the side of the van.

"Ay, guards!" he yelled out, but went unheard due to all the noise the inmates were still making. "Man, there's something stuck on the side of this van and it's smokin'!" he bellowed, finally gaining their attention.

"What!" responded one of the Marshalls.

"I said, it's somethin' stuck to the side of this van, and it's smokin'!" he emphasized.

One of the Marshalls rushed over to further inspect what the inmate was referring to. "What the hell is that!" the guard sounded, observing the smoke coming from some form of apparatus, just as the prisoner proclaimed.

"Officer Manley, you need to pull this van over immediately!" he demanded, just as the smoke turned into sparks. The sudden spurt of sparks instantly caused the guard's eyes to widen in alarm. "Everyone to the other side of the van, now!" he cried out in a voice raw with terror.

Unfortunately, for the group on the van, the predetermined happened simultaneously as in three other locations that were monumental landmarks in Washington, DC. The series of bombs that exploded on the District Court transportation van, Union Station, as well as L'Enfant Plaza quickly had all the powers that be in the metropolitan area on their toes. The blast could be heard for miles, triggering pandemonium. Panic and fear covered the district as the authorities expeditiously stormed the threatened areas.

Law enforcement was quickly and cautiously evacuating the alerted locations. Not wanting to take any chances, the authorities were treating the surprising, frightening incident as a terrorist attack. To all that were involved with the incursion, it was a mission accomplished, but unbeknown to the officers, the occurrences weren't anything more than a distraction for something greater than what anyone could've expected.

A Reading Group Guide

A Gain For A Loss

ABOUT THIS GUIDE

The suggested questions are intended to enhance your group's reading of this book.

Discussion Questions

1. How do you feel about Mike-Mike leaving home to run the streets after knowing what his family had already been through with the death of his little sister?

2. What are your thoughts on Mike-Mike agreeing to something without knowing the ramifications of the commitment?

3. Was Slick wrong for feeling disassociated every time Mike-Mike had to meet Zoe for an important meeting?

4. Do you think Nose overreacted by striking Mike-Mike in the face after finding out about Melvin's death without fully knowing the truth behind it? And was Slick wrong for pulling his gun out on Nose during the incident?

5. If you were in Nose's shoes, would you have thought the same as he after the chain of events that led up to Melvin's death?

6. Do you think that Monique and Mike-Mike could've made a power couple or better off staying friends?

7. Do you think Mike-Mike and Slick brought unwanted attention to themselves by selling the drugs they received

from Zoe for much lower than the going price?

8. What were your thoughts on Malice's character?

9. What do you think Mike-Mike's mother Gloria's reaction is going to be once she finds out the truth behind Anthony's secret?

10. Was Big Herm's deception surprising?

ABOUT THE AUTHOR

Riding high on the success of his debut novel, *CONCRETE JUNGLE*, Darrell 'DB" Bracey, Jr. delivers yet another masterpiece with his sophomore follow-up, *A GAIN FOR A LOSS*. His exceptional focus and drive keeps him in the lab cooking up addictive plots, one of which is the sequel to his premiere project. Bracey's novels skillfully fulfill the reading desires of his targeted audience.

Not the one to allow his current incarceration to deter him from his dreams, in the near future, Bracey plans to transition into the motion-picture industry, where some of his written art can be depicted in film. His tenacious work ethic ensures his success and empowers his steps toward meeting his goals.

When the Washingtonian is not writing, he enjoys watching sports, reading, working out, and bonding with family. For an open line of communication with the author, please follow him on: FACEBOOK @ DARRELL BRACEY, JR. or email him at: authordarellbracey@gmail.com.

Books available at:

www. b n . c o m

 amazon.com.

Made in the USA
Coppell, TX
29 May 2021